About the book

He's a cowboy turned security specialist, haunted by the past.

Ten years ago, Calvin Beckett left Sabrina Holloway at the altar, disappearing without explanation. Blackmailed by his father to abandon Sabrina or see her family ruined, Cal chose to protect her. Walking away from both the love of his life, his family business, and the only safe home he's ever known- the family's sprawling Wyoming ranch, Cal built a new life as a security specialist in the city. But when his father's ruthless efforts to reclaim him intensify, fate throws Sabrina back into his path. As threats escalate, a long-buried secret involving Sabrina's parents comes to light, and Cal realizes their separation was about more than just his father's control. Now, Cal must return to his roots, bringing Sabrina to the family ranch to keep her safe—even if it means risking his heart all over again.

She's a small-town matchmaker who can't find her own happy ending.

Professional matchmaker Sabrina Holloway lives by the motto: if you can't marry, matchmake. After Cal's betrayal, she poured herself into building a career that brings joy to others in their close-knit community. Heartbreak struck again when her father's death left her truly alone in the town she loves. When hired to improve a grumpy security CEO's image and potentially find him the perfect partner, Sabrina is shocked to discover her client is none other than Cal. Suddenly, she's swept back to the ranch she once thought would be her home, forced to confront dangers she never imagined and feelings she thought long buried.

Forced to partner up, Cal and Sabrina craft a fake relationship to outsmart their enemy. As they face their past and an uncertain future, these two lonely souls rediscover their connection to the land, the community, and each other. Working together they realize that the key to defeating their foe might just be embracing the love they left behind. But can they overcome a decade of hurt and the looming threat to both their lives to find their happily ever after under the big Wyoming sky?

The Cowboy's Second Chance Bride

A Wyoming Matchmaker Romance
Book 4

Kristi Rose

Books by Kristi Rose

The Wyoming Matchmaker Series- Whether marriage of convenience or star crossed lovers, everyone earns their happily ever after in this series.

The Cowboy Takes A Bride

The Cowboy's Make Believe Bride

The Cowboy's Runaway Bride

The Cowboy's Second Chance Bride

* * *

The No Strings Attached Series- A flirty, fun chick lit romance series

The Girl He Knows

The Girl He Wants

The Girl He Loves

Beach Town Love- boxset

Audiobooks

* * *

Samantha True Mysteries- These laugh out loud, action pack books take place in the Pacific Northwest. Join Samantha, an adult with dyslexia who's hid behind photography, on her adventures in her new life as a Private Investigator. A job she inherited when her new husband died unexpectedly and left behind a mess and another wife.

One Hit Wonder

All Bets Are Off

Best Laid Plans

Caught Off Guard

Two Time Loser

Dodged A Bullet

Audiobooks

* * *

<u>The Cold Case Mystery Series:</u>

Bone of Contention

Bone to Pick

Audiobooks

* * *

<u>PERFECT PLACE: A Liars Island Suspense</u>

Perfect Place

<u>Audiobook</u>

* * *

<u>Campus Murder Club- The dead are not forgotten</u>

<u>Campus Murder Club</u>

<u>Audiobook Coming soon</u>

* * *

<u>The Meryton Brides Series- A wholesome romance series with a
Pride and Prejudice theme</u>

To Have and To Hold (Book 1)

With This Ring (Book 2)

I Do (Book 3)

Promise Me This (Book 4)

Marry Me, Matchmaker (Book 5)

Honeymoon Postponed (Book 6)

Matchmaker's Guidebook - FREE

* * *

The Second Chance Short Stories can be read alone and go as follows:

Second Chances

Once Again

Reason to Stay

He's the One

Kiss Me Again

or purchased in a bundle for a better discount.

The Coming Home Series: A Collection of 5 Second Chance Short Stories (Can be purchased individually).

Love Comes Home

Open your phone's camera
to scan the QR code and
SAVE

Link will take you to
KristiRoseBooks.com
Buying from me means a
deal for you.

To DHM: How did I get so lucky? every day is a gift.

And for Brynna T. Whose comedic timing is stellar and deadpan expression is masterful. Its fun to witness. That's why I named a character after you. If she has a fraction of your wit then I did a good job.

For Amanda and Rachel H. who helped me remember that community was the roots of this series. I appreciate you both.

Vintage Housewife Books

PO BOX 842

Ridgefield, WA 98642

www.kristirose.net

www.kristirosebooks.com

Publisher's Note: This is a work of fiction. Names, characters, places, and incidents are a product of the author's imagination. Locales and public names are sometimes used for atmospheric purposes. Any resemblance to actual people, living or dead, or to businesses, companies, events, institutions, or locales is completely coincidental.

Book Layout © 2024 Vellum

Cover Design © 2024 The Killion Group

Editing by Red Adept Editing

THE COWBOY'S SECOND CHANCE BRIDE/ Kristi Rose. -- _1st ed._

Chapter One
CAL

There was a popular saying about a person bringing a knife to a gunfight. Usually, I was the guy with the bigger gun, but I'd found myself in the fight of my life with someone attacking my company, my reputation, and my livelihood, and I was the idiot standing there with a freaking butter knife. I never saw this attack coming.

In the last eighteen hours, so much had happened it was hard for me to keep up. I was dog-tired, man. It had been a long time since I'd last slept. A few hours after shit went sideways in Peru, I'd flown back to Seattle at the urgent request of my mother and Paul, my PR guy.

I rubbed the wound on the upper half of my left arm and tried to wrap my mind around all that had happened in such a short time. I was surrounded by my mother, Paul, Jace Shepard—my best friend—and one of the company's field agents and medical expert, Citra Smith. They were all encouraging me to sheath my knife and charge forward with the big guns.

Which was stupid. Did they not know me? Of course, I

was going to strike back and strike hard. But I had to first get a sense of the land mines. And there was this little thing called strategy.

My opponent was wily, cunning, and heavily armed with smart lawyers, and he'd come out swinging, hitting where it hurt the most—my brand and reputation. For a securities expert, trust was of the upmost importance. Clients had to believe we knew what we were doing, that our guidance was solid, and that was never a problem when my company, Optium, only focused on two roles—providing executive protection and training and educating schools on threat assessments.

Up until that moment, all my clients had cared about was me keeping them and their families alive. Even if I had to die to do it. Which was a main reason why I didn't have a personal life. And that had never mattered until eighteen hours earlier, when all of my personal information had been trotted out and showcased to prove Optium had no business launching its new division.

A new division that we'd kept top secret for over a year. A new division that wasn't supposed to launch for another six months. A new division with a secret project that focused on personal safety—at home, in dating, and in internet use— and what to do if you found yourself in a scary situation. There was even a dating app in the works.

All this started because Citra's sister once had a bad experience, and she'd felt helpless. No one should feel helpless. Enter Project ProtectedLove. That was a working title.

Yeah, it was not our area of proficiency, which was why we were taking the time to get it right and have experts test and give input. We were learning to make it our area of expertise.

But none of that mattered. Because when our secret project was leaked, our biggest competitor, Hitchens and Sons, sprang into action, swiping at our jugular by launching a smear campaign to discredit Optium—and me—in order to own the consumer narrative. Also, I was sure they were pissed because in all of our research, we used them as an example of what not to do.

"Have you figured out how Hitchens and Sons got our intellectual property? Was the leak hired by them? Where are we with that?"

PR Paul leaned against the wall. "Took Spoon just under four hours to find the leak."

Benjamin Spoon was Optium's best IT guy. I trusted him with my life. Which was why only Paul, Citra, and I felt comfortable with asking Ben Spoon to find the mole. Because, of course, there had to be an internal mole. How else would Hitchens and Sons have gotten our intellectual property?

"It took Citra less than fifteen minutes to break him," Paul continued.

Citra smiled. "The little weasel. Once Spoon confirmed it, I caught up with him in the break room. He had no idea we were onto him. Nearly pissed his pants when I told him he was caught red-handed, and he almost fainted when I introduced him to our lawyers. He's been holed up since then."

"Fuck," I mumbled, anger welling up and threatening to spill over.

Apparently, someone didn't know the rules of Optium's fight club.

"You ready to hear the worst part?" Paul asked.

"Christ, it gets worse?"

"Guess who turned our employee—found out our mole was having trouble with one of his kids and wanted to send him to a military school. That's all it took."

I knew the answer before Paul said it.

"Your dad. He was also the one to give Hitchens the intellectual property." Paul held up a manila envelope about half an inch thick. "I've got the paper trail right here. That and the mole's confession when Citra cornered him. He was paid handsomely by your father, which is good because he will use it all on lawyers for breaking his NDA. And also, your dad is funding Hitchens's updates on their app."

"Of course he is," my mom mumbled.

I rolled my thumb around my right temple, hoping to ease the tension. Hitchens and Sons already had a foothold in the market. They had customer reviews and had built brand knowledge. With our intellectual property, they could improve their crappy dating app to include better safety systems. If we wanted to do this division and the project, we were seriously behind in the race. Like, several laps behind. This was not good.

"I'm not sure if your dad knows we caught him. We've kept our mole locked up tight," Citra said.

I shook my head. "Dalton isn't going to care if we find out he's behind this. He wants me to know." I rubbed the bandage on my arm again.

Paul cleared his throat. "We have to decide where we go from here. Do we cut our losses or stay in the game?"

PR Paul, as I liked to think of him, was a tall, lean guy with wire-rimmed glasses. He looked average and unremarkable. Neither of those words would describe Paul's personality. He was savvy and cutthroat—just what I and Optium Security needed. In the short six hours since the media had turned on me specifically and on Optium as a side note, Paul had not only worked out the mole and confirmed they looked to be coming from Hitchens and Sons Security but had also learned that these attacks were funded by my dear old dad. And in pure Paul fashion, he'd already devised a solid plan.

Cutting our losses would be a huge financial suck. Losing the edge on our project meant losing a lot of money as well as market share and the first-mover advantage, investment returns, partnership and integration, brand reputation, talent retention, legal and intellectual property issues and lawsuits, positive media attention, data advantages, pricing power, and worst of all... customer trust.

Hands down, had we been able to launch this project on schedule, there was no doubt Optium would have done it with ethics and safety, front and center. All Hitchens and Sons cared about was getting personal data to leverage money. Most people didn't realize Hitchens and Sons also had their hands in the insurance industry, which meant if you tried to get insurance through their company, they could use all the data they collected to charge you higher prices or to reject you altogether. And that was just tip of the iceberg with them.

"You can't just let this go, Cal. You need to fight back!" my mother said.

Morgan Baker-Beckett, my mother, had been gunning for me to take down her estranged husband. And when the attack was launched, she'd jumped on a plane and rushed to my side—only I was in Peru, and she'd gone to our office in Seattle. She'd "thought it best" if she waited here for me.

"Your father will not make this an easy or quick battle. In the thirty-two years of our marriage, I have never seen the man give up or give in."

"Didn't I say I was going to strike back?"

Yes, enemy number one, current and past, was my good old pops. Isn't family great? If I'd had a sense of humor, I would have laughed about the fact that she saw this as a battle, like I did. But I'd lost my sense of humor many years before. My funny bone was a shriveled-up prune of emotion, rotting away deep in the dark recesses of my soul. I lived comfortably with cynicism and snark.

Paul, leaning against the wall, crossed one ankle over the other. "He's done a great job planning this out. We have to give him credit for that. He found your weakness and is using it against you." Paul used his middle finger to push up his glasses. Like me, he had a few choice words for Dalton Beckett.

Jace Shepard scoffed. His nostrils flared in anger.

Tell me about it, buddy. I was just as angry.

Jace had never really liked my dad. When you had a great father like Jace's, dads like mine seemed like fictional villains rather than real-life assholes. Dalton—he didn't deserve to be called dad—had slammed me in the media, saying that a guy who wasn't married and hadn't dated in a decade had no business talking about dating and relationships. He'd said a guy whose house had been broken into the other day couldn't know much about personal security.

Yeah, my apartment had been broken into five days earlier. When Paul told me it looked like all they took was the TV, I'd said, "I don't have a TV."

I hadn't been home yet to check what was missing, but I would have bet a year's salary nothing had been stolen, because I literally had only the essentials—a few clothing items, some cookware, a bed, and a couch. I was never home. I carried my laptop with me.

The day before, I'd taken a bullet for a client when all this bullshit here was going down. And besides that, someone had entered my mom's ranch, broken into my sister's glass-blowing workshop—her livelihood, by the way—and destroyed over a hundred grand in equipment and finished pieces. That had been in the media too. Here I was, supposedly one of the best in that field, yet neither residence had security. It made for a good story. Coincidence? I thought not.

"We're not going to cut our losses. I'm not giving up on this division or this project." I scratched the wound on my upper arm and winced as my fingers tugged on the stitches.

Citra jumped up. "Let me look at this." She gestured for me to take off my shirt, then eased off the slightly stained bandage. As well as being one of my first employees, Citra was an excellent field agent with medical experience, which came in handy if one got shot.

I was that one in this case, by the way. Getting shot sucked. But at least the asset was alive and his stalker was headed to prison.

I wiped a hand down my face, and when I came to my chin, I rubbed at the stubble. I glanced at my watch. Twenty hours of no sleep. Or a proper shave and shower. Did I mention how dog-tired I was?

"Merely a flesh wound," she mumbled in her best Monty Python voice. "I'll give you some antibacterial ointment that should help with the itch. But as you know, itchy is good. However, the stitches the field quack put in are not great." She snorted, letting me know that was an understatement. "They'll give you a gnarly scar."

"I'm told chicks dig scars." I observed the poorly done, uneven stitches. The wound didn't look like a gunshot but more like I'd snagged my arm on a fence or something equally lame.

"Like you care. I'd love to know if you ever showed a chick your scars."

Jace raised one brow. He was like the subconscious part of my brain that I tried to ignore, only I couldn't because his expression always reflected my thoughts. Yeah, yeah—once upon a time there had been a chick. I knew it. He knew it. No one else knew it. Things hadn't ended so well, and that was the end of chicks and showing scars for me.

Citra slapped a clean bandage onto my arm.

"Ow, go easy," I said, partly joking. My arm was a little sore but nothing a pain reliever couldn't ease.

"Next time, don't get shot, and we won't have to do this."

"Well, it was me or the asset, so I picked me. Can you imagine what the papers would be saying had it gone the other way?"

"Calvin," my mother said, drawing my attention back to her. "Why are you so calm? How can you sit there and joke with Citra?" She sat on the couch across from my desk, looking ready to kill. And she had a target— Dalton Beckett, who'd always been the target for all of her feelings. She slapped the leather couch. "I can't believe Dalton is doing this. And I can't believe I'm surprised." She crossed her arms.

"I'm in the business of being proactive, not reactive, so I need time to think and process." I looked at her from under my brow. "But I'm not calm. I'm pissed off as hell."

"As far as the news articles about you on social media go," Paul said, "we've been trying to get the name of the journalist writing all these articles and doing all this posting, but Spoon says he's hidden behind a VPN."

I shifted my focus back to Paul then to Jace, who was sitting quietly by my mom, his expression thunderous.

Paul continued. "Okay, you don't want to lose the project. Good. But this negative press is gonna make the launch of ProtectedLove even harder. I don't think we can afford to wait. We need to launch now." Paul held out his phone. "You know how much social media influences people's beliefs. Well, here's a trending post talking about how you have no family. Who knew being dedicated to your job would be your Achilles heel?"

I pointed to my mother. "I do have family. I have her and my sister."

Paul quirked his brow in disbelief. "I apologize. You want me to correct the post? If we point out your mom and sister, what do you think the first questions will be? When was the last time you were at the ranch? A month, a year? How often do you see your mom and sister?"

Answer: I hadn't been to the ranch in a decade, and in that same span of time, I'd seen Mom and Brynna three times. All those times, they'd sought me out while I was overseas, and the time together had been counted in hours, not days.

I saw his point.

My mother gave me her sad eyes. "Ten years is a long time, Cal."

I had a good reason for that. Just not one most people would care about.

"I have a question," Jace said, holding up a hand. "Why does Cal need to be the face of this project? Can't Optium launch it but have someone else spearhead it?"

Paul shook his head. "Spoon is married, so that's not

gonna work for the dating app. Citra is already doing the LGBTQ portion because—"

"I'm LGBTQ" Citra said proudly.

Jace tossed up his hands in frustration. "Why does his record not count for anything? He's saved dignitaries and high profiles around the world by making sure their security was top-notch. He's a freaking hero for what he does. He's getting an award from the Global Safety Initiative for all his work globally. Why isn't this having the impact it should?"

Hero was a bit much, but I appreciated my friend's defense. "Besides, how does one have a family when one works all the time?" Again, I was the one in this scenario.

Paul looked between Jace and me. "That's called being a workaholic, Cal, and that's just one more flaw to use against you. I've seen smear campaigns work that have made absolutely no sense whatsoever. Dalton and Hitchens are feeding off the fear of others, and once that's on a roll, and confirmation bias kicks in, what's being said becomes the new truth. We have to get ahead of this, more to save the project than anything else. Are you sure you want to save this venture? Because it's not going to be easy."

All eyes swung to me. We'd all worked so hard on this concept, and there was an emotional attachment to it as well. It was the right kind of project. The good kind. The kind that helped and made a difference. The kind that could keep my single sister safe should she ever consider online dating sites as a way to find partners.

Goddamn my father.

"Of course I'm sure. And I heard what you said. You think we need to launch now even though we aren't as ready as we want to be. I worry that launching early will make more problems than solve them."

Paul continued to look cool and calm. "Time is of the essence here. We have a narrow window for taking control, and it's slipping away quickly."

"Your father is a terrible person," muttered Mom.

"Tell me something I don't know." I splayed my hands wide in question. "What I can't figure out is why now."

"Oh, honey, it's not 'why now.' You know he's been gunning for you since you walked away. He's just going all out now because"—she held up one finger—"I just so happen to know he's been having some health issues lately, and I think the fear of passing the family business to someone who is not family spurred him into action."

Since my mother left my father, they'd rarely talked, and when they did, it was through mediators whom I doubted were sharing that kind of info.

"How do you know this?" I asked.

She shrugged one shoulder and looked at her long maroon-painted nails. "Instead of going after you, he should have hired you to teach him some security, for Pete's sake. The man hasn't changed his password in years." She met my gaze. "When you walked away ten years ago, it gave me the courage to do the same. Since then, everything has slowly been eroding around him, and he can see it. He has to go big now. Time's not his friend."

I arched a brow. "How sick is he?" I didn't care, but I didn't not care either. That was the plight of unwanted children.

She waved a dismissive hand. "He's not dying or anything—the man will never die, because Satan is afraid of him. He just needs to eat better and exercise, or his heart will explode."

"Jeez, Ma. That doesn't sound good."

She rolled her eyes. "Well, it won't be for him, because he can't do either of those things consistently. For the humans who know they are mortal, it's all completely reversible and manageable."

Paul cleared his throat, drawing the attention back to him. "Let's talk about the plan. It's sexy and personable. And it will steal the show."

I closed my eyes and leaned back in my chair. "Would you be offended if I said it was a stupid plan?"

Paul chuckled. "No, I've heard that before. And usually, it's the stupid plans that tend to be the most successful. Just one more reason to use it." His brow went up as if he were ready for a challenge.

I pulled myself to the desk and leaned forward on my elbows, my bandage pulling tight, meeting the man's eye. "You really think we need to bring a love consultant on board? Do those even exist? Am I supposed to date or get myself an arranged marriage or something? No offense, Jace."

He smiled. "None taken."

Jace's loving father had put him in a quandary at one time too. A workaholic like me, Jace had been given an ultimatum by his dad, who said he wouldn't leave Jace the family ranch unless he had a better work-life balance. Enter arranged marriage. That was Jace's idea, and it was supposed to last until... well, I wasn't sure when, but it didn't matter because Jace was madly in love with his mail-order bride, Meredith. They were a perfect match.

Paul put his hand on Jace's shoulder. "This is kinda where the idea came from. We bring in a love expert to help you test the app in real time. You know nothing about dating, so no one is gonna buy it if it was just you. But pair you, the security expert, with the love expert, and we have a social media reality show told through reels and posts that people will love to watch. This also builds consumer trust, so even if Hitchens relaunches his revamped product, we have the home-field advantage."

"And maybe you'll get lucky like Jace," Mom said.

"Hard pass, Ma." Yeah, marriage wasn't in the stars for me. There was no way we could do this plan. I would never subject a woman to my company. How awful for them. "Won't anyone I show attention to be caught up in this mess too? That doesn't seem fair. And am I supposed to date with no real intention of it going anywhere? With a love expert over my shoulder? Too weird. See? Stupid plan."

"Do you not want to settle down, Cal?" my mother asked quietly.

I pressed my fingers to my closed eyes. We'd had this discussion so many times. Then I looked back at Paul. I shook my head.

He pushed off the wall with a jerk. "I see where you're coming from. The expert won't be over your shoulder. She or he will be behind the scenes, guiding you on how to navigate the dating landscape. But it has to be you navigating the landscape. It's a true test that way."

"Do love experts really exist? How do you find one of those?" I really thought I had the win here with this one. It's not like these were easy to find.

"We use a matchmaker," he said.

I snapped to attention, my hands slapping down on my desk involuntarily. My gaze jerked toward Jace. He straightened and, with a tiny shake of his head, told me this was the first he'd heard of Paul's plan to use a matchmaker.

"A matchmaker, huh?" Jace asked.

Mom leaned toward Jace. "I gathered a list. Meredith said you two used a friend. We were hoping maybe we could use her too. I like the idea of bringing in someone who has already been vetted."

I shook my head, silently pleading with him to keep his mouth shut. Yeah, Jace had used a matchmaker to find Meredith. But it wasn't matchmakers that were the problem —it was a specific matchmaker I had an issue with. She was a secret and needed to stay that way.

Jace cleared his throat. "Uh, I happen to know the one we used isn't available. I'm not even sure she's in the country." He was talking to my mom but looked at me the entire time.

Paul looked between us, probably trying to listen in on our silent conversation.

I needed to quash this fast. "Can't we use a psychologist or something?"

Paul smiled. "I thought of that, but typically, they're there to deal with dysfunction. A matchmaker is perfect. We need to lean into what's been said. You admit you're a workaholic. You know nothing about dating—that's our expert's job —but the core value of ProtectedLove is the safety of dating in this current age. People are meeting online and getting catfished. How safe is an app? You can't help but wonder about the risks. So you'll be killing two birds with one stone —ensuring dating safety and building your knowledge in this —making you and Optium a good fit for this project and app."

I shook my head. "Why does this feel like it'll go over like a turd in a punch bowl?"

"Because you're a pessimist." This from Jace.

"If you're determined to use a matchmaker, let me see your list. I want a say in the pick."

Paul nodded. "But we need to pick soon."

"I'll text you my list," Mom said.

"I'll get on it ASAP. I know we are battling a ticking clock. I'm still skeptical about this plan working."

Paul's smile was smug. He was very sure of his plan. "We lean into the fact that you can't just stifle the need to protect people. It's who you are. And maybe if Citra's sister is willing, we share her story, which showcases the fact that women are the most vulnerable. How could you not look to find ways to protect them and anyone else who is most at risk of being taken advantage of?"

I stood. I needed to go home and get some sleep. "With all this leaning, it's a wonder I don't fall over flat on my face and all this blows up around me."

"Crisis averted," Jace said.

My mother and Paul clearly thought Jace was talking about the plan, but I knew he wasn't. Jace was talking about them wanting to bring Sabrina in to help. An impossible option. I'm sure deep down Jace would like to see his two closest buds be friendly again, but I'd destroyed any chance of that when I walked away. It didn't matter that I'd done it to protect her. Jace knew Sabrina needed to stay as far away from me as possible.

The trouble was, she was the only girl I'd ever wanted.The one girl I'd thought I would be spending forever with. In my desk drawer, under several files, was a worn-out picture of her, taken the day before we were supposed to get married. She was getting a piggyback ride from me and smiling over my shoulder, looking like all was good in the world. Jace was in the picture too.

Had I known that a few hours later it would all come crashing down... Well, I still wasn't sure what else I could have done. And she hated me now. There was that.

"I get a final say on who the love expert is," I said firmly.

Jace was the only one who knew my father was behind what had happened that day. Bringing Sabrina in would be like pouring fuel on this fire my father had started.

I returned my attention to Paul. "Are we in agreement?" If I could control who the love expert was, maybe this stupid plan was doable.

Paul pushed off the wall. "It's closing in on tomorrow. To stay ahead of this, we need to have some press releases out by six a.m." He looked at his watch. "I'll give you five hours to sleep and get me the name of your pick, and then we have to put this all in motion. It's one thing to make a statement that you're gonna be testing the app, including dating, and tools of the project for flaws. But we need to start showing that before Dalton or anyone else can respond. We need to capture everyone's attention."

I nodded. I could see the merit of Paul's plan. For a second, I considered the advantages of having Sabrina do the job.

Shit, did I really just think that? I must be loopy from lack of sleep. No. Sabrina was a definite no.

I swiped my keys off my desk as I stood, then walked toward the door. I stopped when I got close to Jace and poked a finger in his chest. "I'm counting on you to watch my back here." He would know that meant I wanted him to make sure they didn't catch wind of Sabrina.

Jace gave one sharp nod. "You need me to drive you home?"

I shook my head and started to move away, but Jace

jumped up, reached out, and grabbed me by the shoulder. "I'm glad you're okay. And I'm glad Peru is over. All things aside, you can't keep living like you have nine lives. As I see it, you'll be getting some much-needed downtime."

He gave me a wry smile.

Jace and I had never guided each other wrong, and at the moment, he looked like he'd had more sleep than me, having flown in when he heard I'd been shot. I knew I could count on him.

I headed toward the door. When I got to Paul, I paused and patted the center of his chest with an open hand. "Okay, Paul. Five hours, and we'll pick a love expert."

"You won't regret it," Paul said.

"He doesn't do regret," Jace said. "That's not his hang-up."

I only had one regret, and it ate at me every day. I'd sworn to never have another one. And I wouldn't have any regrets about destroying my father. The man deserved it.

Chapter Two
SABRINA

I was a hard woman to get a meeting with, and I liked it that way. So when the sleek black Bentley with tinted windows pulled up as I was exiting my potential client's penthouse apartment, I didn't think anything of it. That car wasn't there for me. I stepped around the car and looked for my Uber.

"Ms. Holloway?"

I turned to find a tall woman standing beside the back passenger door, one hand on the hood. Evening was giving away to night, with only the streetlamps and the passing headlights of cars offering occasional light. The building's light was pointed toward the doorway.

This was totally an opening for a true-crime story. The night, the poor lighting, a stranger calling my name... Yeah, women serial killers were rare, but not unheard-of.

I put my hand on my phone resting in my raincoat pocket. "I'm sorry?" I hadn't expected someone to call my name.

"You're Sabrina Holloway?" The woman was walking

toward me. "Of course you are. You..." She shook her head. "Sorry, I'm Morgan Barker."

She stuck out her hand. The woman was in her mid-fifties, with blondish silver hair and immaculately applied makeup that drew attention to her blue eyes. When she smiled, a dimple appeared on her right cheek. Something about her seemed familiar, but I couldn't place it.

I looked around, then back at the woman and shook her hand. "How did you find me?" I found it hard to believe my assistant would give out my whereabouts.

"Gossip among my bridge group led me here. Mindy is in that group. You were the matchmaker Jace Shepard used, correct?" She gestured toward the car. "Can we ride and talk? We'll take you back to your hotel."

My Uber pulled up, and I hesitated, taking a step away from her and toward my ride. This situation was highly unusual, and just because the woman had thrown out Jace's name didn't mean she was legit.

"I want to offer you a job." She indicated to the apartment building I had just exited. "Mindy is fickle. She could change her mind in a flash. My offer would be a good backup plan. While Mindy is processing all this, you could be helping me out."

Mindy Fisher was one hundred percent a waffler. I'd picked up on that right away. She'd even canceled our first meeting. But scared people did that, and I believed Mindy wanted love more than she was scared. Mindy was matchable. And I had convinced her of that. She had the contract and was going to sign it once her lawyer reviewed it. But that didn't mean the offer of extra money was something I was willing to look away from. Normally, I was not one to rank money so highly, but that had all changed with my new goal.

"You're looking for a match?" I asked. I'd told Mindy to share my name with any of her friends who might be wanting a match.

Morgan smiled. "No, I'm good, thank you. We're not looking for a match but more to tap into your expertise." She pointed at the car again. "Please."

I assessed Morgan Barker. She didn't seem twitchy even though she kept trying to get me in the car. The Seattle autumn day was a blustery, wet one, and Morgan Barker was dressed perfectly for it in a Burberry raincoat. The woman screamed money. Not that serial killers couldn't be rich. Or fake it. I'd seen enough heist movies to be wary.

But Morgan had piqued my curiosity. Besides, I had a few hours to kill as my flight was scheduled for later that night. And where else did I have to go? Back to my hotel alone so I could get my bags and go to the airport alone so I could then fly home to Texas alone to an empty house. Alone sucked, so much so that I was willing to take my chances with the stranger before me.

I took a picture of the car's tag and sent a text to Jace:

> If I die it's because of you and this is the
> person who did it.

"I'm gonna ride with her," I told the Uber driver. I took my phone out of my raincoat pocket, also Burberry, in case you were wondering, and closed out my ride request. "I canceled the ride but gave you a tip."

The driver nodded and eased back into traffic.

Morgan gave me a bright smile. "I apologize if you catch me staring. You just remind me of someone I lost a long time ago, and it's caught me off guard." Her voice was soft and buttery and filled with kindness. She held her arm out for me to precede her into the car.

As Morgan slipped into the seat next to me, I said, "I hope the person I remind you of was someone you liked." Maybe it was her mortal enemy, and Morgan was totally going to kill me.

Morgan looked away, a wistful expression on her face. "She was the best. We grew up together but lost touch after college. Thank you so much for seeing me on such short notice. I'll get right to it, as time is not on our side." She opened a small cabinet built into the seat in front of her. "Drink?"

I shook my head. "I'm all ears."

"I'm part owner in a company called Optium. Have you heard of it?"

I searched my memory bank. "Optium? I don't think so."

Morgan studied me for a second.

"You're surprised," I said. "Should I know the company?"

"It's just that our CEO is... He's been getting a lot of press lately, and he's a leading expert in the field of security. Optium is a security and personal-protection business. We offer executive professional protection and threat-assessment training for schools and universities—how to recognize signs of impending violence and how to respond. But Optium has been wanting to branch out into the area of personal safety, including home security, self-defense, and dating."

Ah yes, I'd seen something about it in the press. But I'd paid little attention. My clientele didn't use apps. They required far more privacy and vetting due to their status and wealth.

I shook my head. "Sorry."

Morgan nodded, but the surprise in her expression didn't fade. "The program Optium created is twofold. They have a dating app and also provide information about all the ways people can protect themselves, with notifications on where self-defense classes are. And for those who have children, what things you should and should not do, like post first-day-of-school pictures with their name, grade, and school."

I made a note of that, not wanting to make that mistake when I had kids. I was intrigued and wondered what my part in this was going to be.

"In the last eighteen hours, our company has come under attack," she continued.

"Attack? That's ironic for a security company." I adjusted in my seat so I could both see Morgan and make sure the driver wasn't going to pass my hotel.

"Very much so. If I wasn't so invested in the company, I would laugh. We had a breech, and some intellectual property was stolen and given to our competitor. And to add fuel to the fire, a smear campaign has started regarding our CEO. The gist is that while he may be good at protecting high-profile people, what does he know about dating and, specifically, women's safety issues? Now our competitor has a huge advantage because they already have a foot in this market. This attack affects both our reputation and brand, which will bleed over into our executive-protection division."

"That sounds ridiculous. Doesn't Optium's work speak for itself?" I knew as soon as the words were out how stupid they sounded. With the internet and misinformation, no one knew what truth was anymore. People loved a good train wreck, and that was exactly what smear campaigns were.

Morgan chewed her lip. "We've also just had a security

fail with a protection detail. People were hurt. As you can imagine, that doesn't help us either."

"Who would want to hire or use a company with a bad reputation and which has likely lost clients."

"Precisely." She clutched her hands in her lap. "Not to mention how priceless social proof is."

"Sounds personal." And it sounded like this woman was worried. Maybe she had a lot invested in the company. Money made people do crazy things.

"It is. We know who is behind it." Morgan pressed a perfectly manicured finger to her lips as if she were telling herself to not speak. A moment later, she removed the finger. "I'm sorry. I was about to say some unkind things about our attacker. Where was I?"

"You were going to tell me what my role in this would be." Now came the juicy stuff.

"Optium has put a lot of time and money in this new division. We're not willing to lose it now. So the plan is to launch early but test the products and classes in real time, be honest about the flaws and show the fixes. Build customer trust. And since our CEO is a securities expert, and not an expert of relationships or love, we thought to pair him with one. And that one is you."

"Will he be doing the dating? Will he be the one having these in-real-time experiences?" This might be the weirdest potential client ever.

"Yes. I'll be honest. He's not crazy about the idea. He's a lone wolf. But he's the perfect test subject, as he's not dated in long time. He's very rusty. Though if a match were to genuinely happen, no one will really complain." She sounded more like a mother than an employee.

"He might. People don't like getting handled unless they ask for it."

She waved away my words. "Falling in love would be good for him. He's such a loner, and he's not the easiest person to get to know. But that is not the objective. What we want to do is to develop a safe online space for people who are looking to find love... among other things."

"Okay, so how long is this job, and what are the hours? And is it located here?"

This was an interesting proposition, and I was intrigued. I was a pro at helping people find just the right fit for their emergency. Make-believe wives and fiancées were a niche specialty of mine. My success rate of those ending up in happy and fulfilling marriages was over ninety percent, all of whom are still married to this day. But helping the everyday person—that would be a new challenge. My clients had a range of things they wanted in a partner. Often I worked for the wealthy, who put money at the top of their list, believing if each person entered the arrangement with their own money, then the other would be more comfortable signing prenups. And those potential partners were limited. Matching on an app, on the other hand, involved a massive number of people. It was inevitable that things would go wrong.

"We can work all that out tomorrow if you'll meet with us and decide to take the job."

She was hedging.

"What aren't you telling me?" I was the kind of girl who believed in just saying it all up front. When people didn't communicate, lives were ruined and hearts were broken. I should know.

Morgan chuckled. "You have me figured out. I think

maybe I didn't emphasize enough about the... um, shall we say, abrasive exterior of the CEO." She put up both hands to stop any comments. "Don't get me wrong—he's amazing with clients. It's the personal-life stuff where he's a bear. He's resisting this, even though he knows it's the right thing to do."

I liked prickly men. They usually had a story to explain their attitudes, and I was good at finding the right person to heal the wound. And these prickly men were looking to be part of pair. "Do you know what his deal is?"

Morgan reached into the seat cabinet and pulled out a bottle of seltzer. She took a long drink from it before speaking. "Besides a cold and critical father, who I believe to be at the root of all the problems? I can't say. Maybe a lost love, but that could just be rumors."

I pressed my lips together as I studied the woman. My success rate was high because I knew what clients to not take on. This situation was straddling the fence. I wouldn't be matching—I'd be coaching, trying to get a guy to change who didn't want to change. That was hard on a good day, when the guy wanted it, but damn near impossible if he was fighting it.

As much as I liked a good challenge, I did not like one that required me to bang my head against the wall. This situation had the markings of just that, with a difficult CEO who purposefully avoided entanglements. Changing that mindset was sometimes like pushing a two-ton truck up a hill in high heels. Impossible unless you were Superwoman. And I was good—just not that good.

The car pulled into the hotel's porte-cochère and glided to a stop at the sliding glass doors. I squared my shoulders as I prepared to let the woman down, putting on my calm yet compassionate face. I'd found that if I appeared this way, the other party would as well. Crazy how one person's state of mind could affect other people's.

"I'm sorry. I don't think I'm a good fit. I'm not sure—"

"Wait. I have done a terrible job describing him." Morgan picked up her phone and started tapping the screen. "He may sound hopeless, and maybe that's how I think of him, but perhaps fresh eyes would see him in a different light. You could meet him and decide then, no?" She slid the phone across the seat toward me. "He's quite handsome, don't you think?"

I smiled at her as I picked up the phone. It took my brain exactly 1.2 seconds to register the picture. Thank heavens I had already schooled my expression, and praises to my daddy for teaching me how to have a poker face at the tender age of five. Those two skills came together in perfect harmony.

I didn't gasp. I didn't look at Morgan in surprise. I didn't even lick my lips or shudder in revulsion—a reaction I had once upon a time hoped to have if I ever saw his face again.

No. I blinked once. Then again.

Calvin Beckett.

The one and only man who'd broken my heart. That thought made me want to snort in anger. Broken my heart? More like ripped it out and batted it around with a wiffle-ball bat. Those dang holes made the sting hurt a thousand times more.

Before that, our relationship had been perfect, or so I'd thought. Hindsight was twenty-twenty and all that.

So Cal was a security expert. I found that interesting. Apparently, blocking notifications about him on all my devices had panned out. I was totally oblivious to Cal's life, and I wanted it that way. Doing a Google search out of curiosity and finding Cal married—or even worse, married with children—was something I wasn't sure I could cope with. So I'd set my life up to limit, and hopefully negate, my chances of ever having that experience.

Yet here was the universe, delivering the notification in person. That bitch.

I set the phone down and tapped the picture with my nail. "This is your CEO?"

Morgan nodded. "Handsome, right?"

She'd get no commitment from me. "Mmm."

"Do you know him?" She arched one brow in question.

I wondered how much she knew, assuming Jace being her source and all. I glanced at the face that had been such an important part of my life. Man, I hated him. Just as much as I still loved him. There was a fine line between those two emotions.

He'd changed. The lines at the end of his smile used to be deep grooves from his constant laughter and ease. Those were gone. His warm and inviting eyes were shuttered and vacant. Sure, to strangers, the image would look professional and exactly what one would want in a security expert. Cal looked dark, like he knew about the scary things hidden under beds and in closets and that he could single-handedly destroy them. In a movie, he'd play a Navy SEAL or some other sort of badass, with his dark hair, piercing dark-blue eyes, strong jaw, and slightly crooked nose from a few too many bar fights.

But I knew a different side to this face. Like a harlequin's mask, neither side was the real face.

I looked up at Morgan and shook my head. "I don't know this person." I probably never had.

"Oh." Morgan blinked rapidly.

"Why am I having this conversation with you instead of him?"

Is this Cal's way of bringing me back into his life, to teach him to date? I found that hard to believe. He wasn't a cruel person.

She bit her lip and looked like she was considering what to tell me. "He's asked to have final say with hiring a love expert. The company PR guy and I think we need to get this rolling sooner rather than later, and you are the best. Your reputation precedes you. When I heard you were in town, I thought it was a sign that we should ask you, and if we waited for him to weigh in, you'd be gone."

Hmm. Close scrutiny of her expression told me she was telling the truth.

"Well, um, do you think you might be able to help him? Of course, we will pay you. And pay you well. Twenty-five thousand for a minimum of two weeks for your consultation services. Each week after that will be negotiated on a week-by-week basis."

Holy crap. That was half of my goal amount for only two weeks of work. I felt lightheaded just thinking about how quickly I could have that money in my account.

Who cared that I'd spent the first five years after getting dumped by this guy trying to recalibrate and figure out who I was or the last five years trying to forget he existed.

The real question was how badly I wanted to reach my current life-and-money goals. The sooner I reached them, the sooner I could move to step three. And I really, really wanted to move to step three.

I stared at the phone. I'd locked up that hurt a long time ago, knowing if I saw him again, it would all come flooding back. And I'd been right—I was sitting in a soup of memories and heartache at that very minute.

He'd told me it was over and that separating was for the best. That was it. Nothing more.

I'd begged like a fool for further explanation. All I got was a view of his back as he turned and walked out the door. For good. I never saw him again. And though that seemed cruel, in my heart of hearts I knew there had to have been more at play. What hurt was him not believing in us enough to address it as a couple.

Did I have closure? Nope, not a bit. Did I want it? Yep. Was getting it worth the possible setback it might cost me? Heck, yeah, I deserved it. You didn't give someone three years of your life and run off to elope only to be dumped hours before the wedding and then not believe you deserved closure.

And to get paid to get my closure. Boom! I'd never sought him out after he left, believing that the universe would deliver closure. And boy howdy, had it delivered.

Cal needed a rescue, and his company had come to me. Ironic? Coincidence? Did I care? Nope. Lying in my lap was the golden goose.

Okay, but think of the job. Can you be his love expert and help him?

Barf. That's what that thought makes me want to do.

But this was a win-win situation. I'd get my closure, and he'd get the help he needed. Plus, there was the money. Hello. And we were both adults, not emotional college students.

I couldn't see the downside to this. My dad used to say, "The house always wins," and in this scenario, I was the house. I always had the option to walk.

Could you really leave that money behind?

Yes? No? Probably no.

Cal was the past. My goal was my future. I would have to keep that in mind.

I smiled at Morgan. "I don't know if I can help, but I like your idea of meeting him and seeing if we can make something happen."

Oh, something was going to happen all right. And Cal wouldn't see it coming. I got a little bit of pleasure knowing that.

Was I being a little petty? Sure. Did I care? Not too much, actually.

Morgan beamed at me. "Can we pick you up first thing in the morning? We can fly you home after that, considering you are missing your flight tonight." She grimaced. "Timing being what it is and all that."

"Yes, that will work." I was already reaching for both my handbag and the door handle at the same time.

"Excellent. Michael, my driver here, will pick you up at seven a.m. sharp. Thank you so much, Sabrina."

I felt slightly bad not being fully transparent with this woman. But all I had to do was recall the harshness of Cal's words and the anger in his face, and I was able to stuff any second-guessing or misgivings into a deep hole.

"Oh, don't thank me yet. This could all go horribly wrong in a heartbeat." I would have loved to place a high-stakes wager that they were not going to prepare Cal for my visit, and his reaction to me would be all it would take for this plan to crumble. That was going to be the main obstacle to me keeping this job and getting this money.

But, truthfully, I couldn't wait to see his reaction. The anticipation might just kill me.

Chapter Three

SABRINA

B right and early the next morning, on yet another rainy Seattle day, I walked out through my hotel lobby and got into a waiting Bentley. I decided to stop overthinking my choice. I'd spent the majority of the night tossing and turning, playing out a billion scenarios.

I would soon find out if seeing Calvin again ten years later was a good idea. But to prepare myself, I'd written out three scenarios on the hotel's mirror.

- 1. Highly unlikely, but he could drop to his knees, ask for forgiveness, and tell me how much he missed me.
- 2. He could be stunned to see me. We have a cordial conversation, and he either accepts me for the job or tells me he can't work with me. I'd leave with nothing resolved, feeling more like a stranger than a former girlfriend. And without 25K.
- 3. He could get ugly when he sees me.

As the private car sped toward—well, I didn't know what, exactly, or where—I did some more internet searching. With the previous night's investigations, I'd learned the headquarters for Optium was near Pike Place Market, but there was no address or picture. It could be any of the tall buildings or even under the market, for all I knew, which made the experience unnerving and unfamiliar. I always liked to know way more about the person who hired me than I did with this Cal, who felt like a total stranger. I never would have guessed private security could be a career option for him. Jumping in front of bullets had never been something he'd shown an interest in. But realizing this just affirmed that I hadn't known all of Cal—just the part he'd wanted to show me. And the fact that he'd never introduced me to his family, stating they'd had a falling-out, had been a red flag I'd ignored.

Smartly, Optium Security barely had an online profile other than a few podcasts and cable TV shows that Cal had appeared on. And, of course, the first wave of the smear campaign. The article was ugly, the core of it being that while Cal and a few other employees of Optium were protecting a high-profile client, something had gone sideways, and people had been hurt. The article used its one fact, that this had just happened within the last twenty-four hours, to not include any other actual facts but instead use the "situation is evolving and will be updated as more information becomes available" line to let people create their own narratives. A rush to throw shade, in my experience.

Then the article went into Optium's new division of personal safety and how ill-equipped the company was to enter this arena. Nothing I read sounded like the guy I'd once known. I was going to approach this as if he was a stranger, because it seemed he was. And based on the way we'd broken up, he kind of always had been.

Would it even faze him to have his old college girlfriend try to help him in the love department? I was honest enough with myself to admit that if he wasn't, even the slightest bit, I would be hurt. Emotions were tricky, illogical bastards.

Morgan hadn't been kidding when she said Cal was single and had not been in a relationship for some time. In fact, there were no hints of any relationship at all. I tried not to create a story to explain why. That would be super unhealthy even if I did find a bit of satisfaction in knowing he'd been single.

I wasn't one to talk, but I'd dated more than Cal, it would seem.

After opening up my notes app, I clicked on the folder at the top labeled List and other good tidbits. My thumbs hovered over the keyboard. This was the place where I purged my thoughts. Well, here and on the mirrors and windows in my house. A good dry-erase marker and glass provided the best platform for notes. Or words of encouragement. Or reminders of to not be stupid.

What I'd added to the note last night:

Don't forget why you're doing this.

- 1.The money gets you closer to the goal.
- 2. Your goal is your future. Cal is your past.
- 3.Closure is a bonus. Purge your demons.
- 4. You are not the same hopeless romantic he once knew. That girl is G.O.N.E. Gone.

When the majority of your job was to arrange marriage matches built on partnership, love just didn't look like the be-all and end-all. A long time ago, my pain had given way to anger, and though a decade had passed, seeing his image on that phone the previous day had produced a feeling equivalent to getting a large area of hair waxed—a quick and unexpected, yet barely tolerable pain, followed by irritation and tenderness the rest of the day.

Did that mean I was speeding toward a nightmare?

That's cool. No problem. Whatever.

I hoped after today, my old wound would now be a smooth and beautiful, barely noticeable scar. I chewed at a thumbnail. I should just go back to my hotel, grab my bags, go hide at the airport, and catch the first flight home. I should leave well enough alone—find another way to make some extra money.

But the more time it took to raise the money, the further down the adoption list I went. And that meant extending the wait time. And I was so ready for a family. Being a party of one sucked.

The car pulled up in front of a stationery store. We were downtown, so the buildings varied in height, and they nestled one upon the next, making it hard to see where one ended and the other started.

"We're here," the driver said, catching my eye in the rearview mirror.

I pointed to the stationery store, wondering if Cal's office was cloaked by journals and paper goods. "Do I go through there?"

He rolled down the passenger window and leaned across the seat to point. "That door, the black one."

Off to the side of the stationery store and before the next building was a discreet black metal door with no sign or anything. It blended in so well with the black-and-brown brick of the buildings that I'd written it off as insignificant.

"Ah, got it. Thanks." I exited the car and only had a moment's hesitation before opening the heavy black door.

Beyond it was a brightly lit, well-appointed waiting room. I looked back out the door. Now would be the time to bail if I were going to. I met the driver's eyes. He gave me a quick smile and eased the car from the curb and into traffic.

It was do-or-die time. I turned around and walked in.

Behind a desk, a tall, lithe, dark-skinned woman in her mid-twenties stood and held out her hand. "You must be Ms. Holloway. We are expecting you. I'm Citra Jackson."

Her grip was gentle yet firm. My daddy had put a lot of stock in a person's handshake, and I did as well. Citra had a lovely smile and warm eyes. I liked her immediately.

She took my raincoat from me. "I'll take you up."

The lobby was modern and simple. Light tones of beige and grays paired with dark blues had a calming effect. Citra led me through another door, this one also made of metal. Behind the door were a few offices. The elevator was next to the stairs. We took it to the third floor.

I was wearing loose, flowy midnight-blue pants with deep pockets—because if pockets could be had, I wanted them—and a gauzy cream-and-blue polka-dot blouse. I hiked my bag higher on my shoulder and stuck my hands in my pockets to hide my nervousness. Calvin D— for Dumbass— Beckett was about to have a no-good, very bad day?

The elevator door slid open, and I looked directly into an office across the hall. I rolled back my shoulders to ease the tension. It would not be cool for him to see me nervous. This was it, the moment I'd often thought about over the ten years we'd been apart, and... well, I still didn't believe I was actually going to see Cal again.

We entered a dark room. "This is Cal's office. He's in a... meeting, but Paul, that's the PR guy, said to have you wait here. They should be done soon." Citra hung my coat on a coat-tree in the corner, next to another jacket, one that belonged to a dark-gray suit. Cal's, I assumed.

"Can I get you anything to drink?"

"No, thank you." I took a seat on the couch that was perpendicular to Cal's desk.

Citra nodded once. "If you need anything, press one on the phone there"—she pointed to the desk—"and someone will come running."

"Thank you."

Citra left, closing the door behind her. I blew out a slow, steady breath. I was in Cal's office, and any minute now, he would come in and see me. Ten years of avoiding all things Cal was coming to an end.

My hands began to sweat, and I rubbed them together like I was massaging in lotion. I'd found this to be a better solution than wiping them down my pants. Then I used the time to try to figure out this new Cal.

Nothing about this office felt like Cal or smelled like him either. Not that I really could recall the smell—it was more that I remembered how it made me feel. This space was... sterile. It lacked personality and history. A narrow floor-to-ceiling bookcase was tucked between two credenzas. I knew Optium had several large-profile clients, but there were no pictures of them on the bookcase. Instead, I found a handful of copies of hardback books, two different titles. The author was C. D. Beckett.

In my search, I hadn't found that Cal had written any

books. From a PR standpoint, that wasn't good. From a privacy one, the lack of discovery was excellent.

In college, Cal had been a law student. His dad had expected him to work for the family hotel empire, but Cal had been toying with taking over his grandparents' cattle ranch instead. Clearly, he'd taken a sharp left turn away from both of those.

I'd been right when I'd looked at his picture on Morgan Barker's phone. I didn't know this person. This Cal.

Other books lined the shelves: books on weapons, travel guides to various places, and law books. If I hadn't had a past with Cal, and had I not seen a picture of him, I'd have had no idea who this office belonged to or what sort of person he was.

This was not the space of the Cal I knew. My Cal had been neat but not without clutter. He never threw away his notes and often would ask me to organize them in binders for him just in case he needed them later.

This office did not belong to a just-in-case-I-might-need-it person. This guy didn't live in the gray. It was all black and white for him.

From out in the hall, I heard voices. I paused to listen. Two men were coming toward me. I considered going back to the couch but instead went to stand in front of his desk which had me facing the door. Leaning back against it, I crossed my arms.

The door flung open, and Cal Beckett stepped inside, the words he'd been about to say falling away. He stared at me. He blinked once and then again, his mouth ajar.

My heart stuttered, tripping over itself, then righted and resumed its pounding, only quicker this time. All the times I'd pictured this moment, I'd never imagined the power of the feelings that were slamming into me with hurricane force. I was glad I'd been leaning on his desk.

He was just like I remembered but nothing like I remembered, all at the same time. Whatever he had gone through in the last twenty-four hours had left him looking beat-up. He sported a black eye and a split lip, and though I couldn't see any sign of it—which told me it probably wasn't that bad—I knew he'd been shot in the arm.

If I looked hard, closing one eye and squinting with the other, I could see the Cal who'd braided my hair when we watched TV and massaged my feet after a long day. He had the same features: the same dark-blue eyes and chestnut hair. But this Cal was taller and broader and looked meaner. My Cal had been quick to laugh. This guy looked like he hadn't laughed in years. And he was standing so stiff and straight I thought maybe he had a stick up his ass. Across his face flickered short-lived emotions, and had I not been watching, I would have missed them; he'd swiped them away so fast.

I raised a brow. "Cal."

He pointed to me. His shirtsleeve was rolled up and showcased a tanned, heavily corded, muscular arm. This Cal was solid power. He was oversized and could easily be described as having a menacing presence.

His face flushed red, and in a deep, gravelly voice, he said, "No. No. No."

Chapter Four
SABRINA

Your first response is to say no, and you're angry? Like what the hell, man? No to what? To just seeing me? I'm the one hurt here, not you, so this no doesn't make sense.

I smiled, showing him his words hadn't bothered me. When I'd told Morgan I didn't recognize this guy, I'd been right. Whoever this guy was, he was not a happy person.

I pointed at his face and made small circles with my finger. "What happened there?" He didn't need to know I knew.

"I was shot and had to apprehend the suspect single-handedly. He didn't go willingly." He pressed his lips together and gave me a quick scan.

Then he pointed to me, then pointed to the door—the universal sign for get out. I considered showing him a universal sign I knew.

Another guy, one with wire-rimmed glasses and a day's worth of facial hair, came in behind him. "She's our match-maker. She's here to help. Cal, this is—"

"I know who she is, and she needs to leave." He stuck his hands in his pockets. By the bulk they made, I knew they were fisted. "Sabrina, you can't be here," he said curtly.

That wasn't what I'd been expecting. I'd wanted him to be more shocked. Or surprised. Or embarrassed. Instead, he was angry.

Well, guess what, bucko? I'm angry too. I narrowed my eyes.

He stepped back to the door and yelled down the hallway. "Citra, get Michael to take Ms. Holloway back to... wherever it was that he picked her up from, and make sure she isn't seen."

Make sure she isn't seen? What the actual...? There was so much to unpack that I didn't even know where to start.

Cal looked back at me. "You're leaving, and you're leaving now."

Just one stinking minute, buddy. This was supposed to be my moment. I was in charge of when I left, and I hadn't gotten what I'd come for. Plus, I was being paid to be here.

I was about to tell him so when the glasses guy ushered Cal out of the room and slammed the door behind them. I glared at the door. He hadn't seen me in ten years, and he couldn't even muster a civil response to my presence. He jilted me. What right does he have to be angry?

I fumed, my mind racing with the many ways I could murder him. Morgan Barker had said he wasn't easy to get along with, so maybe his staff wouldn't care if I took him out. But not before I gave him a piece of my mind.

The odds of getting that chance looked slim, the odds of getting paid even slimmer. Shoot. Now I was disappointed.

Cal was nothing if not stubborn. That clearly hadn't changed over time. He was not going to let me keep this job.

I pushed off the desk and went to grab my purse. I was a step away when I turned back to his desk, a lovely old heavy mahogany piece with a glass top. It had been put there to protect the wood surface, but I knew the glass had another purpose.

There was really one thing left for me to do before I was whisked away. I wanted this job more than I wanted closure. From my purse, I retrieved an erasable white liquid chalk marker. I uncapped the tip as I moved to stand behind the desk, pushing his office chair out of the way.

Then, on his desk, I wrote the reasons he should keep me for the job. I listed three things I'd observed about him, none of them flattering. Each would be a hindrance to building customer trust.

Because I knew it would challenge him, I wrote, You can behave one of two ways. Your choice. I drew a picture of a donkey with an arrow from the words, and then I drew a rocket for the launch with money signs and stars all around it. I finished it with an arrow to the words.

Outside the door, the men whispered in heated tones. The doorknob jiggled as if someone had placed their hand on it to open but hesitated—a cue that my time was up. I recapped my marker as I moved away from the desk. As the door opened, I dropped onto the couch, stuffing the marker in my pocket.

The glasses guy entered first and smiled at me. Cal stalked in behind him and, without making eye contact, went to his desk. I watched his every step.

He grabbed the back of his office chair to pull it up to the desk and met my gaze, his expression devoid of emotion. "You need to go." He was like a broken record.

The glasses guy sighed. "Cal, we need her, and we just

agreed out there that you would shut up and let me do the talking, remember?"

I grinned.

Cal plopped into his chair and mumbled. "You agreed. I said nothing."

My anger ignited like a quickly lit flare. He was knee-deep in trying to save a part of his business but would rather act like this than ask for or accept my help. The nerve. I made sure my smile never wavered.

The glasses guy stared at Cal. "Are you done?"

Cal waved a dismissive hand.

"Good." He stepped up to me, blocking my view of Cal, and offered his hand. "I apologize. I'm Paul Runyon. I'm the PR exec for Optium. Please don't stand," he said as I moved to get up.

I sank back into the couch but took his hand. "Paul Runyon? Did your parents do that on purpose?" A name like that meant he had to have a good sense of humor.

"Yep."

"Do you still speak to them?"

He looked like a straight-laced guy, but the deep laugh lines around his eyes told me a different story. "They're schoolteachers. They thought it was clever. And having a name like Paul Runyon gave me lots of early practice with handling PR."

I chuckled. "I suppose it would. Sabrina Holloway. It's nice to meet you."

"Did you write on my desk?" Cal barked from behind Paul.

Paul turned toward Cal, and I once again had a view of him. He was tapping the picture of the donkey.

"I am not a..." His finger slid down to the corner of his desk.

"I didn't say you were. I said you had a choice to be one or the other. It's your call."

His cheeks turned pink. Not going to lie, I found that rewarding.

Paul wandered over to the desk and started to read. He covered his mouth as he tried to disguise a laugh with a cough. "She's got you there." He tapped the desk.

Cal looked straight ahead, not making eye contact with anyone. "I am not standoffish."

"We all tell ourselves lies, Calvin." I stood and picked up my purse. "Like, I told myself that maybe we could help each other out. But this isn't going to work." I focused my attention on Paul. "I can't help soften someone's image when there is nothing soft about them." Then I threw in a zinger for funsies. "Never mind trying to find potential compatible matches." I moved to the coat-tree to get my jacket.

Cal shot up from his chair. "You're honestly here to help me date?" He turned to Paul. "You all hired her to match me?"

"Isn't that what you need a love expert for?" I shrugged.

Paul said, "You know you have to try the app, and if something more were to come of it, then what's wrong with that?" He shrugged.

I looked at Paul but pointed to Cal. "I'm very good at what I do, but that? I'm not that good. Meeting people and getting to know them is hard. Relaxing around them takes time and willingness." I shifted my attention to Cal. "Relaxing, for you, is unobtainable." So long as you have that stick shoved up your ass. "Admit it. You don't relax often."

We glared at each other. There was nothing in Cal's look to indicate we had a past, much less one that could have resulted in a happily ever after. It was hard to believe that the shell of the man before me had been my great love. And how was I supposed to work two weeks with him when we couldn't do two minutes? My money goal burst in front of me and was whisked away in the wind. I had to get out of there before my façade cracked.

Chapter Five
CAL

Sabrina Holloway. Boom. She was a roundhouse kick to the solar plexus. I'd walked into my office and nearly tripped over myself when I saw her standing by my desk.

And then I panicked. How she'd come to be here I'd find out later. But she had to go.

And then she was leaving, and I wanted her to stay. She calmly strolled out of my office like there wasn't history between us, and I was no more important to her than a pesky gnat she'd taken a second to squash before moving along. Her backside was just as lovely as her front. Sabrina Holloway had been a knockout in college, but now—holy shit, she took my breath away. I'd walked into my office, never expecting she would be in there, and nearly lost my mind when I saw her. My body immediately betrayed me. My heart jumped into my throat, and my hands itched to renew themselves with how she felt. I wanted to hug her. I wanted to smile and tell her what a shitty twenty-four hours

I'd had. She'd always been a good listener. I experienced a familiar flush of want that I hadn't felt in years.

I should let her go. That was the best—the smartest—move for both of us. I would not drag her into this dogfight with my father. She'd been his target once before. I wouldn't let that happen again.

But it hurt to watch her leave. I'd followed her career over the years, and no matter how many pictures of her I stared at, none captured just how remarkable her midnight hair, blue eyes, and cherry lips were. She was so much better in person.

And she was doing what I wanted. She was leaving.

I pounded my desk twice as I fought the internal struggle between what I wanted and what was right. I wanted her to stay. She needed to leave to stay out of my dad's crosshairs.

I stared at the words she'd written in her loopy cursive: Three things this room tells me about you.

- 1.You're cold inside, which can also mean bitter and lonely.
- How a man constantly surrounded by people could be lonely, I wasn't sure. But bitter, yeah. I was bitter. Other than this company, nothing had turned out the way I wanted. I knew why, and it had been a choice I'd made, but yeah, I was bitter about it.
- 2. There are no pictures to celebrate your business success. None even on your book. I think it's because you're mad at yourself. Is it hard to look in the mirror? How can you open yourself up for dating if this is in the way?

- For me, reflecting meant regretting, and I didn't do that, so looking in the mirror was a waste of time.
- 3. The Cal I knew and the Cal you are today are not the same person. And something tells me this Cal isn't very happy.

She'd gotten all that from my office. Or maybe, like me, she'd done an internet research. Either way, she'd gotten it right. And that infuriated me.

I pounded the desk one more time, then pushed off, giving in to my wants. In six long strides, I was outside my office and closing in behind her as she maniacally pressed the down button as if that would make the elevator car come quicker.

"Would you really be a love consultant for me? Set me up with other women? Watch me date?" I stood perpendicular to her and pressed one hand on the wall by the elevator doors. I leaned closer.

She side-eyed me once, then kept her attention on the elevator. "Why is it you have the slowest elevator on the planet? It's three lousy floors. The Empire State Building's elevators travel twelve hundred feet per minute. Your building is, what, thirty feet? Travels at a sloth's speed."

"The Empire State Building is one hundred two floors. If it didn't travel fast, people on the higher floors would have to live there, going out once a week, or else spend their lives on the elevator. Answer me. You could really set me up?" Each thud of my rapidly beating heart echoed in my ears.

The elevator chimed, and the doors slid open. She walked into the elevator and turned to face me, a haughty look on her face. "Of course. That's my job. That is what I was hired to do. Why wouldn't I be able to?"

I stepped to the threshold and stuck out a hand to stop the door from closing. The last thing I needed was for everyone to find out the extent of our history and jump on it. This train wreck was already off the rails. Bringing Sabrina in was a total derailment catastrophe. So I kept my voice low.

"Because of everything between us." I gestured to her and then to myself. "I'm the guy who took your virginity. That's why."

Her lips parted, hinting at a gasp, her cheeks going pink. Then her eyes narrowed, and I knew I'd sparked her temper. Sabrina had a tell. She stepped forward and rested a slender hand over the left side of my chest. It took everything I had to not flex.

"Calvin." She looked up at me through sooty lashes. "Calvin, Calvin, Calvin." She used my full name because she knew I hated it, and with each iteration she drummed her fingers against my chest in a distracting manner. What she said next gutted me. "You may have been the first explorer, but you weren't the last."

And then, to get me out of the elevator, she shoved me hard, her hand on the center of my chest, pushing me backward. I was over six foot three and a solid two hundred twenty pounds, and she still managed to knock me off-balance. I caught my footing as the doors to the elevator were sliding shut. I could tell by her stance she had a finger on a button, probably the one for closing the doors. She gave me a finger wave right before they snapped together, and the hum of the machine indicated its descent.

I stared at the steel doors. I had no right to be angry. She wasn't my girl anymore. Yet the scenarios my imagination created weren't kind to me. Logically, I knew I'd relinquished any right to have her. And I knew doing so meant she would find happiness elsewhere. I just didn't want to think about it. Each internet search I'd done had been an act of torture. Yes, I was a masochist. With bated breath, I scanned the information from my searches, expecting at any time to see a wedding announcement or Sabrina in the arms of another.

Sabrina Holloway. She'd been everything—breath, laughter, warmth, and hope. I put a hand on my chest over the spot where hers had been and thought I could still feel heat.

"We need her, Cal. We need to get on top of this story," Paul said behind me.

I stared at the closed doors, my racing heart returning to normal under my palm. I let out a slow exhalation, then turned to Paul. "Why do we need her specifically?"

My own father had tried to control me by threatening the one thing I wanted to keep safe. Then, because he still couldn't control me, he'd struck again, only this time, his actions had brought that very person he'd worked so hard to erase from my life right back into it. What a fucking mess.

When Paul didn't answer, I brushed past him as I went into my office. We could not use Sabrina.

Paul followed me in. "She's one of the best. She's got an outstanding reputation, and she's great in front of a camera. She'll do an excellent job up against the media. You should go after her."

I considered enlightening Paul as to how dangerous it would be to have Sabrina associated with the company, then decided against it. It wasn't any of Paul's damn business. She hadn't been the catalyst for my father's recent attack, though she would be adding an accelerant to the fire. Best to just move past this moment.

I cleared my throat. "If she's one of the best, then get another one of the best other than her. Simple." I took a seat behind my desk and avoided all the stuff written on the surface. "Who hired her?"

"Morgan."

The next question was how my mother knew to approach Sabrina. The logical answer was Jace, because when Sabrina and I dated, I'd kept her far from my family. My mom and sister had been living with my dad at the time, and there was no way I was going to subject her to him. My house had been toxic. That was why we'd always spent our free time with her dad.

I couldn't imagine my lifelong friend suggesting the company hire her. Jace was the only person other than me who knew the history. He wouldn't put either of us in this position. He was such a reliable friend that he'd flown in when he heard I'd been shot.

I took out my cell phone and sent Jace a quick text:

> Sabrina just left my office. What do you
> know about that?

> JACE
>
> Holy crap. How'd that go?

> Much like you can imagine

JACE

Your mom asked about her. She knew Sabrina was a matchmaker because she knew that's how Meredith and I met. I told her no way was Sabrina a good idea and she shouldn't be on any list. Paul was there.

I looked up from my phone and glared at Paul. "I'm considering firing you," I growled.

Paul shot me the bird. "Because I tried to hire a matchmaker that you have a personal connection to? That plays out in the media so much better than hiring someone you don't know. That's what you pay me to do. You need to explain to me why you don't want her here."

My phone chimed with a new text.

JACE

I'm sorry, man. That must have sucked.

She's gone now. I scared her off.

I looked at the notes scrawled along the surface of my desk. I should wipe them off. What she'd written wasn't flattering. Yet, for the most part, it was true. I would argue against having a stick up my butt. Having a serious nature was not the same as rigidity. Besides, I was in a business that required me to be serious. With one finger, I traced a word, then a sentence. Sabrina had always been that type—the sort that made lists and reminders. She got immense satisfaction from checking off a box. She took pride in those pointy marks.

"You need to go after her, Cal," Paul said. "We're on borrowed time here. Hitchens has already put out a statement about the improvements their app will have. Plus, we're getting calls from former clients wondering if they should continue to recommend us. The Peru thing didn't help. Some are ticked."

My finger paused on one of the questions she'd written on my desk. Why? Don't I deserve to know that? After all these years she still wanted to know why. And after all these years, I still had no intention of telling her.

And yeah, she was still ticked. My clients were ticked. I was ticked.

I stood. "As they should be."

She really did deserve to know why I'd changed on a dime. But not telling her kept her protected. If she knew, she'd fight back.

"I have to take care of something. Find another matchmaker. Start selling the plan. Just leave Sabrina out of this. Please. Trust me when I say she doesn't solve our problems—she complicates them."

Deserve. She deserved to be loved and cherished. After what I'd done to her, I didn't deserve love. When you abused it the way I had—kicked it hard when it was down—love tended to stay away. And rightly so.

Chapter Six
SABRINA

How to get out of dodge ASAP—in 1 hour or less:

- 1.Get my bags.
- 2.Check out of the hotel.
- 3.Catch the next flight home. Even if I have to have a dozen stops before Dallas, get out of this stupid city now!

Home was where I could safely process all that I was feeling. I told myself that I could never like this new Cal and was lucky we hadn't gotten married. I never could have lived a life with that guy. Even while feeling sorry for him.

Seeing Cal was like experiencing the death of a friend all over again. He looked like the someone I once loved, but he was a doppelgänger, the evil twin version, and I found myself mourning the loss of my friend Cal all over again.

And then there was the guy at the elevator, that Cal had showed a spark of the one I once knew. A flash of something had flitted in his eyes that with anyone else, I would have interpreted as hurt or confusion. But hurting Cal had never been my role, only his.

I speed-walked through the hotel lobby, aiming for the bank of elevators, but stopped short when I caught sight of a long-legged gentleman sitting in a chair near the elevators, holding a Stetson. I made a beeline for him.

"I could punch you in the nose." I stood before him, arms akimbo.

Jace Shepard dropped his hat onto the chair next to him and put up both hands. "I swear, Sabrina, I did not tell Morgan to hire you. I told her you weren't a good fit."

"And yet she sought me out." I narrowed my eyes at him. "Did you know I was in town?"

He shook his head.

"Why are you in town?"

"I came when I heard Cal got shot. I swear he's got a death wish. You know, every year we do a fishing trip. This year, he canceled to take this Peru job, which half his team had voted to not take. And he got shot. So I came to make sure he was okay and then maybe drag him away from here, someplace where I'd hope to knock some sense into him. Now this attack from his dad is just gonna make it all worse." Jace picked up his hat and brushed off the seat next to him.

I sank into it with a weary sigh. "His dad is doing this?" I didn't know why I was surprised. Half my business was from people trying to escape controlling parents.

Jace nodded as he shifted to face me. "I bet you were blindsided by Morgan approaching you." His brow was knitted with concern.

I let my head fall back to rest against the edge of the seat. I looked at the ceiling as I replayed the events in my head. "I knew one day, somehow, our paths would cross again. I just thought it would be different than this. So when Morgan asked me to meet with him, I saw that as a sign."

"Why? Did you think you could get him back?" His voice was soft, the question gentle.

I didn't have to think about that for one second. "Yeah, I'll admit revenge had crossed my mind." I'd called it closure, but revenge would have been sweet.

Jace startled and drew in a breath with a hiss. "Judas Priest, Sabrina, I didn't mean get him back revenge-style. I meant win him back."

I rolled my head to the side to look at him and laughed. "You know, I didn't even think of that. He made it clear back then that he didn't want me." I shrugged a shoulder. "So I let go of that a long time ago."

He placed his hand over mine and squeezed. "I'm sorry if this brought up buried stuff. I really did try to warn them off you. I never want for you to get hurt."

I smiled softly. "I know. And you can make it up to me when I come out there in a few weeks. You can let me take your kids home forever."

"Done," he said with a laugh. "Meredith called this morning. Jonah cut Nathan's hair. She says it looks awful. Big chunks missing everywhere. And this on the heels of the Sharpie incident. We're ready for some peace and quiet."

The Sharpie incident had been the twins drawing all over each other using the colored markers. On their arms, legs, and faces. Know what erases a Sharpie mark? Nothing but time.

"It's like your children aren't supervised." I winked, knowing they were.

"Give them three minutes alone, and they could take down an entire city." He shook his head in resignation.

"Aside from seeing Cal, you know, they offered me twenty-five K for a few weeks of work with him. Change his image and all that."

Jace gave a low whistle. "Damn, that was like offering a map to a lost trail rider. I bet you snatched it up."

"I'm gonna ignore that fact that you might be implying I'm lost with this goal of mine. But yeah, that money would have replenished my empty coffers, which, as you know, is a requirement for the adoption agency."

Jace rubbed at the inner corner of one eye with his thumb while he avoided eye contact. His expression bothered me, like he was trying to hide his pity or poking himself in the eye to keep himself from saying something.

I crossed my arms. "I know y'all don't think I should adopt, but I am tired of being alone. You know this. I have tried waiting. I have tried dating. I've tried in vitro. None of those are working out for me. It's time I take charge of my life." We'd had this discussion a bazillion times.

"It's not that. It's the single parenting. Hell, coparenting is rough. These kids eat us alive every day. You know, my sister refuses to babysit them. They switched out her expensive face cream for mayo."

I smothered a laugh. "That's your kids, Jace. Not all kids are like that."

"Yeah, but you don't get to choose, and you're getting a kid who essentially was abandoned. Mere was reading up on attachment disorder. She said if you do adopt, you're just gonna have to move next door. You can't be all by yourself in Texas."

Tears stung my eyes. "That's so sweet. I just..." I pressed

my hand to my mouth to keep from crying. I really did have great friends.

"Hell, woman, I don't know what part you thought was sweet." He shook his head, confused. "Where are you headed? Want to do..." He glanced at his watch. "Brunch?"

It was my turn to shake my head. "I want to get home. I have to call the potential client I came to town to see, and then I'm going to grab my bags and try to catch the next flight home." I stood, and Jace did too. "I hope you get your fishing trip. I hope Cal survives this smear campaign too. And I hope that's the end of my involvement. I'm going to focus on what's ahead for me. Like trying to find another way to make twenty-five K."

Jace lifted a brow. "What about that matchmaker documentary? Is it going to happen?"

I'd been asked to pair up with my good friend Nick Trask, an A-list actor, and help him find love. A widower for a handful of years, he'd asked me to help him get a second chance at love and had casually mentioned that to a director friend, who was now trying to sell it as reality TV.

"Magic 8 Ball says all signs point to yes." I opened my arms for a hug. "But it won't pay out for a while. Longer than I am willing to wait."

He wrapped me up. "Well, if the Magic 8 Ball says yes, who can argue with that? Can I give you a ride?"

My phone chimed at the same time Jace's did. We pulled them out.

"That's interesting," I said, looking at the screen. "Clever line. Optium says CEO will test dating safety on new app and will use a matchmaker. Ruse or desperation."

Jace looked between his phone and me. "Since when did you turn on notifications for Cal?"

"When Morgan Baker approached me." I tucked my phone back into my purse.

"Will you turn them off again?"

I shrugged. "Maybe. I probably should. Though I'm curious to see how this plays out. You should get to Cal. I'm guessing his PR person released the news about a matchmaker, but the smear campaign is getting the headlines. He could probably use a friend."

He nodded and stuffed his phone into his pocket. He started to turn, then stopped. "Did you ask him why he did what he did back then?"

I knew what Jace was referring to. "Back then" meant when Cal had practically left me at the altar.

"I didn't really get the chance. Why don't you tell me now?" I quirked a brow.

"I only know the basics, and it leads to more questions than answers. Besides, it's his story to tell. But, man, I wish he would tell it." He placed a hand on my shoulder. "Call if you need anything, and I'll still see you next month at the ranch."

I placed a hand over his. I'd once been mad at Jace for knowing what he had known and not telling me, but my father had helped me understand that telling me would have been like picking sides. He was too loyal a friend to both of us to do that. And—I knew this to be the cruelest part of it all —whatever Jace knew, telling me would not make anything better. Jace couldn't fix the break by spilling his guts.

So, whatever it was, it had to be bad. But not knowing nearly drove me mad. When the mind didn't have the slightest idea of what to make of a situation, it created its own narrative. And the story—or the several stories I'd created— had been just awful.

I gave his hand a squeeze. "I'm looking forward to getting away. Cricket and I are already planning some girl-only retreats. So prepare yourself to single parent."

We said our goodbyes, and I watched him walk out of the lobby. Then I went to my room and called my potential client, who didn't answer. The client hadn't responded to the two emails I'd sent either. Rubbing the pads of my fingers over my thumbnail, I considered my next step.

I moved to the window to look outside at the city. Mindy was busy, and it had only been half a day since we'd last talked. This wasn't out of the ordinary, yet my gut told me something was off.

Ha. Something was definitely off. I'd just seen Cal Beckett for the first time in ten years. So, yeah, things were definitely off. And that was likely why my gut was all twisted up.

I pulled out my phone and read the article from the notification earlier:

CEO of Optium, Calvin Beckett, talk show's favorite safety guru, is being called out for profiting from selling families on personal safety while not having a safety plan of his own. The accusation is that Beckett, known for his initiative rewarding women's safety, avoids personal relationships, as he believes a family would be too hard to protect, and that there really is no such thing as safety.

I tucked my phone into my jacket pocket, glad my name hadn't been mentioned. I thought about Cal at the elevator.

"I'm the guy who took your virginity," I mimicked. I threw up my hands in frustration and disbelief. "Well, duh. What did that have to do with anything?" I mean, sure I'd chosen him to give it to. I'd chosen him because he'd be the one. Well, jokes on me.

If that fun fact hadn't meant anything when he was dumping me with no explanation, it certainly meant nothing now. He'd wielded it like a sword intended to cut me. All because he'd been surprised that I had come willingly to match him.

I might not have gotten the closure I'd wanted, but I had gotten under his skin, and I took pleasure in that. The infuriating ass.

Seeing Cal again had been the worst kind of wonderful. He was a glass of cold water, and I'd been parched. As ugly as his reaction had been, seeing him had been weirdly refreshing. I hated myself for feeling that way. But maybe that was the power of first loves.

I stared out at the Seattle skyline, curious to know what had brought him to this city after college, when he was either going back to the family ranch in Wyoming or to Denver, where his dad's company was headquartered. He'd been groomed to do either. Yet he'd gone in a completely different direction. His Wikipedia page said he'd spent four years working for a private security firm before starting his own.

The rumbling of a motorcycle downshifting caught my attention, and I looked toward the street. Three floors up gave me an advantage. I could see both the ground and the skyline.

A motorcycle idled at a red light, and the biker's attention was on my hotel. I didn't need to guess who rode the bike. By the length of his long legs and the way he stretched them out to balance the bike, I could tell it was Cal. There was something so familiar about the way he moved. He'd always had the agility of a cheetah, fluid and smooth and quick to respond. After all these years, I still knew his body.

Jace was right. Cal seemed to have a death wish. Because

who rode a motorcycle when, just hours before, they'd been wounded by gunshot? A person who punished himself with pain, that was who. And his presence was confirmation that I'd gotten to him.

Okay, Calvin Beckett. You're not going to let me walk away with the last word.

I gave him time to park his bike. Game on.

Chapter Seven
SABRINA

I didn't have to see Cal to know where he was. I felt him as soon as I walked out of the hotel. This had always been the magic of Cal. As if he were a proton and I an electron, our opposite charges created an irresistible force of attraction, drawing us together like two halves of a whole.

Without looking over my shoulder, I said, "Why are you here? Gonna make sure I leave your town?"

"Why would you stay?"

"Precisely. My daddy didn't raise a fool." I stopped, feet from the porte-cochère, set down my carry-on bag, and surveyed the street for a taxi. My backup plan was an Uber.

Cal cleared his throat before he spoke, his voice so low I almost didn't hear him. "I was sorry to hear about Travis passing."

I pressed my lips together and swallowed because, even five years later, it still hurt to think about my dad's death. He had been my last living relative. He had been my rock.

Pushing back my grief, I hid it by adding bite to my words. "Funny how I knew nothing about you. I didn't know you had a company or if you'd married or not. I never once googled your name." I looked over my shoulder. "I can see that's not true for you. You were the one that left. Why do you care?"

"I did say I was sorry. You know, back then."

With one exhalation, my grief was replaced by fury. I swiveled, leaving my bag behind, giving him a cold stare as I marched the handful of steps toward him. He had tucked himself off to the side where the shadows gathered and made it difficult for him to be seen through the lobby windows.

When I was barely a foot away I jabbed him in the chest with my finger to punctuate my every word. "'I'm sorry, Reenie, this isn't gonna work. It's best if we go our own ways, Reenie.' That's what you think counts as an apology? That's not an apology—that's a cop-out. You used 'I'm sorry' like a buffer, hoping it would somehow make things better, but it didn't work."

He looked down at my poking finger.

"There I am, thinking we're about to get married. I'm on top of the world, then you show up to say we have to go our own ways when just a few hours earlier we were picking out rings."

The tip of my finger began to throb from the contact, so I flat-palm slapped him square in the solar plexus. He didn't even flinch. I pulled back, preparing to land another. He grabbed my hand, his large one swallowing mine, and held tight. Using his hold, he jerked me closer. Neither of us moved as we stared each other down.

"Stop slapping me," he growled.

"You're more solid than you used to be in college." Solid was an understatement. The man's chest was like a Kevlar vest, tight and hard.

His lips twitched. "A lot less beer pong and far more weight lifting."

I continued to hold his gaze. His eyes were dark and dangerous, a look unfamiliar to me that reflected what I felt: a blue-flame heat burning me from my very center. He'd always made me feel that way. I was surprised he still felt it too.

"Beer pong requires you to be agile and quick. That's probably really hard to do with the pole up your hole."

"You keep bringing up this stick. What's with the fascination of my backside?"

"You're an asshole." I tried to jerk away my hand.

He held tight. "I know."

"Do you not think I deserve to know why, in a span of two hours, everything changed for us?" The space between us was as wide as my forearm.

He still held my fist in his. Energy crackled, causing the hairs on my arms to rise. At the point where we connected, our hands hummed and vibrated. If we'd been energy sticks, we'd have had a meltdown, with so much highly charged current flowing between us.

"It doesn't matter why." His gaze fell to my lips.

So mine did the same to his, and I was instantly vibrating with a need to rise up on my toes and flick my tongue across his lips. I tried to focus on the conversation. "It mattered to me."

"But in the big picture, it doesn't matter. It was just something that had to be done."

We were talking to each other's mouths.

I tugged my fist, trying to dislodge it from his hand again. "It came out of nowhere. And you think I was supposed to shrug and move on?"

He tugged back and brought me closer, my bent arm the only thing between us. Slowly, his gaze traveled back up to meet mine. "But it didn't come out of nowhere. Come on, you know things weren't perfect between us, Reenie. Did it not bother you that I never introduced you to my family?"

Hearing the nickname slip easily from his lips—a nickname given to me by my parents—dredged up another wave of achy longing, reminding me once more what I'd lost.

"You don't get to call me that anymore." I pulled against him.

He held steady.

I narrowed my eyes. "You said you were estranged. I believed you. Should I not have? Besides, no relationship is perfect, and it wasn't my idea to run off to Vegas—it was yours. So tell me why you would do that if you weren't sure."

That made him look away.

We continued to play our push-pull game. Any passerby might pause and question my safety. But I didn't feel scared. I was angry that he talked in riddles, never answering my questions.

"Why did you come, Reenie?" he asked, his voice gravelly. He shifted to lean more toward me.

I pressed my lips into a thin line and glared at him. He was using my nickname to disarm me, to try to melt me into a puddle that he could scoop up and do whatever he wished with.

Well, I was not going to have any of that. I needed to get away. My resolve was wavering again, and I wasn't sure what I would do next. Crying seemed impending and unavoidable. I had one move he'd never expect. I stomped on his foot, making sure to avoid jabbing my heel into him. I was going for distraction more than pain, and my aim was true.

Cal swore as he thrust me away then reached for his foot. But because he'd pulled me close and had been holding my hand, I suddenly found myself off-balance and teetering backward. I tried to adjust by stepping back and windmilling my arms, but the momentum pushing me backwards was stronger than my correction.

"Oh," I called as I reached for something, anything, and found the front of his shirt, clutching it in my fist.

His arms snaked out and caught me, and together we shifted, so I crashed into Cal.

"Oof."

"What was that for?" he growled over my head, his arms tight around me.

I was up against his chest, surrounded by him, overwhelmed with the memory and familiarity of what he felt like pressed to me. Yep, I was going to cry. All of these feelings and memories were too much.

I was acutely aware of how alone I really felt, how long it had been since I'd had a hug that was all-encompassing. How long I'd gone without romantic affection and even sex. Here I was, not really being hugged but held, and I wanted more.

"I'm all done here." I straightened and pressed my palms against his chest to push out of his arms. "The ten years have changed you. You've become hard."

"In my line of business, I had to change. I have to be fit."

That was not what I'd meant, and he knew that. I tilted my head and studied him. "This plan your PR guy has is a good one. I think you know that, but I think trust issues are at play here."

He put his foot down and pushed off the wall, coming

closer to me. "I trust Paul immensely. Even though I think a love expert and me dating is a stupid idea."

I chuckled. "I'm talking about you trusting Paul. Jace says your dad is behind this. He has some powerful alliances and is using them against you. I think that's why you don't trust yourself. You're emotionally involved."

Cal scoffed. His eyes darted from the cab back to me, and he opened his mouth to say something, then shook his head and stuffed his hands into his pockets.

I turned and went back to my overnight bag. Then I stepped toward the street and waved at an approaching taxi. The car pulled to a stop in front of me. I opened the door and moved to get in, stopping to look at Cal one last time. There was something cathartic in being the one doing the leaving this time.

"Take care of yourself, Reenie," he said quietly.

I didn't know what to say to that. I could read a million things into those five words. Could that be regret?

"Good luck to you. You're going to need it. If you don't pull your head out of your ass and fight back, then you've already been beaten." I got into the car.

I meant what I'd said. Events in his world looked to be spiraling out of control, and he didn't have his hand at the helm. I didn't want a front-row seat to watch him crash and burn. I would be too busy trying to stitch up my wound, which seeing him had reopened.

I did need to get a life. But to do so, I had to really and truly let him go, because if I'd learned one thing from this whole event, I'd still been holding on to the dream of him. Not anymore.

Chapter Eight
SABRINA

I woke to pounding on my front door. I'd had a long layover in Denver followed by a flight with engine trouble that resulted in me getting home around four in the morning, and I'd only been asleep—I sat up slightly to look at the clock—four hours.

What maniac is at my door at the ungodly hour of eight? If it was a pest-control guy or solicitor, God help me, I might shoot them, and I wouldn't feel bad about it either. I had a clear No Soliciting sign posted at the start of my very long drive, so for them to ignore it took balls. And stupidity. My house was set so far back off the street, no one would see me take out a solicitor and bury their body.

The pounding continued, followed by two presses to the doorbell in quick succession. Just for that, I wasn't going to answer the door. Instead, I pulled the pillow over my head and cupped it around my ears as I tried to go back to sleep. And the silence was amazing. I drifted off as I mentally gave the person at my door my middle finger.

"Sabrina! Wake up."

I sat up in bed and tossed the pillow in the direction of the man's voice as I screamed. When I saw who was standing there I picked up another pillow and threw it at him.

"What are you doing in my house? Go away, Satan. Haven't we had enough interaction?" I searched my night-stand for something else to throw.

On a ring dangling from Cal's index finger was my hide-a-key. "Why have you kept the hide-a-key in the exact same place for, what, fifteen years now? Do you know how dangerous that is?" He picked up the tossed pillows and threw them back onto the bed.

I pulled the sheets up to clutch them over my chest. "I never once imagined you would be in my house, much less in the position to use the hide-a-key. Now, go let yourself out, and put the key back, and I won't press charges."

He frowned down at me as he stuffed the key into his pocket. "The key is the least of your problems right now."

"Yeah, no shit. You being in here is a huge problem. Get. Out." I pointed a finger toward my bedroom door.

He crossed his arms and stared down at me. "I'm serious. There's something you need to see."

I scoffed. "If we're talking about the bend in your you-know-what, save it. I've seen it. I can confirm it's a bit much but not really an issue, but you should talk to your doctor. If it's still bugging you."

Cal barked out a laugh. "Think about that often, do you?" From the back pocket of his jeans, he pulled out a large, folded manila envelope and tossed it onto my bed. "I'm talking about this."

This was the Cal I knew. The long-legged, jean-clad, T-shirt-wearing type of guy with a quick smile and quicker laugh. He'd never been a suit-and-dress-shoes man. And though he still looked tired, and his frown lines were still deep and prominent, I saw a hint of who he used to be.

I picked up the envelope. "What's this—a list with pictures of women you want to meet? Fat chance. Women like someone with a good sense of humor and who's willing to spend time with them. You're not that guy." I lifted the prongs to open the flap.

"Yesterday, someone—a reporter, I guess—was watching our conversation. I can't determine if they were close enough to hear, but I think likely not because all the speculation made in the included articles are not anywhere near what we discussed."

I raised a brow as I slid out the papers. Cal wiped a hand down his face and sighed. He came to sit on the edge of my bed.

"Nope. Get up. Sit over there." I pointed to a chair across the room.

He smirked. "Afraid to have me near and my curved—"

"Ahh, it's not that at all. It's more like I'm grossed out. This is my favorite comforter of all time, and if your bad juju and presence sully it, I will be devastated, and that will be one more thing I won't forgive you for."

He stood and went to the armchair by the window. "So you haven't forgiven me for Vegas."

"Duh." I rolled my eyes.

"What happened to 'What happens in Vegas stays in Vegas'?"

It was a poor attempt at a joke, and he knew it. I showed him my middle finger.

* * *

CAL

* * *

I dropped into the chair and stretched out my long legs, easing the tightness in my muscles. I'd been up for hours already, trying to get ahead of this story. And her bed looked so cozy and snuggly.

Snuggly? I hadn't thought or said that word in what... a decade?

The minute I'd seen Sabrina in my office, I knew I had to make sure her name wouldn't get tied to mine. My dad would lose his shit, and Sabrina would pay. But when I watched her get into the elevator after not seeing her for ten years, I simply wasn't ready for the moment to end. So, like a horny high schooler, driven by hormones and not logic, I'd gone to her hotel for one more glimpse and hung around outside like a kid with acne and no confidence, when what I really wanted was to spend time getting to know her again, maybe have dinner and catch up. But as long as I kept the truth from her, the odds of a friendly dinner out together was slim to none. I had money on none. Those were the foolish dreams of an unlucky man.

So here we were, and this was the new us. I wiped a hand down my face as I stifled a yawn. A friend of Paul's had given him a heads-up on the story before it broke, giving us time to plan. And while we were talking strategy, all I could think of was what she'd said. How my dad had already beaten me. There was a lot of truth to those words. My dad had already gone too far, interfering in my personal life. Working on the app in real time, exposing that side of myself, just felt like I would be painting a bull's-eye on my back. Yeah, I was aware that really didn't make sense, because going after my business was just as personal. Except that he'd gone after my personal life before, and now there was a wound.

Her words had been the kick in the pants I needed, so I'd changed out of my suit and into my fighting clothes—a pair of worn jeans, a T-shirt, and my cowboy boots. They were the standard brown boots with no extra flourish, but they made me feel like I could kick the shit out of anyone. Then I'd walked into her house, and cruel as it was, I felt more like myself than I had in years. Once upon a time, this place had been a second home to me.

Sabrina hadn't made a sound since opening the envelope. I dropped my hand to study her. She was flipping through the pages in a loop, her eyes darting across them.

She glanced up at me. "They're hinting that you were aggressive with me? How coy of them to not straight-out say 'assault.'" She tossed the papers to the other side of the bed and flopped back down, pulling the covers up to her chin. "I don't see why any of this requires you breaking and entering. And FYI, you could have texted me the links and saved yourself a trip."

"I don't have your number."

It was true. She couldn't argue with that. She looked over the comforter at me and rolled her eyes.

"Don't be a jackass. Jace has my number, and you were with him. Plus, I think in your line of work, it wouldn't be hard to get my number." She went back under the covers. Head and all.

I sighed. "Reenie..."

A raised arm came out from under the comforter and pointed a finger at me. "Do not call me that. It's reserved for my friends."

"And I am not one of them, clearly." I knew I didn't deserve to be.

She flipped the comforter off her head to look at me. "Clearly." Sabrina rolled over and snatched up the articles. "Have you not seen these? You assaulted me. Look at this one. It's obvious you were pushing me down." Her expression straight-faced.

She waved an image of me gripping her arm. Her long jet-black hair hung over her shoulder, reaching all the way to the comforter, part of it falling over her face. I itched to tuck it behind her ear. Touching her the previous day had left me with a lot to unpack. The realization of how much I missed her, how her touch affected me like no other, and how all these years that I'd watched over her from afar had been low on the cruel-punishment scale compared to touching her again.

She held up another picture of her falling back and me reaching for her. "And there's this one too."

"The only person being assaulted in that picture was me. I still have a bruise on the top of my foot from your shoe."

She stuck out her bottom lip to pout. "Boo-hoo, you." Then she held up another picture, this one with her hand on my chest and mine wrapped around her wrist. "How does this even look like assault? Ugh, your dad hates you with a fiery passion. Why is that?" She lifted her elbow to frisbee the photo toward me before plopping back down.

Why indeed. I'd asked myself that since I was ten years old.

I caught the picture as it started to drift down. When this

picture was taken, assault had been the furthest thing from my mind. Can she read that in my expression? I wanted to ask Jace what he saw on my face when he looked at the pictures, but that would be opening up a can of worms. I'd long sworn to Jace that my feelings for her didn't matter, and they didn't.

Of course I had feelings for Sabrina. I'd loved her once upon a time. And I found her fucking hot as hell, then and now. She was totally my type. But love or no love, it didn't matter. I was her kryptonite. Eventually, being with me would have destroyed her.

When she'd touched me yesterday, though, I'd felt a gaping hole in my soul, an emptiness I'd pretended wasn't there. Maybe she could see that in my face. I'd never wanted anyone but her. But sometimes I wondered if I felt that way because I knew I couldn't have her.

For the last ten years, I had worked from two principles. One, I would never subject anyone to my family. That itself was a prison sentence. And two, I would never ask another woman to be a part of my life if she would always be the runner-up to a ghost from the past. That was why I'd stayed single. That was why I was a workaholic.

I looked at the photo. Embarrassed by my wistful expression, I squirmed in the chair, then placed the picture on the floor. "These accusations really make a mockery of the app. An abuser using safety as something to hide behind. Like I'm some sort of con. They make me look like a hypocrite of epic proportions. Did you see the other fun spin that we hired you, and because I got aggressive with you, now you won't work with me? Notice that you've been named? The armchair experts in the comment section have a lot to say."

"Ugh." She pulled the covers up over her head again.

"This is why I didn't want you involved, Reenie. I don't want to bring you down with me."

She grunted, then sighed and from under the covers and said, "This isn't your fault." Had the room not been so quiet, I might not have heard it.

"Pained you to say that, didn't it?"

"You will never know how much."

I took in her long form stretched out but hidden under the comforter. "Do you still sleep with your toes linked?" I'd never known anyone else who went to sleep with their big toes hooked together.

"You don't know me anymore, Cal. I left that Reenie behind in Vegas." She was still under the sheets, and though I couldn't see her face, I heard the hint of sadness in her voice.

"I'm holding a press conference. I want you there to show that we aren't working together and that I didn't assault you."

She snorted. "Because no woman has ever been forced to stand before a crowd and lie about something like that. There is no way anyone will believe me. That's a dumb idea. Leave the key on the counter, and don't let the door hit you in the ass." She yawned.

I stood quietly and moved to the edge of the bed to position myself beside her crossed feet. I don't know her, my ass. I picked up the edge of the comforter with both hands and, in one swift jerk, flung the comforter off her and onto the floor.

I pointed to her toes. "You do still sleep with your toes hooked. You big weirdo."

Sabrina bolted upright. "What the hell is wrong with you!" she yelled. "All I want to do is sleep."

"We have a press conference to do and our names to separate. Trust me, you need to do this." I pointed toward her en-suite bathroom.

"Trust you? Ha. Not on your heinous life, buddy!" But she got up and went into the bathroom, slamming the door behind her.

Chapter Nine
SABRINA

Because I felt petulant, I debated wearing long sleeves and slacks just to make it look like I might be hiding something, but I really hated assumed-to-be-true narratives and the ethically deprived people who created them. And judging by the number of missed calls and texts I had, many people I knew were buying into it.

So instead I wore a gauzy white sleeveless top and a dark-brown above-the-knee skirt, both showing off a lot of my legs and arms. I put my hair up in a high ponytail to show off my neck as well. I kept my makeup light and my lipstick glossy and natural. Hearing Cal banging around in my kitchen rankled me, so I quietly slipped out of my house to make a quick stop by his car with a liquid chalk marker. I really had thought, when I left yesterday, I wouldn't see him again.

Fooled you, said the universe.

Then I joined Cal in my kitchen. He'd taken the liberty of making coffee, and his familiarity with my kitchen unnerved me, reminding me of our past and all the times he'd spent here with both me and Dad. I made a mental note to reorganize my cabinets so next time he'd be thrown off.

Ahh. What was I saying? There will not be a next time. We were going to part ways after this press conference, and that would be that. I would go back to my life of pretending Calvin Beckett didn't exist.

Take that, universe.

"You're wearing that?" I scanned him up and down.

"Yeah, I thought a suit and tie might make me look like a douche. Not that what I wear will matter. They'll say what they want." He pushed a mug of coffee toward me.

My eyes narrowed. He'd dolled it up for me just how I liked it. I wanted to throat-punch him for always subtly reminding me of his familiarity.

I picked up the mug and dumped the coffee into the sink. "I don't drink it like that anymore." Liar, liar.

I poured a fresh cup of coffee, leaving it naked, then turned to face him as I leaned against the counter. I took a sip and strained to keep my eye from twitching. Black coffee was bitter and disgusting.

His lips pursed. "I reserved a conference room at the hotel where I'm staying. You want to ride with me or follow?"

"Follow, of course."

"If you don't use creamer, why do you have"—he gestured to my fridge—"crème brûlée in your fridge?"

"For company. I'm not a barbarian." I took another sip and felt my lip curling in disgust. I pressed my lips together tightly. Not only had he ruined my sleep, but now he was ruining my coffee as well. He was a plague on my life.

"If you're ready, we can leave. After the presser, I want

to talk to you about the lack of security at your house." He stood, gave me a nod, and headed toward the front door.

"Just go away, Cal. Seriously."

"Don't tell me I don't know you, Reenie. I know as soon as I'm outside, you're gonna dump a ton of creamer in that coffee. Straight black made your eye twitch." He tossed this over his shoulder and followed it with a chuckle.

I gave him my favorite middle finger and sent angry energy waves in his direction. Cal laughed all the way out the door. I waited until I heard it close before I added the necessary goods to my coffee, then hid the evidence in a dark travel mug.

After grabbing my large black tote that also worked as a purse, I locked my front door and went out to the garage, where my black SUV waited. I didn't get any farther than backing out when I was forced to stop because both Cal's rental and his body were blocking my way. His arms were crossed over his chest.

I gave him a finger wave, clicked the button to bring the window down, and stuck my head out. "Is there a problem?" I bit my cheeks to keep from laughing.

"How am I supposed to drive with that written on my windshield?" He jerked his head toward his car.

"I thought it best we come out strong. Make a bold statement."

"And writing 'This moron doesn't beat me,' and signing your name and drawing an arrow pointing to the driver's side is your bold statement?"

"Too strong?" I let a chuckle escape.

"Perhaps it implies other morons do." He snickered. "You and those markers. I'm going to take them away from you." He was a tall, rigid pole of pent-up... something. Anger was not the word, because laughter was starting to seep out of him.

"Bah." I waved a hand, dismissing his words. "After today, I'll be out of your hair, and you'll never see me and my markers again. The hose is on the side of the house. I'll wait here."

I pointed to the side I was talking about, then closed my window. I hoped he would spray himself accidentally. I was looking for proof that the universe was on my side.

As usual, the universe let me down. He wet the window, then put the wipers on as he continued to spray the windshield. My words were erased in mere seconds. I shrugged. At least I'd had a good five minutes of irritating him.

I followed him to a popular five-star hotel in downtown Dallas. After leaving my car with the valet, I met him in the foyer and followed him to a small conference space where Paul Not-a-Lumberjack Runyon waited for us.

"The room is full. We start in five minutes." He turned to me. "It's nice to see you again. Thank you for coming."

I asked the question that had been on my mind. "Why do a conference here and not in Seattle?"

"We've done security teaching at all the colleges here, as well as for the pro sports teams, and personal security for many of the billionaires who live here—even the well-known political ones. In Dallas, we have a lot of allies but also a lot of people who want answers. This is the quickest way to get those answers to them."

He was talking about presidents and presidential candidates. No wonder Cal was worried about their reputation. Anonymity was power. Keeping secrets from the enemy was instrumental in providing protection and safety countermeasures to attacks. This smear campaign was ripping the anonymity away and, therefore, scaring potential clients and was lobbing financial hits, all while discrediting Cal's company.

I got hung up on another tidbit. Cal had been in Dallas several times over the last decade. I'd never heard about it, and we'd never accidentally come across each other. I should have been glad about that, but I was disappointed. And that made me a ginormous moron. All these years, I'd purposefully kept any mention of him from crossing my screen, and I was sad that had worked? I wanted to slap myself in the face and knock some good sense into myself.

Good luck with that, my inner voice said.

Oh, shut up.

Cal went to check on the attendance while Paul reviewed some of the stock questions they anticipated would be asked and his suggested responses. I gave my nod of approval to all but the last one. That I had declined working with them because it didn't align with my plans.

"Yes, when Morgan initially offered me the job, I turned her down. Yet, when she told me how much it paid, I reconsidered. I'm working toward a goal, and that money would have taken me far. And truthfully, if the job was still available, I would likely take it. I can't lie out there and say I didn't want the job, because I did. I can't say it doesn't align because I'm branching out to do a documentary. But I can say that the timing isn't best for me right now because there's truth to that. Semantics, ya know."

Paul nodded, studying me. I could tell the gears in his head were grinding, and I was curious as to what they might be coming up with.

Cal interrupted us. "Come with me." He held out a hand. "Paul's going in ahead of us."

I smacked his hand away. "Just go. I'll be behind you."

I couldn't bring myself to say "follow," because it was like saying I'd follow him anywhere. Being around Cal was messing with my good sense, and the sooner this presser was over, the sooner he would get out of my life, and I could go back to pretending he never existed. I could get back to me.

He led me to a side door, then turned to me. "Since you won't walk in with me, how about ahead of me? Certainly not behind me."

Why does that stupid sentence make me think of sex? Clearly, I was sleep-deprived. Nothing about that sentence was sexy. I smacked myself in the chest, hoping to knock the horny right out of me.

"You okay?" He quirked a brow.

"You give me indigestion." I waved for him to open the door.

He did and, with great flair, held out an arm for me to precede him.

I rolled my eyes and walked in, chin held high. The clicking of cameras filled the space as soon as we entered.

* * *

CAL

* * *

She walked across the room like a queen. There was a confidence about her that made others curious to know her. Goddammit, she was heady stuff.

I took a seat at the table Paul had set up and expected

Sabrina to sit next to me, but she didn't. She stood beside me. It was a power move, and I liked it.

I cleared my throat. "Well, you know me. You know Ms. Holloway here." I gestured to Sabrina, who nodded at the crowd, a glowing smile on her face. "I'm not going to make a statement, because we've already done that. Like we said, Ms. Holloway and I have known each other since college. Those pictures can be interpreted a million different ways, and apparently, the photographer didn't eavesdrop on the conversation, or they would have had context. I'll open the floor to questions."

"I have something to say." Sabrina approached the table and leaned down close to the mic.

Her shoulder brushed up against my arm, and I could smell her perfume, a scent that was unfamiliar. She'd always been a vanilla-and-sweet-pea girl, innocence and sweetness. But now she smelled... spicy. Warm and sexy with a hint of pepper. Which fit perfectly with her sharp mouth and marker words.

"Hi," she said. "Even if the photographer, shame on that person, did hear what we were saying, they chose to disregard it for clickbait. And now, because of their lack of ethics and morals, I am wasting my day proving to you all that Calvin Beckett here is a good man. Something that does not need proof, considering all the good work he's done. But I'm a Texan and hospitable, if nothing else, so let's get down to making you all feel better about someone else's lies." She patted me twice on the shoulder as she straightened and moved back.

Instantly, hands shot up, and questions were blurted out.

"You went to college together?" And variants of that question on repeat.

"When you say you knew each other in college, what does that look like?" asked a tall man in the back.

"Studying, drinking, laughing, and hanging out," I said.

Some other versions were "How intimate were you?" "How long did you know each other in college?" and "How did you meet?"

"I heard you dated," said a woman in the front.

"Who asked out whom?"

"How long did you date?"

"How did you meet?"

Again, I responded, keeping my answers simple. "Yes, we dated."

There were some questions designed specifically for Sabrina. She came to stand close to me to answer, draping her arm around the back of my chair, her hand on my shoulder. Her body language said she wasn't afraid of me.

"What does a professional matchmaker really do?"

"Can you tell us of any celebrity matches you've made?"

"Aren't you dating Nick Trask, the actor?"

Jace had paired Sabrina's name with the A-list actor a few times. He'd said they were just friends. I'd never had the balls to ask if there was more. I had no right to know. But that didn't mean I wasn't curious. I held my breath and waited for her to answer.

"If I told you Nick and I were simply the closest of friends, would you believe me?" Sabrina followed it with a lighthearted laugh. "Because that's the truth."

I let out a slow exhalation, berating myself for even caring.

"Back to your relationship in college. Is it because the two of you broke up—didn't have an amicable split—that you were aggressive with Ms. Holloway? How does that look for a man who wants to teach women self-defense, who wants to help people find a safe space with dating? Can you be trusted to do that?" This came from a beady-eyed jackass right up front.

Sabrina stiffened beside me. Only I could hear the sharp intake of breath, and I knew, because I knew her, that she was ticked. A glance in her direction showed she was staring down the reporter. I swore the scent of her perfume got spicier from her quick flash of anger. Like me, Sabrina knew this guy was here to cause more trouble. Chances were he was the source of this article or knew who was.

I leaned forward to respond, but Sabrina stopped me by putting a hand over the mic. "I've got this one." She angled her body toward the reporter and, instead of sitting next to me, perched a hip on the table and rested, one leg swinging casually, the hem of her skirt rising just a bit. She put a hand on my shoulder. "Look again, Mr.—"

"Smith."

"Yes, of course. 'Smith.'" The way she drew out his name had a few of the people in the room laughing. "Take another look at those pictures, Mr. Smith. Anyone can add their own narrative to an image. I think there are even contests called 'caption this image' where people win prize money. The caption to our image is a bad one. Unimaginative. Given by someone with a negative outlook. Likely a lonely person who goes home to an empty house with a take-out bag and sits in front of the TV, dripping mustard on their tie, mad at the world because they don't have what others do."

The way she stared at Mr. Smith's tie had others craning to see if there was a mustard stain. Even Smith looked down. Her fingers lightly rested on my shoulder, her thumb caressing it slowly.

"Look at it again," she continued. "Go ahead. I'll wait."

Many looked at their phones, presumably to review the image.

"That's not aggression, Mr. Smith. That's restrained passion."

I stiffened, and she squeezed my shoulder in response.

"Restrained?" someone in the gallery called out.

Sabrina moved her hand from my shoulder to pick up the pad of paper in front of me. She began to fan herself even though the room was a comfortable temperature. "We have a history, and try as we might, there's no denying what's between us. In that picture"—she nodded to the group—"you see two adults struggling to not engage in what could have been described as a very heated public display of affection."

Many in the crowd laughed, and more pictures were taken.

"I see it," someone said. Others murmured their agreement.

What had Sabrina just done? Now we were connected romantically. A new rekindling of our past. This was not going to be good. This was going to be worse than bad. I had not spent the last ten years in a lonely personal hell just to have all of it to unravel now.

I stood suddenly and met her gaze. I sucked in a breath. Dear Lord. She was giving me that look—the one I still saw in my mind's eye—and it drove me mad. It was a look of hot need, and if we'd been anyone else and in a different time, I would have seen her hot need and raised it by one intense longing, which would only lead to me showing the crowd what a real public display of affection looked like right there on the cloth-covered conference table. The heat of her body and lure of her perfume were intoxicating. I was drunk from her nearness. I knew my face showed it. Add that to the coyness in her words, and this moment painted a story that the press would run with: that we were hot for each other.

The press would dig into our past. They would look for anything they could spin negatively to drag her down. She might have bested Mr. Smith just now, but his employer, likely someone with connections to my dad, would strike back with a vengeance. This I knew for certain because for all the people who loved a love story, many others liked a dumpster fire. My father was still out there trying to destroy me. And he most definitely did not want a Sabrina-and-Cal love story.

I needed to end this now and get her as far away from me as I could.

I took the pad from her and tossed it onto the table, which bumped the mic. It made a short but uncomfortable pitchy squeal that I ignored as I snatched up her hand in mine. I pulled her toward the exit. I needed to get away and regroup. I needed her to not say another word.

"Thanks for coming," I said as I nearly dragged her out of the room.

A few people hooted.

Once outside the door, I looked for another room to go to, one that would give us privacy.

"Cal, what are you doing?"

I found the door to a closet and pushed her in, closing it behind us. Fortunately, the light was on, dim though it was.

"What have you just done, Reenie? I was trying to separate your name from mine."

"That smug little weasel was there just to bring you down."

"So let him try. But you just gave him more to talk about. You did the opposite of what I wanted."

"Too late now, and who cares?" She planted her fists on her hips. "You're acting like a tool right now. You bust into my house, you drag me down here to prove you're not a wife beater, and when I give them something juicy to bite into, you freak out and pull me out of the room."

She was toe to toe with me and not backing down. This was a new version of Sabrina. She was strong, confident, and deadly. She would lay waste to a man with that beautiful, bewitching smile of hers, those sparking blue eyes, and her sharp words. I stared at her mouth.

"Which, by the way, just made what I said look factual. Now they think you've dragged me off, caveman style, to have your way with me." She tapped me in the chest to make her point, drawing my attention away from my randy thoughts and her delectable mouth.

Jeez, I'd missed her. No one had held a candle to this woman in front of me. Even her flaws were perfect.

But I knew she had a point. "I care about you being dragged into this."

"So you said. Well, I don't, so let's move on."

"You should care," I said in a low voice. She was so near I could taste her breath, coffee and crème brûlée creamer.

"Why should I care? Is there something about you I don't know? Are you a murderer? A serial rapist? Do you kick kittens and run dogfighting rings?"

"If I said yes, would you go out there and tell them you were joking?"

She snorted.

"Tell them I hit you. Tell them anything to separate us."

She reared back. "I don't understand you. I'm sorry that being associated with me is such a dire situation for you."

"You just had to show them they were wrong, not give them more to feast on."

She stared up at me, searching my face for answers I wasn't about to give her. Then she shook her head as she pushed me to the side and rushed out of the closet.

I wiped a hand down my face. Fuck. How am I supposed to protect her from my father now?

Chapter Ten
SABRINA

I rushed down the hallway, back toward the conference space. I was going to find my purse and get as far away from Calvin Beckett as I could. Gads, this seemed to be a recurring theme these days. See Cal, get away from Cal. Swear to never see Cal again. Repeat.

Today, though, I meant it. I'd done my part, and now we could go our separate ways and forget the other existed. He was infuriating. He'd asked for my help but wasn't happy with what I gave. Didn't he realize that if we weren't seen together again, the murmur of us would eventually die down?

Good riddance.

Paul came out from the conference-room side door, carrying my purse and wearing a giant smile. He laughed happily. "Sabrina, you are amazing. You're in the wrong business because you should be in PR."

I lifted the strap of my bag off his shoulder. "I kinda think what I do is PR."

"If you ever want to change it up, I'll hire you in a hot minute."

"Well, I'm glad someone appreciates me." I didn't have to look over my shoulder to know Cal was coming up behind me. It was like my body was tuned into his pheromones and signaled whenever he was near, with goose bumps, twisty tingles in the stomach, or a head-to-toe flush.

Paul whipped out his phone. "Look at the headlines. Already, the narrative is starting to shift."

Cal groaned.

"My work here is done." I stuck my hand out to Paul. "It was nice to meet you."

He shook his head as he put his hand in mine, not to shake but to pull me alongside him. He began moving toward the elevators. "No, no, you can't leave. Let's go up to the suite and talk."

"Let her leave." Cal came up between us and pushed Paul away, breaking his connection with me.

"She can't leave." Paul moved around to Cal to reach me.

"Why not?" Cal and I asked simultaneously.

"I will explain it all upstairs in private." He gestured around the space before cupping one of his ears as if to say the walls were listening.

I looked longingly at the lobby, where my exit was. If I made a break for it, Paul would try to chase me, but Cal would stop him. So it would be an easy getaway. But there were a few reporters from the press conference lingering, and if I were to make a mad dash, that wouldn't look good.

The elevator doors opened on a chime, and Paul pushed me in. We rode up to the tenth-floor suite in silence. Once there, I took a seat on a chair closest to the door. Marking the time, I made an escape plan. In ten minutes, I would be out of here regardless, and I'd stick my finger down my throat to induce vomit if I had to. Barfing was a surefire way to get out of a situation.

Cal moved to stand at the large windows overlooking the city, his back to me, giving me the luxury of studying him without his awareness. He'd been a big guy in college, tall with broad shoulders. He'd been a swimmer. He'd liked horses, cowboy boots, and beer. But this Cal was somehow even larger. There wasn't an ounce of fat on him. Carbs probably didn't cross that unsmiling mouth. With his arms crossed, his T-shirt pulled tight, outlining the ridges and valleys of his back muscles, and dang— if he wasn't ripped, then I wasn't the daughter of a gambler.

Paul plopped onto the couch. "Well, having Cal use the app is out of the question now."

"Thank fuck," mumbled Cal.

"You two need to be seen together rekindling," Paul continued.

"No," Cal said.

Paul lifted an arm and stretched it across the back of the couch. "Hear me out. Sabrina still needs to come on board as our love expert, but how tacky would it be to have her try and match you after what happened today? No need to answer because it would be super tacky and a terrible idea. What we do now is have the two of you work together on the dating part of the app, as originally planned, but now we have you two test stage two of the app."

"No," Cal repeated.

This response was on a loop. Wind. Repeat.

"Stage two?" I asked.

"What we think is so great about the app is not only the dating-safety aspect but also how the app fits with all stages of life. Match with someone? Now you have to figure out what to do. The app looks at both your profiles and locations and generates a list of options that are ranked for personal safety, location safety, etcetera. The options allow for intimacy calibrations. But let's say you're married. The app can do the same for you as a couple—and, if you have kids, activities for them and school ratings. Searching for a house? We got you covered."

I gaped. "That's wonderful, and a lot. A *lot* lot. Know what I mean?"

Paul smiled. "Sure, it's a big reach, and we weren't looking to do it all at once. That's why launching now is imperative. The sooner we get stage one up and running, the sooner we can move on. But now I think we need to do both simultaneously. You two have changed the narrative to our benefit, and we want to capitalize on that."

"It's still a no," Cal said.

Hope flared in me. Not romantic hope. Sure, I was attracted to Cal—always had been, probably always would be—but I didn't trust him with my heart anymore, and then there was the whole forgiveness part. To know the job was on the table still, though, that in two weeks, I could be halfway to my money goal. That made my stomach flutter with possibilities.

Cal was what was standing in my way. His tight expression and rigid shoulders expressed his resistance. Paul was going to have to be the one to change his mind. If I told Cal I wanted this job and why, he would probably give me the money and send me on my way. Which, come to think of it, wouldn't be all that bad. It would certainly be easy for me.

But I would never be able to take it. Money needed to be earned, and any money given freely by Cal would feel like guilt money. So I played it cool. I took out my phone and started scrolling through my calendar and then my emails. Now that I was home, I had to get back on track in case this opportunity fell through again.

"Give me one good reason why this is a bad idea, Cal?" Paul said.

"I can give you a hundred, but how about this—it will make Sabrina a target. He will come after her just as hard as he is coming after me." Cal turned slightly away from the window. "I'm going to make a wild guess about this, but I think Sabrina would not like to see her livelihood and good name trashed." Cal then turned fully to me; his eyes met mine briefly before he searched my face, looking for only he knew what. He stuffed his hands in his pockets, his Adam's apple bobbing as he swallowed, keeping time with his flexing jaw. "Am I wrong?"

I shook my head. "I think an attack could be launched at me, but I don't think it would stick. All my business comes from word of mouth. That won't change."

Cal looked up at the ceiling as if he was working something out. Perhaps picking his words. He pulled a hand from his pocket to wipe it down his face and rub his chin. He looked exhausted, a complete contrast to how he'd appeared in my room earlier that day. Then he returned his attention to me.

"Reenie, the sole purpose of this attack is to destroy me. In my books, I talk briefly about personal safety. On a large scale, I work toward school safety. All those people who have worked with me or have read my books are questioning the advice I've given them, the programs I've taught, compromising their decision-making and putting them in harm's way. I want to help people get out of violent situations.

Doing so, or fighting back against a stalker, takes a fortitude many people don't have, and this 'exposé' will make them question my advice and maybe take poor advice from someone less ethical than I am. People could die because of this. All because one man wants to ruin me. He will not stop there. He will come after you. He won't quit until he's destroyed everything you love. I can't have that on my conscious too."

I gasped, fully understanding what Cal was feeling. "Why? I don't understand how... I met your dad once, and I never suspected..."

I didn't know how to finish that. I never knew he was so evil. I'd never thought that way about people. Guys like Dalton were only seen on true-crime shows. I'd spent all of five minutes in his presence and by accident. He hadn't been very friendly. Cordial, sure, but there'd been no warmth. I'd been shocked that my sweet and loving Cal could have come from him. But I hadn't known he was a man who wanted to annihilate his own child.

"It's a story for another day. The longer you are here, the bigger the target on your back gets." Cal looked anguished, as if the weight of what could happen to others because of this attack was eating him alive.

The urge to soothe him was strong, but he would never accept it. And I should never offer it. We did not have that type of relationship anymore. I wouldn't even say we were friends. But my heart ached as I watched him hurt, to be on the sidelines of this attack.

"What can he do to me? He can't go after my clients, because there is no way he could know who they are. So he'll tell people I'm the daughter of a professional gambler? Big deal. I'm not ashamed of that."

"He'll do more than that. I can promise you that. His imagination for destruction is far more creative than mine."

I wasn't sure what the break between Cal and his father had been, but Cal had gone in a completely unexpected direction since college. "Is this because you didn't join the family business?" I asked.

He crossed his arms and gave a quick, slight nod. Which showcased his hot bod. This new Cal was hot, hot, hot. He did not deserve to look so good. Now was not the time to get distracted.

I cleared my throat. "Well, your dad is a dipshit. Going after you like this isn't going to help his cause."

His lips twitched, but he managed to suppress his grin.

"Why didn't you go into the family business?" I continued. "I thought you were all set to do that after law school."

He looked away. "Another long story."

I huffed in frustration. "Make it short. Give me the CliffsNotes version." The tension in the room was thick and heating up the space. Or maybe that was my body's response to eyeing him up.

"I decided I didn't want to work with him. There was a moment when I saw what my future looked like, and I didn't like it. So I broke off and did my own thing. I never took the bar exam either."

He made it sound like it was no big deal, and maybe it wasn't to him. But to me, well, his simple statement sent a barb through my heart and dug a deeper gouge in the already ripped-open wound he'd given me. Maybe when he'd had his glimpse into the future, he'd realized he didn't like what he saw with me either.

"I see," I said, trying to keep my voice steady.

I looked at my phone and attempted to focus on my

emails, trying to get my wits about me. Maybe Cal was right to say I shouldn't be here, not because I was worried about his dad but because moments like this were too hard. They left me feeling raw and exposed, and even the light brush of my clothes against my skin hurt.

A subject line caught my eye. I tapped on the email from my client Mindy. Less than twenty-four hours had passed since she'd paid the deposit and taken the forms to fill out to start the process. Sure, she'd been a little scared, but she'd expressed both her firm desire and her excitement to work with me, and now... she was bailing. Telling me she'd had a change of heart.

I couldn't believe it. I gave a small, quiet, derisive laugh. Surely, the timing was a coincidence. I stuck my phone into my bag.

"What?" Cal took a step toward me.

"Nothing." I used my best poker face to cover the lie and drew Paul into the conversation. He'd been watching us with a curious expression on his face. "When you say 'rekindle,' what do you have in mind? How do you want that to be seen?"

Cal moved to my chair and stuck out his hand. "Give me your phone."

I swatted him away. "Go away, bad dream. I'm not giving you my phone." I stared up at him and narrowed my eyes. I had to shift to my side to get the full picture, or else I'd be staring up into his nose. "You are making a big deal out of absolute zero. I saw a meme or read a headline about us, or it could have been a host of things. Why are you acting like a straight-up weirdo?"

Paul cleared his throat. "Like I said, with stage two, we

see you guys dating. Rekindling. We let the app plot out some outings or events and have you two go together."

Cal lunged just as I swiveled to the side, turning my back to him. I snaked my hand into my purse and covertly tried to tuck the phone into my bra. His long arms were reaching over me as I bent to protect my purse and front. I jumped from the chair and skirted away from him, going to stand behind the couch, putting Paul and the furniture between us.

"What has gotten into you? Why are you obsessed with my phone?" I kept my purse over my front as a decoy.

"I'm curious about what you saw that made you frown, and I know that laugh."

"What are you talking about, you loon?"

He moved across from me. "That 'I can't believe this' laugh that you follow up with a rant."

I rolled my eyes. "Like you know me so well. Maybe that laugh has changed. I haven't followed it up with a rant, so clearly you're wrong."

"Reenie," he growled.

I went back to Paul. "You were saying, Paul? Something about outings and events? You want us to appear like a couple?"

"Or two people entertaining the idea of becoming a couple." His attention swiveled between Cal and me.

"If there is nothing on your phone, then why can't I see it?" His hands were on his hips.

"Maybe I got a naughty message from my boyfriend." I quirked a brow.

"Didn't you say you weren't dating that blond actor?" He quirked a brow to match mine.

"Maybe my boyfriend isn't Nick." I kept my eyes on his. It was a battle of wills, and I was determined to win.

"So he sent you a breakup text because had it been naughty, you would have blushed." He took a step toward me and the couch.

"Puh-lease. You really are under the illusion that I am the girl you used to know." I took a step back.

If he saw the email, he would one hundred percent blame himself and loudly proclaim, *I told you so.*

He clenched and unclenched his fist, and I knew he was about to leap. His tells were still the same. He would clench his fist as he made his plan, then unclench when he had it figured out. He was going to come over the couch like a field-and-track runner in the hurdles. And he would be able to clear it easily. We'd done this tango before.

"How long do you think we need to pretend, Paul? I say 'pretend' because we wouldn't really be dating." I wanted Cal distracted by Paul's proposition.

"Just a few weeks—like eight to twelve—and then you guys can break up and go your separate ways," Paul said.

"That's two to three months. Saying it in terms of weeks does not make it feel less like an eternity. Have you not seen us? We can't be together more than a few hours." I did the math in my head. Twenty-five K for two weeks of work, times six, would be one hundred fifty thousand dollars. If we pretended for two months, the amount went down by fifty K.

Sweet Jesus. My heart skipped a beat.

Goal achieved. Next level unlocked. I couldn't even wrap my mind around it, the prospect was so unreal.

Cal and I swayed, moving from side to side, mirroring each other. "What do you say about that, Cal? You and I pretend to be dating again?" I asked.

Cal launched, but I saw it coming when he had no response to my use of the word again. He took two long steps, then pushed off the edge of the couch to go over.

In any relationship, it seemed there was always one person more in love than the other. I'd been the more-in-love one, and I had devoured all-things-Cal like an addict does a drug. I knew how to anticipate him more than he did me. As he came over, I ducked down and went under. He literally leaped over me.

I burst out laughing. "You're a jackass," I said, skirting the couch. "Look at how you're behaving."

I was halfway back to my chair when a long arm snaked out and jerked the purse from my hands. I gave a scream of protest. Cal's other hand grabbed me by the elbow and dragged me toward him. He tossed my purse to the ground as he wrapped one arm around my waist and pulled me up against him. His body was a hard wall.

"I know whatever it is you're hiding has to do with this whole situation. And I'm sorry to do this, Reenie, but I need to say I told you so." And he plunged a hand down the front of my shirt and slipped out my phone from between my breasts.

Chapter Eleven
CAL

She was like a bad recording on repeat. "You don't know me; I'm not the same, blah blah blah."

Yeah, some things about her were different. Some things weren't. Hiding things in her bra had been her standard go-to in college. And by the way she clung to the purse, holding it in front of her chest, I knew she'd tucked her phone down her shirt.

I had one arm around her and the other down her shirt. Her hair was in my face and smelled like peppermint. She fit next to me perfectly. My chin was at her temple. The feel of her took me to a place I long thought had shriveled up and blown away. But as my knuckles brushed the smooth skin of her breast, my fingers scraping the lace of her bra, I was cata-pulted back in time to a place where I could drink from her sweetness because I had an open invitation.

Now, she was probably going to stomp on my other foot. As she should.

I have no right to touch her.

God help me, I wanted to touch her more. To run my

thumb across her bottom lip. To taste the coffee she'd had earlier. To lose my hands in her hair as I tasted her skin.

I had to get away from her. If she knew what she still did to me, she could break me in two. And I would deserve it.

As I slipped out the phone, I spun her away and held the phone high, out of her reach.

"I got some great pictures of that," Paul said.

"What?" Sabrina and I asked simultaneously, our attention swiveling to him.

Paul pointed a finger and moved it back and forth from me to Sabrina. "Whatever that was, I caught it in pictures, and it looks good. Sabrina, you have an Instagram account, right? You should post this." He turned the phone so we both could see it.

I leaned forward as did Sabrina. Dammit if we didn't look good together. The image showed what could be interpreted as her leaning into me with one of my arms around her waist and the other across her front, as if I were pulling her in to kiss her from behind on the temple. Her hands were on the arm over her chest, and the camera caught her laughter. No sound was needed. The image looked romantic as fuck.

"We do a handful of these pictures paired with showing what dates the app suggested you two try, and I think we come out ahead on several fronts," Paul continued. "The app gets tested, we improve your image, and I think this will work sufficiently to distract your dad, so we can make some counterattacks. Hitchens won't have anything this great either. Come on. You both know I'm right."

Sabrina straightened first and pointed to her phone. "A client I signed canceled. They had a change of heart.

Yesterday they were gung ho, and today not so much. Cold feet."

I handed the phone to her. "I told you so."

She gave a clipped, bitter laugh. "I knew you would think it had something to do with you, but this client had been hemming and hawing for weeks now. Only yesterday did they decide to take the leap. And maybe they did get cold feet when they saw the articles about us. Who cares? If they're that skittish, I can't help them find a good match."

I pointed to Paul's phone. "Images like that will only represent more of a challenge for my dad. He loves a good fight."

"Then we should give him one." Sabrina held up her phone. "If there is a slight chance, and I don't believe there is, that your dad had anything to do with my client, then I want to fight back. How dare he?" She stuck a hand on her hip, her eyes flashing with anger.

"What do you mean *again*?" I asked.

"What are you talking about?"

"You said 'pretend to be dating again.'"

Her smile was wry. "Heard that, did you? Then. Now. What does real even mean? Do you really want to have this argument?"

No. No, I did not. I wanted to go back to a time when our lives were separate and she was safe.

I dropped onto the couch next to Paul, winced, and scratched my brow. "I no more want to revisit the past than I want to have to argue about why this pretend dating is a bad idea. Sorry. I don't want to play fake house with you, Reenie. I just don't. Not even to test the app."

I met her gaze and held it. I didn't want to hurt her, but I knew if this train continued to barrel down the track without a conductor, we were going to crash, and people—maybe both of us—were going to get hurt. Hadn't I hurt her enough already?

Paul leaned forward. "Well, it's Sabrina or no one. There is no changing that after today's press conference."

It had always been Sabrina or no one. That was the irony of this situation. Even now, looking at her from across the room, I could feel the pull of her: my unexplained need that made me want to touch her all day, every day. Not grope her —not that I wouldn't mind getting handsy with Sabrina—but tucking her hair behind her ears, running my thumb across her cheek, holding her hand. Those innocuous moments had always given me enough of a fix to last until I could touch her again.

"Would it make you feel better to know you'll be paying me and paying me well? Because I did just lose a client and that income, and I have some goals I'm trying to hit."

"What goals?"

"None-of-your-business goals."

I shook my head. "Does it seem weird to pay the woman I am supposed to be dating? Can you imagine the field day my father would have?"

Paul grunted in agreement. "We're not paying her to date you. We're paying her for her expertise."

"Nope, not gonna work. Let's just call it," I said.

She met my gaze and held steady. "Believe it or not, I don't want to play house with you either. I have a possible documentary deal coming up. I was going to go to Jace and Meredith's and take some downtime. I have some deadlines to meet and things to do, and you aren't one of them. Pretending I enjoy your company so much that I want to climb you like a tree is not going to be easy for me. It'll be stressful and uncomfortable because you aren't the easiest man to be around. But I do not like to be handled. And I dislike it even more than I dislike you. And you need this. Your company needs this. Do this for all the people out there getting bad advice. For all the women who are scared and don't know what to do. We take a few pictures together on 'dates'"—she did air quotes—"I drop them on my socials, and we're as good as gold."

I groaned. With Sabrina teetering toward Paul's ideas, this whole thing felt like it was getting out of control. Was it just yesterday I flew in from Peru? In twenty-four hours, my life had gone upside down in a way I never could have imagined.

* * *

Sabrina

* * *

Cal was trying to do that Jedi mind trick where if he stared long enough, he believed it would make a person feel uncomfortable enough to blurt out what they were thinking.

Well, you've got another think coming, buddy.

This wasn't my first Calvin Beckett rodeo; only this time, I wore spurs, and I was going to make him buck. One look at that picture had firmed my resolve. Cal was still attracted to me. Anyone who knew him could see it on his face, plain as day. I'd taken one look at that image and knew I could give back to Cal a little of what he had given me when he'd left. Maybe not heartbreak but longing. Oh, how I'd missed him. Missed his hand in mine. Missed the comfort of his hug.

When my dad had died, I hadn't gone through it alone—I'd had friends around me—but that's when I'd felt Cal's absence the most and really could have used a hug from Cal back then. He had a way of wrapping me up tightly, his big arms around me, that made me feel like everything was going to be okay. He gave me strength somehow. But I hadn't even had his friendship to call on back then. Nope. Nothing.

I wanted him to remember how good we'd been together. I wanted to know leaving me hadn't been easy. And when this was all over, maybe the wound in my heart would be a little smaller. The universe was handing me the perfect opportunity to remind him of what once was.

We were to spend copious amounts of time together. Fake date, if you will. Easy-peasy.

Easy-peasy? Who am I kidding?

I pushed away the thoughts. It wasn't like I would fall in love with him, because I'd never fallen out of love with him. I'd just come to understand we weren't meant to be.

I'd believed what Cal and I had together was unlike what most people had. That was what made it hurt all the more. At the end, he'd walked away so easily that he seemed to have not felt like I did.

But that picture told otherwise. All I had to do was be myself to remind him of our time together. And getting paid too? Well, that was like winning the lottery. With Mindy bailing, the loss of income would push my adoption goal back at least six months. And that just made me feel like I was living in a world where all the things I wanted weren't for me. I was so tired of that feeling. So tired.

I narrowed my eyes and met his. We were in a stare down. My lips twitched with a restrained smile. "You said you had another idea, Paul, besides us playing pretend?"

In my peripheral vision, I could see Paul look between us. Then he said, "Well, sorta. Sabrina, you mentioned that you were headed to Wyoming for a break. Why not take this 'romance'"—he did bunny ears—"back to your ranch, Cal. Show people the Cal who isn't always talking about the scary stuff. Show people that they can live life well and do it with peace of mind because they know how to handle themselves."

"No," said Cal.

"Yes," I said at the same time.

I released my restrained smile and let my lips curve. "Wow, you are just the king of Nopeville, aren't you? It's your default answer."

"No, it's not."

I laughed. "Are you sure? Kinda sounds like it is."

Cal wiped a hand down his face in frustration. "There are—"

"Things you have to do to save your work, and being at the ranch isn't one of them," I said, mimicking him.

"You've been shot, yeah, you're all but healed up, but that doesn't mean you don't need some decompression time," Paul added. "When was the last time you and Jace went fishing? You could do that while you're home. You could also look at the ranch's security. Now that there's been a break-in and all."

Resignation passed over Cal's face. He knew Paul had him there.

"Paul's right, Calvin. We take a trip to Wyoming. I get to see my friends, and we can do this." I pointed to each of us as I made a circle. "I won't be in your space any more than I have to, and I'll be making trips to LA since I already have scheduled meetings. We can ask my friends to test the app too. This will help me look at how the app's algorithm is doing with matching. I actually don't see this being a big deal or hard at all. My vote is to do it. Knowing it twists a knife in your dad gives me great pleasure."

I couldn't help but wonder if I'd just jinxed myself. As soon as I'd agreed, a brush of cold air tickled down my spine as if sending a warning. I'd been cavalier in saying I didn't see it as a big deal.

Easy-peasy, you said?

Yeah, I was lying. Spending any time with Cal was a big deal to my wounded heart and pride.

Chapter Twelve
CAL

Home. When people asked me "Where's home?" I would cycle through all the places I'd spent time growing up. I once asked Jace what he called home, and he said he'd always thought of his childhood bedroom on his family ranch, but now that he was married, he thought of the kitchen of that same ranch because that was where he pictured his wife and kids.

Those images weren't anything I had. Home, during the school season, was the all-boys boarding school I went to, with its dorms and narrow bed in a room with five other boys. For breaks, I went to the big house my parents had outside Denver. I didn't have a kid's bedroom like most of my friends. Sure, it was decorated like a boy's room, but it was never filled with stuff I liked or played with. Just things I couldn't touch.

When I thought of the one place I was the happiest growing up, it was my maternal grandparents' place, the Rolling Thunder Ranch. I hadn't been there in a decade. When I'd walked away from my dad and Sabrina, I left behind everyone and everything. The ranch had been in our family for generations, and the sprawling two-story eight-bedroom home had been my place of refuge. A place to escape my dad. When my mom had left my dad ten years ago, she moved to the ranch for good.

Currently, home was an apartment in Seattle with a view of the sound, when the day wasn't cloudy and rainy. But I was rarely there. I preferred to be in the office, at the gym, or on an assignment. I'd traveled so much that hotels felt the same as my apartment, only my apartment had more clothes and hotels had more food. And a TV.

I could thank my dad for all that. He'd taught me how to be a minimalist.

Although Sabrina claimed she was willing to be a part of this battle, she hadn't spoken to me on the plane. She'd kept her laptop open for the entire trip. She'd even sat next to Paul.

And I was fine with that, dammit. I'd only looked in her direction for a large portion of the flight because the side of the plane she was on had the most scenic views. That was what I'd said when she asked.

"Not mid-flight," had been her response.

I'd had to turn my back to her then. I was in a weird place with Sabrina. I didn't want to say I liked it because, well... I just didn't want to say that.

But I didn't not like it.

A few years after I'd left her in Vegas I set up Google alerts to ping me if she was ever in the news. Those little unexpected notifications that would slide across my screen had the power to cause a brief arrhythmia. Each time, I half expected the notification to be her engagement or wedding announcement. Each time, I was relieved when it wasn't.

I pushed a hand through my hair and tried to wrap my mind around how quickly my life had done a one eighty. My dad had to be choking on his spite. There was a bit of satisfaction in knowing that. And it was fitting that Sabrina got to play a part in it as well.

"Hello, dipshit. You just gonna sit there all day?" Sabrina asked.

I turned to find her standing by my seat. "Dipshit?"

"I tried all the names. Dipshit was the one that worked. Weird that." She gestured to the front of the plane. "We're here and ready to disembark. Where were you? Were you planning an escape? That you'd stay on and have your pilot fly you back to Seattle and bail on us?"

We'd taken my company jet, which seated sixteen and had sleeping quarters. Both the pilot and flight attendant were staring at me with smiles that asked questions more than projected kindness. They were stuck on board until I got off. I was holding everyone up.

How long was I in a fugue?

I quickly stood and immediately towered over Sabrina. "I doubt you used any other name to get my attention."

"It's your word against mine." She turned on her heel and strode out of the plane. Dressed in figure-fitting dark jeans, a gauzy white blouse, and turquoise cowboy boots, she looked like a rich girl who'd grown up out West. Her long black hair was in a thick braid down her back, and I wanted to tug on it like a dumb middle schooler who didn't know how to talk to girls so antagonized them instead.

I had single-handedly built a multimillion-dollar business in under ten years, and this leggy woman with a pink birthmark where her spine ended and her ass began had turned me into a dimwit. As I watched her ass sway seductively, I couldn't burn away the memories of all the times I'd kissed said birthmark. I hoped this fake dating would kill me and put me out of my misery. I was in a paradoxical hell. I wanted to be around her and dreaded it at the same time.

I grunted in self-derision. "Dammit all," I mumbled.

"What's that?" she asked as she took the stairs down to the tarmac, glancing over her shoulder with a bewitching smile.

I caught a waft of her spicy perfume. My dick twitched. "I think I left something back at the office."

I was so attracted to her it was stupid. I always had been, from the minute I'd seen her thirteen years ago at a party at some dumb frat house. And here she was, better than ever. God help me.

"You're not at work, Cal. Forget about it."

I wished I could. I really wished I could.

Paul was already across the tarmac of the private airport, where a large, black SUV was waiting for us. My mother had thought ahead. I opened the back cargo space and started throwing bags in. I needed to get to the ranch and away from everyone.

I was about to close the hatch when Sabrina grabbed my arm. "Wait. Let's get a picture." She spun me around so the airplane was behind us. And behind that were the mountains. She stood slightly in front of me but to my side and held out an arm to take a selfie.

She looked over her shoulder at me. "Get in the frame, Cal. All I can see is your big, dumb chest."

"You think my chest is big?" I leaned over her shoulder.

"And dumb." She smiled and took the shot. She studied it before giving a one-shoulder shrug. "It'll have to do. I'll hashtag it 'getting my getaway on.' Oh, look," she said, opening up my app, ProtectedLove. We'd put the beta on our phones before making the trip. "Over a hundred people have signed up to test the app." She tapped her screen. "And just like we asked, a bunch are from this area. That's encouraging."

She was thinking about the job, and here I was thinking about her body.

"Get in the car." I gave her a nudge in the back to get her moving. But instead of going around to the right, she took the back seat directly behind the driver's seat, where I was sitting.

"I can't wait to see where you became you, Calvin," she said.

Hard money on her kicking the back of my seat the entire hour drive to the ranch.

"I didn't always live out here. I spent a lot of time in a boarding school, but this is where I came back to when I wasn't in school and didn't have to be with my parents." Essentially, when I was allowed. I always had to downplay my love for the ranch because to like it meant my father would take it away.

In the three years we'd dated, I'd never once even thought to bring Sabrina here. I hadn't wanted the ugliness of my homelife to touch her, and though the ranch was, for all intents and purposes, a happy place, it also served as a reminder of all the things I didn't have and the thing every kid wanted—a happy, safe home. So in college, when we'd had a chance to go home, I'd always picked Sabrina's Texas ranch, my other refuge.

I caught her eye in the rearview mirror. "My mom and sister live full time on the ranch."

She nodded and didn't ask any other questions, which

surprised me. She'd never met my family except for the one time she met my dad. I'd explained about being estranged from my dad, and she'd accepted that with blind faith. I sometimes wondered how my life would have turned out had I married Sabrina in Vegas and my dad met her afterward. Would Dalton still have gone on the attack? Would he have come between us and broken down all we had?

"I contacted a very good friend of mine, a reporter out here." She put a hand up to stop Paul. "I was off the record. I trust her immensely. I told her about the app, and she signed up. She said she'll help with some press with whatever we need. Do a story if we want. She knows what's up, and she suggested that she take pictures of the first date we select from the app. I don't know if you've played around with the app, Cal, since we put in our info, but one suggestion was that we take out horses and go sightseeing, and I really liked that. It's a great first date."

"That's a terrible first-date suggestion. That stranger could murder you," I grumbled. Sure, there was truth to it being somewhat unsafe, but my reaction was more related to how quickly I wanted to do this.

"You're not a stranger. That's why the app suggested it. Whoever added the section to explain why the activity was being suggested was a genius."

"That would be Citra," Paul said.

Sabrina leaned between the seats. "You have horses, Cal?"

I nodded. "It's a ranch, so..."

She rolled her eyes. "Maybe not everyone uses horses. I saw a show once where a guy used a drone to survey his land and corral sheep."

"A drone?" Paul asked.

"Yeah. It even barked to help move the sheep."

I smirked. "I saw the same show. No one uses drones. That was just for TV."

"Some people use ATVs. I have one on my ranch." She sat back and crossed her arms. "It was a fair question."

She was annoyed with me. Good, I could live with that. Annoyed I could handle. Nice made me a weak-kneed jackass.

"You are so prickly," she mumbled.

* * *

Sabrina

* * *

We fell into silence. Exhausted, I closed my eyes, rested my head against the window, and took a catnap. Only hours earlier, I'd been in my bed in Texas when Cal had barged in.

I woke when the SUV slowed and made a left turn. I blinked several times to clear the fuzz from my head. He'd turned onto a private road and crossed under a large ranch arch made from insanely large timbers. A sign declaring The Rolling Thunder Ranch swung softly in the breeze from the cross timber. I sat up and looked out the window. Miles and miles of deep-green land spread out around us. To the right was the backdrop of blue-and-brown mountains shaded by white, puffy cotton-ball clouds in a baby-blue sky.

I'd been to Wyoming several times because my friends Jace, Meredith, Cricket, Cori, and Fort lived out here. I never got tired of the view. And this one looked strikingly familiar.

"How far away do you live from Jace?" I asked.

I knew they'd been friends before college and were both from Wyoming. I knew he'd been to boarding school, though I'd thought it was only his high school years so he could get into an Ivy League college. Which he did. And then turned down to go to a state school in Texas.

But ranches were vast and isolating. When I was at Jace's, I'd never thought about who was out there beyond the fences because I knew they rarely ran into people unless they went into town.

"He's the next town over, a little over an hour."

"How far away from Wolf's Creek are you?" Wolf's Creek was where Cori and Fort lived. And Shane and Ellie. Wolf's Creek was my favorite.

"This is Wolf's Creek," he said as we crept along the road.

I sat upright. "Shut up—it is not!" How many times had I been out here and never once run into him or heard his name or any hint of him? Millions, that was how many. Millions.

"It is."

"You know Fort Besingame?"

Cal shook his head. "I haven't been back here in years."

"How could you not come home to this? It's stunning. Already, I feel a thousand times lighter, like I can handle anything. Looking at this view is like doing deep meditation. It's good for the soul." One more opportunity our paths had run close together but never crossed.

The ranch itself was two stories and sprawling with a wraparound porch. There were three barns and lots of corrals. Cattle grazed in a field far off. The house had dark timber trim and accents, contrasting with a whitewashed house that was all big windows and sunshine.

He pulled up to the side of the house near a garage and sighed heavily, not moving. "It is spectacular, isn't it?" He seemed to be soaking it in.

"And I thought I had something special in Texas." I got out, stretching like a cat after a nap in the sun.

He got out beside me, and I bumped into him as I lifted my hands high over my head. I froze and gave him a side-eye as I felt the rush of heat I always got when I touched Cal. Then I did a quick few sidesteps to move away, arms still in the air to finish my stretch. Cal chuckled.

Footsteps on the porch drew my attention. I was fixing my shirt, which was only partially tucked in, when I looked up and saw Morgan, the coworker who had started this whole nonsense.

I pointed at her. "I know you." To Cal, I said, "This is the person who asked to hire me."

"So I was told." He gestured to the older woman. "Sabrina, this woman, full of trickery and hidden agendas, is my mother, Morgan Beckett."

"But I go by my maiden name now, Barker."

"Your mother?" I remembered how the woman had stared at me so curiously when we'd met. What were her full intentions? Morgan had to have known of our past when she tried to hire me. I turned to Paul, who was unloading the bags. "I owe you a twenty. You were right—he is human." To Cal, I said, "I thought you'd been hatched from an egg like all cold-blooded snakes."

Morgan slapped her hands together in pleasure. "You are such a delight, Sabrina. I cannot wait to get to know you better."

Cal groaned. "She's not going to be here for long, Mom."

Morgan put her hands on her hips, her smile large.

"Well, don't just stand there, Calvin. Bring your friend in, and let's make her comfortable."

Cal moved up the stairs next to me and gave me the side-eye. "We're not friends. Just two people who once knew each other."

I gave him a wicked smile. So my line about us not having a friendship had hit a nerve. "Mere acquaintances."

The space between his brows made a divot as his gaze roved all over my face, probably trying to figure me out. Good. I liked my Cal Beckett unnerved, with a side of confusion.

Chapter Thirteen
SABRINA

The Rolling Thunder Ranch was like a breath of fresh air or a hug from a stranger that felt familiar and comfortable. Weirdly okay.

Cal's family was a delight. Aside from his mother and his younger sister, Brynna, there was the housekeeper, Mrs. Claudia, and a seven-year-old named Rod who I thought might be her grandson. This kid was destined to be a cowboy, based on the way he hooked his thumbs over his waistband belt and spit every few minutes.

"Too much time with the ranch hands," Mrs. Claudia scolded, but that didn't stop him.

When Cal had told me he and his family no longer spoke, that had been sufficient for me. But it would seem in the last decade, something had shifted. Watching them, I witnessed a comfort between Cal and his mother and good-natured banter between him and his sister. Cal explained that Brynna, seven years her senior, was a glassblower and that one of the barns was actually her workshop. Brynna had to have been around sixteen when Cal and I were dating—a child.

How could he possibly have been cut off from her?

Brynna quickly gave me a tour of her amazing work. She was quiet, but her personality was reflected in the art she created—bold colors woven between softer ones. It wasn't until I saw a vase that looked similar to one I had in my house that I put the pieces together. Brynna Beckett's work was in some of the finest galleries. A few years back, I'd bought some pieces, not knowing she was Cal's sister.

Overall, the vibe at the ranch was welcoming and warm. Moments like this were the hardest for me. Though I enjoyed them, I was acutely aware of what I didn't have—a family. Living relatives. Loneliness crept into these lovely moments and pulled at me. They made me feel itchy, which then made me get restless and needy with wanting to act on my adoption plan. The adoption was something that simply could not be rushed, but boy I wish I could rush it. I was ready.

We spent the rest of the day getting settled, talking over our next move and, for me, getting caught up on sleep. The next morning, we were set to meet Cricket and Cori to put the plan in motion. Cricket was going to do an interview, and Cori was taking pictures, which was a huge relief because everyone knew the deal, and it wasn't like we were lying to them too. And that had been my caveat. I didn't want to straight-up lie to people. The beauty of social media was that you could put something out there, and let people add their own narratives, since they were going to do it anyway.

I ran outside to greet them when I heard Cricket's pickup come down the long drive. No sooner had they parked than they were out of the vehicle, and we were all hugging each other's necks. I'd known Cori since we were kids, my dad having done a short gambling stint in the small town where she'd grown up. That was where I had come to know Fort as well. And when he'd needed a pretend fiancée, and Cori had needed to escape said small town, where her daddy had left a wake of angry people, I'd put them together. Now they were happily married with two kids, one just six weeks old.

Cori looked tired but blissed out.

"I'm so happy to see you two," I said. I really did have the best friends.

"We're happy you're here. We've been looking forward to your visit for a while," Cori said, still hugging me.

"And the fact that you came even earlier and we get to help you guys out with this problem is even better," Cricket said with her arm around both of us.

"It's been forever since I've done something for myself that wasn't kid related. I love them—don't get me wrong—but it's nice to have adult time," Cori said as we pulled apart. She picked up her camera bag. I loved that Cricket had asked her to be our photographer.

"Who knew your past was just right down the road?" Cricket said with a wag of her brows.

"Not me," I said. "But Jace knew."

"He's wicked good at keeping secrets," Cricket said.

"No kidding. Come on. Let's get some coffee and map this out." I gestured to the house.

Inside, I poured us some coffee. Paul soon came into the room. Cricket got immediately down to business, happily volunteering to be our first single to test the app. She'd also been monitoring the news landscape for us.

"So far, nothing has changed," Cricket said. "The interview you all did yesterday in Texas is still the topic, as is the Instagram Sabrina posted. Nick has been peppered with questions, but he's handling it like the pro he is. I did find a blog making some broad accusations about your dad and possible tax issues. I'm not sure where that's going or if it'll get picked up, but I assume it will."

"My dad?"

Paul chimed in. "Cal did say nothing would be off-limits. You have to be prepared for this, Sabrina."

"I am. Well, I guess I'm getting there. But it's really odd to see someone go after a person who is deceased."

"I'll show you what I write up before I publish so maybe we can try to anticipate any spin-off questions. Sound good?" Cricket asked.

Paul and I nodded.

"I'm also going to write about the app. Dating in a remote small town is not easy."

" 'Scuse me, ma'am."

I turned to find little Rod standing in the doorway. "Hi," I said.

"I was told to saddle up some horses but not which ones. I'm assuming the giant quarter horse, but which horse would you like? There's a paint that's not too sluggish and not too testy that I like. Want me to saddle her for you?"

Dear Lord, he was adorable. Cori fairly cooed next to me from his adorableness, this child-man.

"That works for me. I defer to you, Rod."

He tipped his hat at me, and Cricket smothered a chuckle with a cough.

"Can I get some coffee to go, please, Mrs. Claudia?" he asked.

The housekeeper-cook had been busy with biscuits.

She slapped a hand on the counter. "No, sir, you may not have some coffee. You are too young. But once you get that horse saddled, you come back, and I'll give you a hot biscuit."

"But all ranch hands drink coffee," he protested.

She came around the counter and shooed him away with a tea towel. "I'll put fresh strawberry jam on one side of that biscuit and that chocolate stuff you like on the other. Now, git."

He started to leave but stopped. "You mean Nutella?" His eyes were wide with excitement.

"That's it." She waved her towel at him again.

"Deal." He dashed out the door.

"Little stinker," she said with a chuckle.

"What a cutie," Cricket said. "He's doing real well with you, Mrs. Claudia. He's lucky to have you."

She tsk-tsked but went back to her work.

Paul glanced at his watch. "We have to get this show on the road. Cal has a meeting this afternoon with some clients. You all go on out, and I'll go find him."

I feigned indignation. "Get this show on the road?" The show was the first fake date for Cal and me. "Is this how you approach dating, Paul?" I shook my head. "You make it sound so romantic. Thumbs-down. One star on this date. App fail."

Paul laughed. "Just be glad I was the one that said it and not Cal." He winked and left the room.

I headed out with my two friends. "So, care to share, Sabrina?" Cori asked.

"Nope, it's old news."

"How about some new news?" Cricket asked. "I mean, I knew what happened back then because you mentioned it briefly, but I'll admit, now that I know who the other party is, it's obvious you two are perfect for each other."

"You've never met him," I scoffed.

"Oh, I know, but I've read a lot, and those pictures of you two..." She pretended to fan herself.

"Agreed," Cori chimed in. "That look he was giving you in that last picture, that's the look Fort gave me that got me pregnant. You be careful."

The hotel picture. That was what she was talking about. That same picture had told me there were still feelings.

I looked out across the lovely landscape. "Yeah, I'm not really worried about the getting-pregnant part."

Cori stopped in her tracks. "Oh, Sabrina, I'm so sorry. I wasn't thinking. All I really meant was that's usually when he sexes me up. It's a hot look."

Both Cori, Cricket, and Meredith knew I had severe endometriosis, which meant my chances of conceiving were slim to none because of the abnormal tissue growing outside my uterus. I'd spent a good chunk of my savings on various treatments and trying in vitro with a sperm donor. Nothing had happened except the dwindling bank account. Hence the need for more money. I couldn't get on the adoption list until I had fifty K in the bank.

"It's okay. You didn't say anything wrong, I'm just super-sensitive." I gave her arm a squeeze.

"Rightly so," Cricket said. "But Cori's right. Be careful here. This guy hurt you once. Chances are it could happen again. And you deserve some happiness. You've had enough heartbreak."

Cricket caught my eye, and I knew she was talking about herself just as much as she was talking about me. She'd fallen in love with her deceased sister's husband, a man she emphatically stated was off-limits. Reason number one for trying Cal's app—she was ready to find a love that was her own.

"Though he is superhot," Cori said. "Too bad you can't keep it casual, because otherwise, I say you just hit that, as the guys say, and have some fun."

We both looked at her, shocked.

"Sorry, hormones," she said sheepishly.

"You're telling me to go wild, and Cricket is telling me to be careful. Angel and devil. But here's the deal. Yeah, we have chemistry. But we're different people with different lives, and I don't think either of us fits into the other's. This here"—I swept my hand to indicate all that was the ranch—"is pretend. It's a job. And it will end."

And yeah, Cal was hot. And I had thought about hitting that, as Cori had put it. And then I thought I should poke my eyes out so I wouldn't have to see him anymore, and maybe those naughty thoughts would stop. But each time I had a steamy thought, I reminded myself of one simple fact: this would all be coming to an end.

Chapter Fourteen

SABRINA

Standing outside with the horse Rod had saddled for me, I was laughing with Cori as she used me as a test subject to warm up her "shutter finger." I was making goofy faces and poses. Being outside with the sun and a cool breeze, with nothing to do but be right here, was like having a massive weight lifted off me. Or at least the weight had shifted to the side and was temporarily forgotten. I wasn't at an event, networking. I wasn't staring at my depleted savings account, wondering how I was going to fill it in a timely manner. I wasn't alone. Sometimes I got caught up in all I needed to do, forgetting the right now. Which reaffirmed my decision to adopt but also reminded me that I sorely neglected downtime and self-care.

But also, this moment was taking me closer to my goals. Which was a win. This didn't feel like work.

Cal strode across the yard toward the corral. He was in dark jeans and an autumn-colored flannel shirt with a T-shirt underneath and was carrying a brown Stetson. And was that a hint of a smile on his face? Well, hot dang, it sure looked like one.

If I'd forgotten to prioritize downtime, Cal had downright cut it from his life. The previous night at dinner, the stories from Brynna, Mrs. Claudia, and Cal's mother about the ranch and the town had worked him over in the best possible way. He'd left Peru and that attack behind and joined us in Wyoming. His shoulders had visibly relaxed, and the frown between his eyes had softened.

I beamed my brightest smile at him. "Morning, sunshine."

He walked to the fence and leaned against it, one booted leg up on the low rail. He flicked his fingers at me. "Come here."

I shook my head. "What for?"

There was a mischievous glint in his eyes. He must have seen the message I'd left on his mirror and jumped back on his pole. I wasn't going to apologize. I was here to make his life miserable, all while helping him out. That was the only way to balance this weird-ass situation I was in.

"Reenie."

I had to give him credit. The man could suppress a grin really well. I crossed my arms and arched one brow.

"I didn't figure you for a chicken," he said, crooking a finger at me as he stuck his Stetson on his head.

Dear Lord, he looked like a sexy bandit out to steal all the ladies' jewels and hearts. I strolled toward him and got as close as I could with the fence between us, without bumping noses.

I mimicked his position and put my foot on the lower rung. "Something the matter?"

He looked over his shoulder at my friends, who were

loading up the ATV they were going to use to follow us. His gaze swung back to mine and held it. "I got your message on the mirror last night. Is this going to be a thing?"

"What do you mean by 'a thing'?"

"Something that happens a lot."

I shrugged one shoulder. "Maybe. Depends. If the spirit moves me."

"And the spirit moved you to give me a list of why we will never be friends?" His gaze bounced to my lips, then quickly back up again.

"Well, of course. When you told your mom we weren't friends, I thought maybe you needed to have some whys in your back pocket in case she asked. This way, we'll be on the same page if she asks me too. And it wasn't a list."

"There were three reasons. That's a list." He held up three fingers.

I gave a dismissive wave. "That's the start of a list. Five is more like a real list."

"We aren't friends because I'm too tall?" He arched a brow and... yep, there it was, a tiny little twitch of the lips.

"Yes. Look at my posture right now. I have to crane my neck to look up at you, and it's eventually going to become an issue where I might need physical therapy and weekly massages." I paused and held up a finger. "No. My bad. Can't use weekly massages as a negative because that would actually be a perk."

I poked his rock-hard chest, mostly because I still couldn't believe he was so solid, and this had become a fun habit. I thought about that solid chest of his too much. I was so very curious to see it in real life, not just picture it in my mind's eye. I was a fool.

He leaned in, and I caught a whiff of him. He smelled

fresh, like soap. But not one of those dull bars that people just grabbed at random. No, this scent reminded me of the tall trees and the mountains around me and the blue sky above me. He smelled like the outdoors. Cedar and...

I couldn't put my finger on it. I drew in another breath, savoring it. My knees got weak. Like, I actually swooned.

Dear God, I swooned. What the actual hell is wrong with me? All from whiffing this guy. I rested more on the fence and tried to get a hold of myself.

"You aren't so short, you know," he said.

I blinked at him prettily as I scrambled for words. "That's just because you see me as larger than life."

"And we aren't friends because I think dolled-up coffee is the equivalent of a milkshake?"

I reached up to tighten my ponytail. "Breve, latte—those are not milkshakes. They are coffee art, and aficionados everywhere are appalled by your insult."

He rolled his eyes. "They'll survive. You think your friend is a good enough photographer to pull this off; make us look like something we aren't?" It almost sounded like he was fishing.

"Yeah, totally. Cori knows what she's doing. Have faith." I patted him on the arm.

"Let's get this done, then." He pushed up to climb over the fence, and I had to back up and move to the side to get out of his way. In two moves, he was over it and dropping down beside me. "Want me to get your horse for you, or you got it?"

Though the brim of his Stetson cast a shadow across his eyes, it did nothing to tamp down the steely look in them.

"I got it." I shook away the heady feeling that was swirling around me. "Actually, Rod got him."

Eye contact was bad, bad, bad. When he looked at me, my stomach got all zingy, like a swarm of bees were in there bumping against each other. Being near him made my body vibrate. And remembering our past made my heart sting. And then there was the swooning, for crying out loud.

"But we should make a short video about this. Tell the people what we're doing and why we're doing it. You know, for the app," I said.

He agreed and just stood there, so I whipped out my phone and made a quick video about our first date, explaining that because we knew each other, going off together in an isolated place wasn't scary. Trust had been established. Cal listed reasons why this wouldn't be a good idea for the first twenty dates. His point about not really knowing someone after just a handful of dates, even when you felt like you knew them, hit home. And then we were done with that part.

"Ma'am." He tipped his hat, then strode out to the larger of the two horses.

I called out, "What about the third reason? Do you want to discuss that?" I smirked.

"Nope," he said over his shoulder. "Not much I can do about that, can I?"

* * *

CAL

* * *

When I'd turned in the previous night, I'd been caught off

guard by Sabrina's loopy and pretty handwriting on my mirror.

Top three reasons you aren't friend material:

1. You're too tall.

I smiled at that. She used to like that I was tall. I didn't really think that was a reason.

2. You call dolled-up coffee "milkshakes."

The horror.
My smile hitched a tad higher.

3. And oh yeah, that whole "broke my heart" thing.

My smile fell.

When it came down to it, what I'd done had created a barrier the size of the Grand Canyon between us. She might be here, helping me, laughing with my family at dinner, but for her, being here was just a job. The shit-ton of hurt resting in that canyon made traversing our past damn near impossible.

Then I'd gone outside and seen her in the corral with the paint. Sabrina wore dark jeans over turquoise boots and a turquoise shirt tied at the waist—showing off every damn curve—and her hair was up in a long, bouncy ponytail. She was laughing with her friends and teasing the kid Rod. I had a flashback to a time in college when we'd gone back to her ranch to see a new horse her dad had purchased. We'd sat on the fence, our thighs pressed together, my arm around her waist as we watched her dad and the horse get to know each other. Then she'd turned toward me, tucked her face into the curve of my neck, and delivered the softest three kisses along my jawline.

"One because you're so tall, two for the way you smell, and three for the way you love me," she'd whispered in my ear. I'd come undone, and had her dad not been there, I would have climbed off that fence, picked her up to straddle me, then showed her right then and there all the ways I did love her.

Seeing her in the corral and having that memory, I did exactly what I said I wasn't going to do—brought up the note on my mirror.

"Ready?" Cricket called from the ATV.

I looked to Sabrina, who nodded and mounted her horse. I grabbed the reins to my seventeen-hands quarter horse, tall to accommodate my height, and was up and galloping toward Sabrina and the gate in seconds.

Cricket stood up in her seat in the ATV. "How about taking us down toward No Man's Lake?"

I gave her a thumbs-up and took the lead. As we rode through the woods and the valley that gave way to the mountains, I found the weight of the stress ball that had been sitting on my chest easing. I'd stayed away from the ranch and my family because, in the past, I found that the quiet and slower pace only opened the door to memories and regrets. I loved Jace and his family, but even with them, I had a limit—after two nights, my mood would sour dramatically as I faced the other side of what life had to offer. I didn't see an option for that side unless I did exactly as my father wanted, including dating and marrying whomever he chose.

I glanced over my shoulder at Sabrina. Her face showed all the pleasure she was experiencing. I'd loved that about her. She'd never been one to hide her feelings if she didn't have to. This new Sabrina hid more than she showed. Except at the moment. The beauty and wonder of the scenery were mirrored in her expression of awe. She leaned forward and rubbed a hand across her paint's nose, whispering words that I assumed were filled with love and kindness because that was who she was.

The ATV was everywhere—ahead of us, then pausing to get behind. Cricket did a good job of not getting in our faces. We came around a bend forty minutes after leaving the ranch, and the space opened up to a glacial blue lake with the mountains reflected in the water.

Sabrina gasped. "This is incredible."

"It's one of my favorites," Cricket said. "It's very popular."

"Mine too. I won a photography contest once with this scenery. Just stunning," said Cori. Apparently, she'd known Sabrina since they were kids. That was kind of cool.

"Funny how popular it is and yet how remote it feels." I shifted in the saddle and let the reins rest across my legs.

Cricket chuckled. "Yeah, in all the years I've come out here, I've never run into anyone. I think that's the magic of the lake. Let's get a few shots here, and I'll ask a few questions. I'm going to run the article as a behind-the-scenes test of the app." She winked at me. "And then we can call it a day, and you both can do what you want."

My eyes swung to Sabrina's. I liked the idea of alone time, just the two of us.

Sabrina didn't look at me. "I have a Zoom meeting with the director of that documentary in a few hours, so this is probably as far as I'll explore today."

Yeah, I had a meeting this afternoon too. Funny how I'd forgotten that just now.

Cricket shrugged as if to say *your loss*, then got to directing the photographer on what shots she wanted. "Hey, Cal? I can call you that, right? You haven't been on a date in how long? This is for the article."

"Uhh, it's been awhile. I'm really not sure of the date." I bent over to check a saddlebag, not the least bit ready to see anyone's expression or for them to see mine."

"Was it even this year?" Cricket asked.

"What's the next question?" This from Sabrina.

Thank fuck.

"Well, I know Sabrina's been on some dates recently, and I'm not sure about Cal. But this date is more like an excursion. Are you really comfortable being out here together, and can you picture doing this with someone you recently dated?"

I looked at Sabrina. She adjusted her hat. "To be honest, no. I can't see myself doing this with any of the guys I dated previously. Maybe it's because Cal and I used to go riding for fun when we dated, so this feels familiar, normal."

"I think that's why the app suggested it," I said.

Cricket gave us a thumbs-up. "One point for the app." She continued with the questions and asked me for tips about wildlife safety. Then she stared at her phone a second. She looked at Sabrina. "About that blog I mentioned. The one hinting at your dad's tax issues."

Sabrina turned to me. "It hasn't been picked up by any papers yet," she said as though trying to reassure me. I'd warned her about this happening.

Cricket put out a hand to stop Sabrina. "I just got an alert. It's getting traction. I think we should have a response.

I can put out a statement. Before we rode out, Paul and I agreed that we don't want to make a big deal about it, but we don't want to ignore it either."

Sabrina groaned as she dismounted and gave her horse a quick rub along the neck. "My dad never had any issues with taxes. Being diligent with taxes was nonnegotiable for him. It won't stick."

I dismounted as well. "It's part of the smear campaign. It doesn't have to be true to stick." I told you so. I opened my mouth to tell her that but stopped because she had one finger pointed at me.

"Don't say it."

"I don't have to. But I can see on your face how upset you are. Meaning the article has done its job."

Instantly, she wiped her feelings away and hid behind her poker face. "I know you all said he would go after my dad, and I thought I was prepared, but I'm not going to lie. It hurts having him attacked."

I opened my mouth to apologize, but she began wagging her finger at me.

"Don't say it!" she cried.

"I wasn't going to tell you I told you so." I stepped toward her, wanting to wrap her in my arms and hold her until the awful feeling she was experiencing dissipated.

"You were going to say you were sorry, but you don't have to apologize for someone else's actions. I don't want to hear an apology. I want to fight back." She clenched her fists and held them up to her mouth as if they were keeping all the feeling words from escaping.

I wanted to find my father and pound his face in. Well, that was something I'd wanted to do every day, but watching Sabrina get pulled under this deadly current was hard as hell, a special kind of torture, just as I'd known it would be.

"Reenie." I stood in front of her, rubbing a hand down her upper arm as I searched for words of comfort.

"Reenie?" Cricket asked.

Cori gasped. "Her dad used to call her that. I had totally forgotten until I heard it just now."

I watched Sabrina cycle through her feelings.

"Ahhh," said Cricket with a chuckle. "We're gonna head out. We'll see you tomorrow. Hurry, Cori, get on the ATV."

Sabrina looked around me to them and shook her head. "You both are so obvious!" she called.

"Obviously wonderful friends!" Cori called back. Then she yawned and waved. "See ya." They crept away. When they hit the valley, the sound of the ATV gunning it echoed across the land.

"What was that about?" I asked.

Her fists were still clenched. I eased my hands over hers and slowly worked to pry her fingers apart.

"They're being stupid. Ignore them."

"Reenie, it's going to get uglier." My fingers were entwined with hers, her arms between us. "We can stop this anytime."

As I squeezed gently, an electric warmth shot up my arms and spread through my body. I felt our energy surge through me, and it was like a caveman-style drug making me feel horny and protective at the same time. My eyes did a quick dart to her lips, which were red from the wind and lingering lipstick.

She shook her head. "I was just caught off guard by the intensity of my feelings. There's no validity to the claim, and it can't hurt my dad. Just me. Now that this Band-Aid has been ripped off, I won't be blindsided by the next one."

"I will never hold it against you should you decide to quit at any time. Got it?"

"I'm not a quitter. But thank you." She smiled, but her eyes spoke to her sadness.

Off in the distance, an elk made a loud, wailing bugle sound. Sabrina jumped toward me. I twisted to the side to grab her horse's reins, catching them just as the mare was about to take flight.

"Oh no!" Sabrina pointed to my horse beating feet out of the valley. "For such a large horse, he really is a scaredy-cat, isn't he?"

I handed her the reins, then put two fingers in my mouth and gave a low whistle. "This usually brings him back."

"So he's done this before?" She arched a brow as she ran her hand up and down her paint's neck.

"Once or twice." I waited a beat and whistled again.

Nothing.

"Looks like he's gone gone."

"Ha," she said. "You think?"

"Don't laugh. We're going to have to ride back. Together."

Her smile widened as she mounted her horse. "You say that like it's a bad thing. Two people can share a horse without it meaning anything, right, Cal?"

Either she did not feel our chemistry, or she was a master at hiding it. I would put my money on the latter. She might not want to be with me—breaking her heart had likely sealed our fate of being apart—but that didn't mean we still didn't have chemistry.

Sabrina patted the front of her saddle. "You can ride bitch."

I gave her my *Are you kidding me?* look.

Her smile widened. "You can't ride the skirt. Your feet will drag. You're too tall."

"Seems to be an issue for you," I said.

"Not me. It's not my problem. It's yours."

I studied her before making my decision. She was going to torture me regardless—sharing space did that to me. So I might as well do it in comfort. I grabbed the pommel like I was going to pull myself up in front of her but instead snaked my other arm around her waist and pulled her off.

She cried out. "Cal, what are you doing?" She toppled onto me, all legs and arms. I spun around, righted her, then planted her on her feet before snatching the reins she'd let go of and quickly mounting her mare.

"Now, who's going to ride bitch?" I quirked a brow, my smile splitting my face.

She glanced at the rump, likely weighing her options.

"Sure, you can ride there," I said. "We both know that's not comfortable, but at least your legs won't drag." I held out my hand to pull her up. "Your choice."

She took my hand. "You're an asshole." She stuck her foot in the stirrup over mine and let me lift her.

"So you've said." I adjusted on the saddle so she had some space in front, but it was small, and when Sabrina took her seat, she was square in my lap. Her back was flush against my chest. Her spicy scent enveloped me. I closed my eyes and tried to gather my wits.

She looked over her shoulder and said in a husky, quiet voice, "Is there a problem?"

Hell yeah, there was a problem. Sabrina bouncing in my

lap the forty-minute ride home was going to kill me. I was going to literally die from either a heart attack or an aneurysm. There was no way my blood pressure wasn't absurdly high at the moment. I considered telling her I would slide back onto the rump, but she was right. My feet would drag, and my weight on the back part of the horse wouldn't be good either.

"There's no problem," I said.

Yet. Give this ride ten minutes max, and we were going to have a problem. A hard one at that. It was going to be right there between us.

Chapter Fifteen

CAL

I was caught between a rock and a hard place. No pun intended. I squirmed in the saddle, trying to give my crotch more room to breathe.

The natural canter of the horse meant we continued to bounce against each other. If I had the horse book it back to the ranch, then at least we would get home quicker and end this torture. But going fast meant less chance of controlling our body contact. Yet if we took a leisurely ride, my body would probably explode from all the building pressure.

And it wasn't just pressure in my pants that was building. This was just pressure on top of already mounting pressure. The pressure to stay one step ahead of my dad meant fighting a constant headache. I could feel in my bones that all we'd experienced thus far was equivalent to a predator baiting his prey, and the shitstorm was about to blow into town. The distraction of Sabrina in my lap was one I didn't need.

My hands were on the reins, bringing my arms to circle around her, my forearms rested on both my thighs and part of hers. My hands were close to her knees. And though I was touching her, I wanted to really touch her. My hands itched to rediscover her curves and valleys. Christ, I missed her. And for all the times I'd internet searched her or heard stories from Jace and gotten those pangs of longing, they were nothing like what I was feeling at the moment.

Total gut punch.

Back then, I'd reasoned that as long as there was space between us, and our last time together had been that awful breakup, she was safe from me and my family, and I was able to balance my wants and must dos.

But hell, must do had taken on a whole new meaning. As in, I must do anything to keep her near me. I must do anything to protect her. And my favorite—I must do her.

She looked over her shoulder, her lips turned down.

"What?" I checked my appendages to make sure they hadn't gotten a mind of their own and started feeling her up. Nope, all good.

She leaned back and turned a little so I could hear her better. "I thought your dad would come at me about my career, not my dad. I'm still kinda reeling, to be honest." She straightened and faced forward.

I leaned toward her. "I don't know what you want me to say. You won't let me apologize."

Her ponytail was near my cheek—I was that close— and I drew in this new warm scent of her. She was sultry and mysterious, and as much as I knew her, I also knew I didn't know her at all. This was a new Sabrina, and I liked it. Is her favorite kissing spot still right behind the earlobe? If I turned my head ever so slightly toward her, I could brush...

I ground my teeth together. Brush nothing. I needed a

cold shower and a punch in the nose. This was Sabrina, and she didn't deserve mixed signals.

"He knows I'll do everything to protect you." I hadn't meant to say it. Something about the slow canter, our synced rhythm, and her being technically in my arms had short-circuited my brain, and I'd forgotten there were things I didn't want her to know.

She gave me a curious look over her shoulder. "That's stupid. Our breakup was ugly, and we haven't seen each other in over ten years. Why would he even think that?"

Pressing my lips together to keep any other revealing statements from flowing out, I looked over her shoulder, not meeting her eyes.

"Cal?" She shifted so she could turn more, and now her sweet ass was rubbing against my thigh.

Why did we have to travel so far from the ranch? I wondered if it might be worth walking the rest of the way.

"Calvin!" she snapped.

"What?" I gave her eyes a quick drive-by, hoping she'd take that as enough eye contact.

Sabrina grunted in frustration, then as if performing acrobatics on a horse, shuffled in her seat, swung her legs around, and before I knew it, she had turned herself around to face me, riding backward.

"What are you doing?" I asked. This was not going to go well. I could feel that in my gut. We were either going to fight or do something far more stupid.

"What are you not telling me?" She narrowed her eyes.

"Not telling you about what?" I was going have to play the long game here and hope she gave up.

She shook her head. "You forget that I know you, Cal. So don't think I'm going to play the deliberately obtuse game with you. Why would your father assume you would protect me? It's been a decade. We haven't seen each other, or even spoken one word to each other, in years."

Her new position put her closer. Her legs were over the tops of my thighs, and I could see down her shirt... if I wanted. She was that close. Does it not bother her to be like this? Is she not acutely aware of the attraction that remains between us? She'd told the reporters it was restrained passion, and to me, that had been a perfect summation. Walking away from her had been an exercise in restraint. Sitting here, touching her, watching her—it was all restraint. It was enough to break a man.

She gripped the side of the saddle and looked ridiculous bopping up and down in rhythm with the horse's canter, a scowl on her face. My arms were still around her, holding the reins, our canter slow and lazy. Seducing us. Or maybe that was just me.

But this situation needed a quick shift, and I was the man to do it. Her position gave me an idea. In hindsight, it might not have been a good one.

I leaned in and closed my arms around her.

"What are you doing?" She bent back, her hands grabbing my biceps.

"What are you doing?" I made a point of staring at her from top to lap, to draw her attention to all the ways our bodies were touching.

Her eyes went wide.

"Maybe you should turn back around," I said.

"Maybe you should answer my question." She met my arched brow with one of her own.

"What question?" I smirked.

* * *

SABRINA

* * *

The man was exasperating. That seemed to be a running theme with Cal Beckett 2.0. My Cal, college Cal, had been tactfully honest, which I had found refreshing.

That was why I'd turned around in the saddle. For a moment there, he was my Cal. The feel of him behind me was as familiar to me as if it were my own body. I'd watched his hands loosely hold the reins, and I knew those hands. Knew the scar across the knuckles of his three middle fingers on his left hand, from an accident he'd had as a child. I knew the feel of the scar when our hands were entwined. And for a moment, I forgot where I was, or maybe I just lost the last ten years because so much was familiar, and it felt so good. Familiarity was comfort, and I sorely missed it.

Then I mentioned my father, and all the loneliness of the years washed over me. My mother had died when I was three, and though I had her parents, they passed when I was a teen, leaving me with just my dad—until I met Cal. With him, I saw more. I saw a growing family, and I hoped and wished and crossed my fingers because, dear Lord, I wanted that. I dreamed of so many wants with Cal that I felt greedy, but I never once thought I was asking for too much. Until it was all taken away. Cal left. My dad died. My uterus betrayed me. And I was... alone. Really, truly, deeply without.

And then Cal had said his dad had targeted me because he knew Cal would protect me. Why would a man who walked away protect me? And why would his dad think he would do that?

I caught his eye and held it. "You keep saying stuff about protecting me. You can't protect me from what your dad and his cohorts plan to do. You can't protect me from the press or whatever. And it's not your job to protect me. You gave up that right in Vegas."

He was the first to break eye contact as he looked over my shoulder, a stubborn set to his jaw, the muscle in his cheek popping. He was trying to find the right words. I knew him. I knew how to interpret that look.

He cleared his throat. "Whether you see me as a friend or not, I will always protect you. It's what I do. Just because we couldn't be together anymore didn't mean I stopped caring for you."

"If you still care for me, then tell me why we broke up in Vegas."

He shook his head. "I'm not sure it matters anymore."

"What if it matters to me?"

"Reenie?" He sounded aggrieved.

I reached out and touched the scar that ran under his chin and toward his jawline. "Remember when you got this? We went to the Caribbean for spring break."

His eyes flicked to mine, skimmed past my lips, then looked away. "Your dad was there at a tournament."

I gave a small smile. "Yeah, he was kicking ass, chalking up the wins." He'd won enough to pay my tuition for the next year, had I needed it, but my grandparents had funded my college.

A smile teased at Cal's lips. "Watching him play was amazing. And we ran into some others from school down there, and one was a girl Jace liked. Remember that?"

I barked out a laugh and nodded. "I wasn't legal drinking age, so you kept ordering me virgin drinks, then swapping a few of them with Jace's. He didn't know—he was so caught up in that girl."

He nodded, a smile fully on his face. Lord, he was beautiful when he smiled. "But you told him she liked the guy that was in their group, and he liked her. They just hadn't found the courage to take the next step yet. Even then, you could read people. You were a matchmaker, and you didn't even know it."

I had always been really good setting up couples. I just sucked at it when it came to me.

"And we swam with the dolphin, and afterward, I was ready to switch my degree to marine biology just so I could swim with dolphins for a living," I said.

Cal tipped his head back and laughed. "You were obsessed with that dolphin. You said Capri-Sun was your spirit animal." His voice was deep with a hint of scratchiness yet smooth and comforting as well.

My heart was bulging with happiness from the memory. My head was calling me a fool for going down memory lane.

"Capricious," I said, committing to being a fool. "His name was Capricious."

He met my gaze, the corners of his eyes crinkling with pleasure. "That's right. I don't know why I can't remember that."

"Because you were jealous," I said, recalling all the fake fights we'd had about me and the dolphin.

He searched my face for a beat, then wiped a hand across his scar. "I was only jealous of how much of your time that dolphin was taking. You went to the dolphin, and Jace and I went to the Jet Skis and acted like fools. Racing and being stupid guys. That Jet Ski bucked me off like a bull does a rider."

I followed his fingers across his scar. "Who knew water could cut like this?"

He grabbed my hand in his, and we held each other's gaze. "What are we doing here?" Cal asked, his eyes flicking to the space between us.

"What do you mean?" The shift in conversation had me confused.

"Sitting like this? What do you want from me with this?" His voice was raw.

"I want the truth. I want to know why you keep me in the dark about that night."

He transferred the reins to one hand, then slid the other down my back and stopped at the top of my butt. He looked up and met my gaze, his eyes shadowed by his Stetson, but I saw a flash of something, remorse maybe, in his gray eyes. Then he jerked me toward him until I was practically sitting on top of him. Driven by reflex, I gasped at the sudden closeness and clutched his shoulders to steady myself. There wasn't a hint of daylight between our bodies.

"Sitting like that makes me want to do this." He clutched me tighter. "And this." His head dipped low, putting his mouth close to my neck. His hot breath warmed the spot behind my ear.

Because my body was a traitorous bitch, I shifted to give him access and so his Stetson wouldn't bump me and come off. I dug my fingers into his shoulders as my heart thudded loudly in my ears.

"But I can't do this," he whispered. "That wouldn't be right. Because what would follow? A fling?" He shook his head. "I couldn't live with that. Not a relationship—I don't want one. That means when we're done with this job, we go back to our lives. The one where you're not in mine and I'm not in yours because our time together has passed."

Like a bucket of cold water had been dumped on my head, I came back to reality. I pushed away from him and did the same swivel in the saddle I'd done before, putting my back to him. We rode the rest of the way in silence.

Chapter Sixteen
CAL

With my job, I sometimes had to stay up for forty-eight hours straight. I sometimes didn't get to shower for twice as long as that. I'd done a few days without food and slept out in the rain because that was the safest place to be. But no night in the history of the time since I'd owned Optium had I had a night as tough as last night.

A person could temporarily satiate hunger with thirst, and eventually, they would stop noticing the body odor. But trying to tamp down desire and push aside want, that was damn near impossible.

Sleep was elusive, and when I did manage to doze off, I had sex dreams. I hadn't had a sex dream since I was a teen, but that night made up for it in spades. When I was awake, all I could think about was Sabrina's touch and the feel of her in my arms while sitting on my lap. Which just led to having sex dreams, jerking off, and repeating. The only solution was to take cold showers repeatedly in an attempt to purge.

I stepped out of the cold shower, wrapped one towel

around my waist, and dried my hair with another. It was time to face the day, and I was dreading it. I had to go out there and act the same way I'd been acting for the last ten years—as if I didn't give a shit.

But the ranch was big enough I could probably avoid Sabrina all day if I tried. A man could hope. My dick needed a break.

Dressed, I made my way downstairs and into the kitchen to seek out coffee. When I walked by Sabrina's room, her door was closed, so maybe she was still sleeping. It was fairly early.

Mom and Mrs. Claudia were in the kitchen, and biscuits and gravy were on the stove. Things were looking up already. Rod was at the island, chowing down. He put his hand up for a high five while shoveling food into his mouth with the other hand.

"Can I get some of that?" I asked, pointing to Rod's plate.

"Coming right up," Mrs. Claudia said, then seconds later slid a heap of goodness in front of me.

"What's on the agenda for the day?" I asked, glancing at the hallway to see if anyone was coming. If I ate fast, I might get outside without seeing her. Yeah, I was a coward.

"They're bringing in the cows who are ready to birth," said Mom.

"I can help with that." I nodded.

"They already left," Rod said.

"I can catch up with them," I told him.

He gave me a *whatever* look.

My heart skittered when I heard someone come down the hall but sighed with relief when Brynna came around the corner. She swiped a biscuit as she poured coffee into a mug.

"Hey, thought I'd come by today and see how your work's going." I smiled at my sister.

"Nope. I am in the middle of a project, and I don't want any interruptions. If you interrupt me, I will scar you with a hot iron." She gave me the stink eye.

"A *no, thank you* would have sufficed." I stabbed my fork into a biscuit.

My mom stopped in front of me, wiping her hands with a towel. "What's going on here? Is your arm bugging you?" She eyed where the bullet had grazed me.

"Nothing is going on, and no, my arm is fine. It's practically healed. I'm just ready to get out there and do some work."

My mother narrowed her eyes. "So if your arm is fine, then what was keeping you up last night? You took several showers. I assumed you were working out some aches."

"What are you talking about?" I feigned innocence.

"This house has old pipes. I heard them rumbling off and on all night." She quirked a brow.

Brynna snickered. "I bet I can guess what's going on." She wiggled her brows at me.

"I'm still stiff and sore from Peru." I shrugged. My face, my arm, and even the road rash were healing nicely. The bruises were fading.

"Yeah, that's it. Stiff from Peru." Brynna snorted and raised her coffee mug to me.

Mom returned her attention to me. "Why don't you just take it easy today?"

"Because I can't just be idle. I need to be doing something, and weren't you the one always asking me to come home? I think even once you said there were things I could do here that needed attention. Well, here I am. And I want to do something." I turned to Rod. "What are you doing today?"

He placed his fork on the table next to his clean plate and wiped his mouth. "I'm going to school. You can come with me if you want, but I'm not sure how that would fly with the other adults." He took a drink of something that looked suspiciously like coffee. "But you should probably stay here with people your own age." He got up and put his dishes in the sink, then snatched up a backpack by the door before exiting.

"He'll be back at four if you want to play then," Brynna said with a laugh. "You are so pathetic."

"Don't I know it," I said sourly. "I'm going to ride out to the herd and help with the heifers." I returned my focus to breakfast.

"Nope," Paul said, coming into the kitchen, carrying his laptop. "Looks like the second wave of attacks has been launched." He put the laptop on the counter and swiveled it so I could see the screen:

"Security CEO Jeopardizes Client's Life."

The article proceeded to break down what had happened in Peru. Logically, I knew I hadn't put the asset in danger, and things could go sideways when assets didn't always follow the rules. I'd taken a bullet to the shoulder as proof. And the asset had come out unscathed.

I looked up at Paul. "Okay, we figured the Peru stuff would get some attention. Put out the press release like we talked about, and let's move on."

"Already did that." Paul pointed at the laptop. "Click on another one of the open tabs."

Four were open. The first was the article I was looking at. I clicked the second.

"Early Reviews of Optium's Safety App ProtectedLove Are Positive. Is It Because They're Bought and They're Bots?"

"Wow, I bet that writer thinks he's clever with his play on words." That headline required an eye roll. I clicked the third tab.

Optium's Matchmaker Ruse Exposed.

If they are dating, then why is Sabrina Holloway trying to adopt a child and be a single parent?

I pointed at the screen. "Utter lies. Let's see if we can sue or something."

Paul shook his head. "I was just talking with Sabrina. While some of the information isn't correct, most of the article is factual. The article names the agency she's working with and even shows some of the private documents Sabrina completed with them. Which we can totally go after them for because of HIPPA and privacy laws. But the adoption agency has already put out a statement they were hacked, and now lots of their customers are scared and panicking. This article might have single-handedly put them out of business."

"You meant the hack did that." Sabrina is trying to adopt a kid? I wasn't sure what to make of that.

"They were hacked for the purpose of this article. You and I know it. And mostly people don't care, but it's being used to discredit both you and that presser we did in Dallas. It also sparked a conversation on talk shows about singles adopting kids. And as to be expected, some people in the comments admire Sabrina, and others are tearing her to pieces."

I brushed my hand over my chin as I worked to find the next step.

"There's another tab," Paul said.

And by the look on his face, I knew this wasn't going to be good either. I clicked the tab and was instantly greeted with a picture of Travis at a poker table. The lighting was poor, the image grainy, his cards were on the table, his fingers were on his cards, and a lot of chips were beside him. The picture made Travis look...

My mom came up behind me. "Oh, that is not a good picture of Travis. It makes him look smarmy. Deceitful."

"Crooked," I said. Sabrina had to be feeling like she was drowning:

"Professional Gambler Travis Holloway's Estate Being Investigated for Tax Evasion."

"This isn't good." I stood, ready to go to her.

Paul put out his hand. "She's really upset and said she needs some time to herself. She'll come downstairs when she's ready to see people."

So much for avoiding her. Soon I would find myself pacing outside her door, anxious to see how she was holding up. And here I'd spent the night cold showering, all while her life was unraveling.

Chapter Seventeen
SABRINA

Could a person get dehydrated and need medical intervention from crying? Because I honestly felt like there were no more fluids in me. My stomach hurt, my head hurt, and my heart was broken. I was too exhausted to get water, but I was thirsty and kept licking my dry lips with my dry tongue.

I woke to the pinging of messages on my phone. All from Cricket. She had been the one to see the articles and alert me. I ran down the hall and woke up Paul. In real time, we watched comment after comment get posted. They talked about me like I wasn't a person who had feelings and desires and whose feelings and desires they were currently mocking and judging. To be fair, some were defending me. But nice voices always got lost in the louder, negative ones.

That was when Paul made me go back to my room. I thought about waking Cal instead, but I knew he would need to loop Paul in, so I cut out the middleman, maybe partly because I didn't want to have the adoption conversation with Cal. I was relieved knowing Cal hadn't pursued the path of family and kids. If he had, how could I not believe he'd been right to dump me because I never would have been able to give him kids.

And yeah, when I pictured what life would be like when this job ended, I pictured him going back to his death-wish lifestyle, and I would go back to mine, only with adding a baby. For some reason I couldn't explain, I didn't want Cal to know about my reproductive issues.

When I thought things couldn't get worse, which was such a cliché but only because it was true, my adoption coordinator called me. Mrs. Monighan and I had been on this journey together from day one. I had cried in her office while filling out the paperwork. She'd been the gentle guide I needed.

"Sabrina." The way she said my name was not gentle at all but cold. Practical. All business.

"Yes, hello, Mrs. Monighan. I was going to call, but I was waiting until my lawyer and PR person had done due diligence so I could pass along what they found."

"I understand. I'm calling to let you know the agency has frozen your application."

"What does that mean?" I'd been sitting in a chair by the window, looking out across the vast landscape of the mountains, feeling almost like I was out of my body. But her comment drew me back in and snapped me to attention.

"It means right now that we will not be moving to the next step." She almost sounded like a recording, her voice a monotone.

"For how long? And then when it's unfrozen, do I start at the bottom of the list again?"

"Indefinitely."

I bent over, resting my chest against my legs, a cheek on

my knee, as I faced the window and felt faint. "Is there a policy on what indefinitely looks like and how to unfreeze?"

"It's being crafted as we speak."

Which meant freezes weren't a thing. So why don't they just drop me?

I would find out later that they froze me out because dropping me could have exposed them to legal issues, and with being hacked, they were already facing a lot of those.

"Mrs. Monighan, I'm not the one who hacked the company. Why is this affecting my application?"

"We were hacked because of you." She cleared her throat, and when she spoke again, it was in a whisper. "They see you as a risk. Having it known that the information of hundreds of private adoptions is in the hands of a hacker has made our families panic. Which has made our board panic, and you are the scapegoat."

The sudden switch in tone and divulging of information made me think her call was being monitored on her side of the wire.

"So essentially, we are through."

"I'm so sorry, hon. And you should know a few of our board members sit on boards for other adoption companies, so you might have a hard time with some of them too. When you're researching who to go to, make sure you look at their board."

Tears ran down my temple onto my knee, burning a path down my leg to my ankle. All I could do was sniff in response.

"I am so sorry." She cleared her throat and said in her robot voice, "Have a good day, Ms. Holloway." And hung up.

I stayed like that until my legs started to tingle, no more tears were coming out, and the sun was sliding lower in the sky. I stood up slowly and looked around, stunned by how quickly my life had fallen apart.

That was when the next stage of grief hit me—anger. I stomped my feet into my cowboy boots while still dressed in my capri yoga pants and a maroon sleep shirt that had a Labradoodle on the front with a ball in his mouth and the words Fetching Tired underneath.

I was so tired. I wanted to hide in the bed with the covers over my head until someone fixed this. But I had to get out of the room. Suddenly, I couldn't breathe.

I whipped open the door and came face-to-face with Cal. He opened his mouth, and I said, "Nope, not yet."

I brushed past him as I rushed down the stairs and out the door. I headed straight to the corral, where some horses were grazing. When I got to the fence, I hung my top half over the upper bar and closed my eyes, trying to take in deep breaths.

Apparently, you could still cry when you were dehydrated. Cal joined me but faced the horses, not looking at me once. He didn't say anything, just stood next to me while I cried. I wasn't sure how long we stood there before he climbed up the fence to sit on the top bar. A few minutes later, I did the same. As I was climbing up, he glanced at me, paused at my shirt, and gave a slight smile. Then he looked away once I settled next to him.

The paint I'd ridden came over, and I started petting her muzzle. "I don't want to talk about it."

"Okay," he said.

"But you can say *I told you so*."

"About what?"

I sniffed. I had been so cavalier about taking on his dad that I really hadn't given Cal's warning its due. "You were right about me not being able to handle this. Your dad hit me right where it hurts the most."

"I never said you couldn't handle it. I'm sorry about those articles today."

"I don't think I can do this." I stared at the horse but saw the quick side-eye he gave me.

"Okay, it's over. Done. We'll make a statement. I'll talk to Paul right away." But he didn't move off the fence.

"But then again, it's stupid to quit now, because the worst has happened. What more can happen?" I probably shouldn't have said those last few words.

"That's a fact." Cal nodded.

"Facts!" I held up one finger. "No one cares about facts. But here are some fun facts. I have three. One, even after a ton of treatments, I was still not able to get pregnant. Which leads me to two: I have depleted my savings account, even used some of my dad's life insurance money for three shots of in vitro that all failed. And the third fact is this is hard proof that the universe hates me." I now held up three fingers.

"That's not really a fact."

I thrusted up my arm, one finger pointed to the sky and exclaimed, "Fact! I am so angry I could punch Calvin Beckett in the face. You'd think he'd just let me rant instead of chiming in." I put my face to the paint's muzzle and scratched his ears. They were very soft and soothing.

He cleared his throat. "Uh..." He scooted away.

I turned to him then. He looked as sad as I felt. And the intensity of it was the same as that picture Paul had taken of us at the hotel. That had been deep longing. And this was deep sadness. He hurt for me. Which made our break all the more confusing, but whatever. We were together right now, and this was one of those moments when I needed someone, and had I been alone, I would have thought of him and wanted one of his healing hugs.

"I bet you have a lot of questions for me." I threw him a bone.

"Only one."

"Which is…?"

"This thing you have, what you had the surgery for… is it serious?"

"It's not terminal, if that's what you're asking. Endometriosis."

He nodded. I narrowed my eyes. He wanted to ask another question but kept it back.

"Just ask," I said irritably.

"You need a hug?"

That was not what I was expecting. The man had just learned I was trying to be a single mom and hadn't asked one question about that. He had to be curious. But that was for later. He'd offered me a hug, and I desperately wanted one.

I nodded, and he scooted closer to me and wrapped a long arm around my shoulders, drawing me into his side. Then his other arm came around, and somehow, there on the fence, sitting by my side, Cal gave me exactly what I needed —comfort. He held me and maybe even kissed my head, but I was trying really hard to not cry again because I was sick of it. He let me pull away when I was ready, his hands brushing across my body as I straightened, then across my hair and my shoulder, with a gentle swipe over my cheeks to wipe away the tears.

He nodded once as he met my eyes. "If you ever want to talk, I would like to know the whole story." He jumped down off the fence into the corral. "Let me know if you decide to stay." And with that, he walked away.

I stayed on the fence and watched the horses. Some of the ranch hands were driving in cattle, and Cal had gone to help guide them in. He looked so natural, and his body looked looser and more relaxed. The ranch suited him. I was so captivated watching Cal, marveling at the subtle change, that I didn't even notice Rod climbing up beside me.

"My favorite is when the calves are born." He took a large square wrapped in a paper towel out of his jacket pocket and started unwrapping it.

"You've been here when calves have been born?"

"Sure. My dad has worked this ranch for years." He displayed a piece of what looked to be banana bread.

"Which one is your dad?"

"He's not here. He took off for a bit." He looked at me, his eyes sweeping across my face. "You look like you're having a bad day. Want some?" He held out his bread. "It's really good. Mrs. Claudia makes it for me and gives me a big slice when I have a bad day."

I confirmed his statement with a head nod. "I lost something I really wanted. What about you?"

"I failed a math test. I hate math. I don't get it."

"I'm actually pretty good at math. I can help if you want." I took the piece he was offering. It was still warm. "What do you mean, your dad takes off for a bit?"

"Sometimes he gets itchy legs—that's what he calls it—and will take off for a while. But he always comes back."

"Do you always stay with Mrs. Claudia when he does?"

Rod nodded.

"Do you have any other family?"

"Nope, my mom's in heaven, and there ain't no grandparents."

Rod was kind of like me. His lack of family was something I was familiar with.

"My mom and dad are in heaven with my grandparents. It's just me," I told him.

He broke off another piece. "Are you scared?" His eyes grew large with wonder.

Lonely was always the word that came to mind... but scared... I hadn't really thought about it that way. "You know what? Sometimes I do get scared."

"What do you do?" He paused his eating as he waited for me to answer.

"Well, I'm lucky and have really good friends. They're almost like family. Like Mrs. Claudia is for you."

He nodded again and looked to be tucking away that tidbit of info for later use.

How hard must it be to have his dad get itchy legs without any warning and uproot this kid's life. Yeah, things in my life sucked at the moment, but I'd always had the security and safety of my family. I hoped that Rod's dad would return while I was here. I had a strong urge to give him a piece of my mind.

Chapter Eighteen
SABRINA

The bad press was getting worse for both me and Cal. Paul clicked through various tabs on his computer, tsk-tsking and shaking his head. I had read a few. Most of the articles about Cal were much of the same—slamming his company and the app and throwing shade on what had happened in Peru—all designed to discredit him.

The articles that included me were about my dad and speculation about the life of a professional gambler. They tried to make it look terrible by saying we moved a lot, and I had grown up in casinos—which wasn't a lie. After Mom died, we had moved a lot, and I had spent a lot of time in casinos, but I'd also learned to ride horses and had become a strong swimmer. When I was old enough, I worked at some of the casino hotels as a lifeguard. I also graduated from high school with excellent grades, but of course, that wasn't mentioned at all.

The beta test of the app was slogging along. There had

been an initial mass sign-up in the low hundreds, not in the thousands like Cal had expected. But the sign-ups had slowed. Cricket's article about our date and using the app had gotten buried under my adoption story.

The reporter from the press conference who had irritated me with his innuendos was Jonathon Smith. He had dug up some college classmates who'd verified that yes, Cal and I had dated, but we'd broken up and instantly dropped out of each other's lives. The questions regarding our breakup were paired with creative sentences that hinted at an ugly undercurrent of abuse and cheating. It didn't matter that the reporter left the assumptions open for the reader to make. And his attack on my father was just as ugly. Accusations of card counting, underreporting winnings, colluding with dealers to fix games, and even using technology to spy. The last one was laughable. Dad was the least techy person I knew. He'd never upgraded from a flip phone and, up until his death, still handwrote letters and used snail mail. What bothered me the most was that Dad wasn't able to defend his reputation, and I knew that even if all this was retracted by the paper, some people out there would believe it regardless. That alone made me want to weep with regret. This was happening because of me.

I found a silver lining in the fact that Dad wasn't here to see it. I'd been raised to believe justice would prevail, and that same belief was applied to truth. The truth would come out. I had nothing to fear there.

Cricket sat across from me and chewed the end of a ballpoint pen. She was waiting for an answer. The question was, how did I want to respond?

"I'm just not sure," I told Cricket. I'd been asking myself

that same question for the last sixteen hours. I'd only slept out of sheer exhaustion. I picked up a paperclip off Cal's desk and started to unwind it. "I'm too close to this, too emotional. I need distance."

"How do you get that? Because the sooner we respond, the better."

Paul agreed from across the room. He was reading articles and scribbling notes. At least he had ideas on how to respond to the articles about Cal.

"Usually, I go for a ride or a drive, but the weather..." I pointed to the window, which showed dark clouds and a steady rain. "Let's talk about something else. Maybe if I distract myself that way..."

"I went on my first date—you know, the one I got by using the app."

I threw up my hands in frustration. "Why didn't you tell me? How was it? What was he like? Will you do another?"

She laughed. "I didn't tell you because you have been having a rough few days. But Paul, Cal, and I did a short interview about it, and it's getting good traction on Instagram. I had a nice time, and I'm thinking about a second date. He's already asked."

Encouraged, I turned to Paul. "I don't think you need me for this app." Cricket had found success, even if it was just one date, without my intervention.

"Actually, that guide you created on how to build a profile was great," Cricket said. "I built it, then read the guide and completely changed it based on what you said. I would have never thought about putting some of those keywords in my profile. I think that's why this match was really good."

"Now, if we can get some good press on it, that would be great." Paul sighed.

Cricket slapped her hand on the desk. "I have the best idea!"

She had our attention.

"Okay, Sabrina needs to do something physical to work out her thoughts," Cricket continued. "Cal needs to be out there doing his job, and you two need to be seen together. Plus, there's the app work. It's Saturday, and people are stuck inside. Why not host an impromptu self-defense class at the community center this afternoon? We have a fair number of single women and older women who can attend. We can get students, shop owners, and whoever. We can even set up a babysitting program for those with no childcare."

Paul stood and gaped at Cricket. "Can you pull this off?" He looked at his watch. "And get people there, say, by three? Enough people, Cricket, not ten. We need numbers."

She nodded. "Yes, because we need something like this in this community. We're not free from the ills of society just because we're a small town. I bet I can even get people from Bison's Prairie to come over."

"I actually love the idea. Cal needs to get back to doing what he loves. This in-between is eating at him," I said. Paul was nodding.

Cricket picked up her phone and did a quick text. When she finished, she smiled up at them. "We should have an answer in less than five minutes."

I was about to ask who she'd texted when her phone chimed. She glanced at it, then beamed up at me and Paul.

"Fort just gave the thumbs-up. He said he will call Cody, who manages the community center, and get it set up."

"Fort?" Paul asked.

"The sheriff," I said with a smile. "Cricket, you are a genius." I leaned across the table, clasped my friend's face between my hands, and kissed her on the forehead. "An absolute genius. I love this idea. What do you need me to do?"

"I'm going to prep Cal." Paul hurried from the room.

I waited for Cricket to tell me what to do.

"Start texting people and let them know what's going down. Start with Meredith. She can text people over there, and maybe they'll drive over. I'll put it on the website and send out notifications." She reached for her bag and laptop.

We had a plan and were putting it into action.

At three in the afternoon, Cal stood in front of a crowd of fifty or more, a mix of all ages and genders. Cricket had been right. People from neighboring towns had driven over to attend the class. I was excited to watch Cal do his thing. I wanted to know this other side of him. He was dressed casually in dark jeans, running shoes, and a blue jacket over a gray T-shirt. He looked almost nondescript, and I wondered if that was by design.

Cal explained who he was and what he did. He talked briefly about the app and how they could use it for personal safety. Then he ran through some scenarios and asked the crowd how they would respond. This got them really engaged.

"What do you do when it's nighttime, and you hear something outside?"

"Make sure it's not a bear!" someone hollered.

"Once you rule out that it's not a bear," Cal said. "Because sitting there paralyzed and waiting to see what happens may not be the best response. What do you do when you're walking to your car, and it looks like you're alone, but you can sense someone nearby? Or how about when the person walking toward you gives you a bad vibe?"

"What exactly is a bad vibe?" a guy in the row behind Sabrina asked.

"All the women in this room know what I mean about a bad vibe. Intuition. We develop that over time, but society has a way of trying to make people feel bad for listening to it. Often, women ignore that bad vibe because they feel their response isn't socially acceptable. Let me give you a few examples." He walked over to a woman in scrubs. "Ever have to stay late at work with a coworker you distrust? Or work with someone whose ego does not accept 'no'? And your gut keeps you on high alert?"

She nodded.

He moved to a young girl, a high school student. "Ever feel pressured to take a drink from someone you don't know or who gives you the creeps? Or maybe you feel pressured to get into a car with a friend of a friend, despite feeling uneasy." She nodded and swiped a finger under her eye as if Cal had struck home with that one, bringing her to tears.

He stood near a middle-aged man. "Ever tell your kids to give someone a hug, like a relative they barely know, and they resist but you make them? That's teaching them to ignore their instincts. That's teaching them that being uncomfortable is just something they have to live with. And it's not." He moved back to look at the crowd. "When I was a young teen, my dad's mother passed away. At the funeral, he made my sister and I go up and kiss her goodbye. It was open casket."

Only a few people in the group gasped. One person called out, "Yeah, but that's creepy because she was dead."

Cal nodded. "Yep, that was part of it. The other part was that my grandmother was a mean-spirited woman. She looked for reasons to hit us. Even animals avoided her. My mom said the first time my grandmother held me, I wailed uncontrollably. Same for my sister. That's intuition. There's an observation part to that as well, but I'll get to that. My point is if your first reaction is to back up, say no, or run—listen to it."

He walked over to a mother who was cradling a baby. "Ever been loading up groceries and strangers come to help?"

She nodded and smiled. "All the time. People in this town are so kind."

"Ever been worried about it? Ever got a bad feeling as it was happening?"

She shook her head. "Of course not."

"What would you do if you did?"

She shrugged.

"That happened to me," another woman said. "I was in the city and stopped by a big-box store. I had my kids with me, and this guy, I had seen him in the store and felt like he was following me. But that made no sense. Why would he do that? He checked out when I did. At my car, he stopped to offer to help me unload. I didn't know what to do. Should I let him while I put my kids in the car?" The woman rubbed up and down her arms as if remembering he was giving her the creeps. "I said 'No, thanks,' but he insisted, said he knew how hard it was to do these thing with kids, and he just wanted to help. If the couple in the truck next to us hadn't come out, I don't know what I would have done. The stranger loaded my car but didn't leave, and I had two littles still sitting in the cart. Thankfully, the gentleman next to us heard me telling the stranger thanks and that I could take it from here. I'll admit I said it pretty loud." She paused to take a breath.

Someone from the crowd asked, "What happened next?"

The woman crossed her arms and gave a shiver. "He wouldn't leave, and I just got scared, so I told him that. I said, 'Thanks for the help, but you are making me uncomfortable.' That's when the guy next to us turned his attention to me. He asked if I needed help. Thank the Lord he was a big guy too. The stranger took off. The couple watched me load the kids and gave me a piece of paper with the stranger's make, model, and license number. They told me to drive around a few times to make sure he wasn't following me before I went home. All I could think about was how there are stretches on the road home that are long and not a town or house for miles. Sometimes you're lucky if you see another car. I was really scared. Truthfully, I didn't know what to do." She shrugged, palms up, looking uncertain, and the woman next to her gave her a hug.

Cal gave her a warm smile. "You did a few things right. And you did nothing wrong. You spoke up. You were loud. You called him out. You got his vehicle information. If you ever find yourself in that situation, listen to your gut. As you're checking out, tell the cashier your observations and fear. Sometimes they'll call a manager, and that person will escort you out. Sometimes you can wait at the customer-service desk for the creep to leave. Typically, a good manager will make sure the creeper has driven away before escorting you out. Any decent person would. Better to look foolish than to be dead or sexually assaulted."

This went on for a few more examples. The crowd was entranced. Cal was good at what he did. He was genuine. He didn't make people feel bad about their reactions. He simply explained the alternatives and backed them up with real stories. There was a case in Wisconsin about a woman being attacked in a parking garage. He quoted sexual-assault statistics. He wasn't fearmongering but fact laying.

He was powerful, and he had found his calling. Cal had gone to law school because that was what his dad wanted, and Cal needed to take over the family business. He'd never seemed happy with the choice, just matter-of-fact about it. But this man here, he loved what he did. He came alive. I now saw why saving this app was so important and why we needed one like it. If everyone who was interested in the app could spend half an hour with Cal, there would be no hesitation to join. No issues with trust. He genuinely cared about people.

"Let's talk about awareness. Ever heard of the Color Code of Awareness? It was created by a former marine colonel Jeff Cooper, and it describes the different states of alertness."

A few vets in the crowd raised their hands.

"White, yellow, orange, and red. Right now most of you are in white. Totally unaware. Prime targets for a surprise or attack. You aren't paying attention to your surroundings." He explained the other colors.

"Let's get into some basic self-defense." He pointed to the woman who had shared her story. "You're on a run or you're at the store. Or maybe you're coming off a bad date, and the person will not leave. What do you do?" He took off his jacket and tucked it into a duffel bag, then walked over to me, extending his hand. "Will you be my assistant?"

"Of course." I jumped up excitedly and took his hand. I, too, had experienced situations like he'd described.

He led me by the hand to the center of the crowd. "Ya'll, this is Sabrina. We have known each other since college and have recently reconnected. So keep in mind there is some familiarity here, but there is also some uncertainty, which will affect how she reacts. I tell you this because, often, the situation you will find yourself in will be with an acquaintance, at the very least." He squeezed my hand as he turned to me. "Have you taken any self-defense courses?"

I grimaced. "No, but I run and have decent core strength."

"Big whoop," he said. "Chances are you're gonna need more than that." The crowd chuckled, and he turned to them. "I am going to show you some basic moves, but everyone really needs to take a more comprehensive self-defense course. If there isn't one locally, I can do one here at any time. They usually last longer than the time we have allotted today."

He faced me. "Okay, we're going to learn the palm heel strike, knee strike, elbow strike, and how to break common holds. I'll show you how to do each one, and then you get to practice on me." He gave a quick demo of each move.

I clasped my hands together excitedly. "Oh, this is going to be wonderful" Taking my cues from him, I turned to the crowd. "You know he broke up with me in college, and now I get to hit him, and it's legal. If this isn't karma, I don't know what is."

The crowd laughed.

Cal gave me a wide smile. "You seem a little too excited

to do this." He glanced at my shoes. "Luck might be on my side because you left your heels at home. Don't forget I have a wound." He tapped his arm, where there was now a healthy-looking scab.

"Wound shmound. Let's start with the knee strike," I said with a laugh.

Chapter Nineteen
CAL

Choke hold, wrist grab, bear hug from behind, hair grab, shirt grab, and headlock. I had never been so excited to be a victim or a creeper. My dad should put that in his smear campaign.

In each of these scenarios, there was a bonus—I got to touch Sabrina. I got to be close and hold her. I got to... Wait. Those felt like the thoughts of a creeper. Sure, I had her consent, but it felt a little pervy to be so excited to fake attack a woman just to get her to touch me.

Dammit, I was just so happy to be around her, and loved seeing her have a good time, and especially loved that I was teaching her a skill that could protect her. Nothing about that was creepy.

The stress of the last few days showed on her face—the dark circles under her eyes, the pinch of worry between her brows—but as she bounced from foot to foot in front of me, her ponytail high and swinging, there was a large, open smile on her face. Smiling was something she hadn't done since the latest batch of articles had hit.

"Is it wrong that I'm excited to have the chance to knee you in the junk?" She beamed as she bounced from foot to foot.

"I'm sure I deserve it." I gestured for her to come at me. She did but came in soft. Cute. She was all talk and really didn't want to hurt me.

"We're gonna do it again. Come in hard. Don't be afraid; that's what this suit is for." I was dressed in a padded suit that made me look like the Michelin Man and crushing on this woman so hard that I was excited to let her dick-punch me. And in front of a large crowd. The turnout was spectacular, and the participants were engaged.

My family had been in this town for generations, yet I only knew people who worked on the ranch. That fact did not escape me—just more proof that I had closed myself off. Sabrina was a visitor to the town and had a network of friends. She was tight with the sheriff and his wife, Cori; the vet's wife, Hannah; a park ranger and his wife, Ellie; and of course, Cricket. Where Sabrina went, life happened. Considering how alone she might have felt, she still surrounded herself with people she loved. Even though I had family, for the past ten years, there had been no real life to my life. All I did was work and called it living? I'd closed myself off from any attachments.

"Do I have to put my hands on your shoulders to kick your man parts?" Sabrina asked, bouncing around like a boxer.

"It's really hard to put some oomph into it if you don't." I held up a finger and turned to the crowd. "Listen, this is for everyone but especially women. If the predator thinks he can overpower you, he's going to put his hands on you, or he's going to be close enough to put a gun in your face. Do not get moved to another location. It's okay to fight back. I'm going to come at Reenie from behind, trying to use surprise to get her."

"Show me what you got," she challenged, a twinkle in her eyes.

I faced her and signaled for her to turn away and start walking.

The first evolution didn't go so well for Sabrina. Full understanding dawned across her face, her amusement replaced with determination as she realized just how easily getting overtaken could be. Then she practiced the moves a few more times and started to improve.

At one point, I had my arm around her in a mock choke hold when she tapped me gently on the forearm to get me to pause. "I know this is practice, but even in practice, being grabbed like this is unnerving. I know you. I have known you for years now, and I trust you, and yet I still feel trapped and worried that I won't be able to get away. It's very sobering."

She trusted me. I blew out a breath I didn't know I'd been holding. Part of her forgiving me would be to trust me again. And we were on that path.

"Imagine if this was real life. We are not educating people enough. I think self-defense should be taught in middle school PE classes. You ready?" I asked.

She straightened up and squared her shoulders, gave a quick nod, then twisted my arm and flipped around when I loosened my hold, ending with a knee to my groin.

Reflexively, I dropped to my knees. The padding was good, more than enough, but my body wanted to close in on itself as I thought about how bad that would have felt.

I stood and gave her a high five. She was beaming and radiant.

"Let's partner up and practice on each other. Without making actual hits, though. Oh, and one last question; what color was the jacket I was wearing when we first started?"

People shouted out colors. They were just going through the rainbow.

I held up a hand to get their attention. "Not knowing is a clear example of the white level: oblivious to your surroundings. If you said blue, come stand by me." A handful of people, a mix of ages and genders, moved to stand next to me. "You all are at the yellow level," I told them. "Calm but alert. Aware. Congrats." I turned back to the crowd. "This is where you want to be at all times. Slow down and stop to take a moment to survey your surroundings when you are out. That will pay off in dividends."

For the rest of the afternoon, people practiced, and I moved around, showing them how to perfect the move. At dinnertime, as the group dispersed, some lingering, an older woman about my mom's age approached me. She was worrying her hands, her expression tight.

"Excuse me. I have a question. What do you do if someone won't leave you alone?" Her eyes darted over her shoulder, and I followed her gaze to a young woman in scrubs talking to Hannah, the veterinarian's wife.

"Can you explain what you mean by not leaving you alone?" I gestured for her to take a seat, which she did. She rubbed her hands down her legs nervously.

"It's my daughter. All I know is that she went on one date with a guy, and he shows up at her place at all hours, won't leave her alone. Calls her incessantly with no concern for time. She said he's also been showing up when she goes out with her friends."

"Does your daughter live here in town?"

She nodded.

I made eye contact with Fort, the sheriff, and with a quirk of the head, told him to come over. "Let's get your daughter over here so we can all talk."

The woman shook her head. "She thinks she's got it all under control. But I'm scared. I was reading up on stuff online and..." She pressed a hand to her mouth.

Fort took a seat on the other side of the woman. "What's going on, Sally?"

Sally shook her head, so I brought him up to speed.

The sheriff gave a heavy sigh. "Is it one of the hired hands that have come in with the Nickelson ranch?"

"I think so," said Sally.

Fort explained that one of the locals had sold out to a billionaire looking for a pet project, and the staff he'd brought in had had a tough time learning about what they were and weren't entitled to. He signaled for the daughter to join them. She came over and stood in front of her mother, with her hands on her hips. Sabrina joined them and took a seat by my side.

"What did you tell them, Ma?" The daughter was clearly irritated.

"Casey," Fort said. "I'm curious why your mom seems worried about this guy and you don't."

"It's so embarrassing," Casey said.

I stood and offered Casey my seat. "That's exactly what he's using to manipulate you. Your embarrassment, being self-conscious. I bet he even says things that hint to your being bitchy. Things like 'I'm just being nice' and 'I'm sorry if you are misunderstanding me.'"

She nodded.

"When people get scammed out of money online, who

do they tell? Usually no one because they are embarrassed. But did you know you can report the scammer to the FTC, your local police, and even your bank? That's the same thing in your case. There are steps to take and acts to put into place to protect you and stand up to him."

"File a report with me, and I'll ride out myself and have a talk with him," Fort said.

"Which could escalate him. Before Fort does that, make sure you're secure. Take a picture of him to your work, and tell them he is not allowed near you. Let's talk about your routine and home security."

Casey nodded and took her mom's hand.

They went over everything. I even offered to drive to her apartment, check it out, and install the motion detector and cameras, but the woman said some family would help. I hoped they wouldn't waste a moment. But this right here was why I wanted this app to be successful. With the app, people too afraid to ask for help could get solid information about what to do without stumbling across the misinformation the internet was wont to offer.

Fort said he'd drive by and check things out, as well, and to call if they had any issues. He would drive to the ranch in two days' time.

I caught Sabrina's eye. Her face showed her pride and admiration, and I knew that, yeah, I'd gone into personal safety because I'd liked it but also because I'd felt useless when it came to protecting her, my mother, and my sister from my father, so I'd set out to protect everyone else. But this look Sabrina was giving me—it was everything. It was better than money, time on a morning TV show, or a book deal. The ease on Sally's face when they started talking strategy was the reward too.

Dammit all. This was what life was all about, helping people and getting an adoring look from the woman I loved and had never stopped loving. My company be damned. I was going to fight for Sabrina. There was no use pretending that I didn't want a life with her.

Chapter Twenty

SABRINA

The community center was almost empty. Some people had stayed behind, including Meredith, Hannah, Cori, Cricket, Fort, Cal, and I. We were cleaning up when Jace walked in. It was the first time in a decade that I had been in the same room with Jace and Cal. Jace walked up to me and gave me a hug.

"This is kinda weird for me," he said, pointing between me and Cal. "Having you both in the same room."

"Remember when it used to be normal?"

"Barely." After he was done hugging me, he reached for his wife, grabbed her by the arm, and snaked her into his.

"Where are the children?" she asked after giving him a longer-than-normal casual kiss on the lips.

"Who knows? They've taken over the ranch. I packed our things. We should go on the lam now before they catch up with us an make us come home." He buried his face in her hair. "I'm so scared of them. Hold me."

Cal chuckled and slapped Jace on the back. "We should all get some dinner together."

I had a glimpse into what my life might have been like had Cal and I not broken up. But maybe that was just wishful thinking or the imagination of a girl who liked romance novels. Real life was clearly not always so pretty.

"Oh, that sounds fun," Cori said.

Cricket shook her head. "The diner had to close early because they are hosting a rehearsal dinner, so the only place that's got good food is Bruno's bar. And tonight just happens to be line dancing night."

Bruno's used to be a titty bar, but during the COVID-19 pandemic it had become more family friendly. Cricket said Bruno made more money now than he had before, which was why he kept the family-friendly theme.

Had I been a cat, my ear would have perked up and twitched. Reflexively I looked at Cal, who was looking at me, a question in his eyes. Someone groaned.

"No," Jace said, pointing at both of us. "Nope. No. No way."

"Is it country-music line dancing?" I asked.

"Or a variety of music genres?" Cal asked.

"There are some things that should be left in the past, and this is one of them." Jace was still pointing fingers at us, his voice uncharacteristically loud.

I waved a dismissive hand in his direction. "Oh, come on. You act like we tortured you with line dancing. You had fun." I turned to Cal. "He's totally overreacting."

"He might be acting that way because the last time I went line dancing was with him, and he drank too much, then threw up all down the front of his shirt."

"Gross." Meredith gave her husband a grimace.

Jace pointed to Cal. "I got sick because this asshole turned it into a drinking game."

"It's not my fault you have two left feet and you can't say no to a bet." Cal stuffed his hands into his pockets and beamed at Jace.

The change in him was stunning really. Even if he put on his suit and dress shoes, he would still look different from the Cal I saw that first day in his office. His face was softer, his shoulders were more relaxed, and he was quicker to joke and smile.

Meredith held up a hand to pause the conversation. She turned to her husband. "Are you saying all this time we've been together, you could line dance, but haven't ever taken me?"

Jace pointed to Cal. "Didn't you hear what he said? I had to drink because I was so bad at it."

"He confuses his left and right," I fake-whispered.

"I do not," Jace said.

Cricket held up two hands. "Hold on a sec. Are you telling me that you, Sabrina, and you, Cal"—she pointed to each of us—"like to line dance?"

"He loooves it," I said, jerking my thumb in Cal's direction. Sure, I'd taught him, but the student had become the teacher.

Cal shrugged. "Big guys often don't look good dancing club style, but a guy of any size can pull off a line dance. But I don't really do it anymore."

"Oh my God, we are so going, and dang it, I'm without my camera." Cori wrapped her arms around her husband.

"Your phone's camera will be perfect," Cricket said.

"I'm warning you all now; do not go line dancing with these two!" Jace called.

"I think Jace might be right. Line dancing might not be a good idea," Cal said.

"Seriously?" I asked Cal. "Are you saying that because you are an old fuddy-duddy or because you're chicken?"

"Do not challenge him, Sabrina," Jace groaned.

"Fuddy-duddy?" Cal asked. "I think only fuddy-duddies use the term fuddy-duddy. I'm not being fussy. It's just that it's been a long time, and we were in college then."

"Exactly," Jace said. "Good call."

"Shut up," Meredith told him.

I kept my eyes on Cal. "Oh, so there's an age restriction to line dancing? I think you're just saying all that because you're chicken. Or maybe it's because you think you've got this image to protect, Mr. Serious-About-Law-and-Order."

"Nothing wrong with that image," Fort mumbled.

I continued. "So serious that you have lost your sense of humor. You're as fun as soaking-wet jeans on a cold day."

"Well, that's not fun at all," Cal said sarcastically.

I gave him a loose eye roll. "But it's true, right? You know another reason why we shouldn't do this? Because I think if your dad actually saw you having fun, it would make his head implode. And if you really truly relax, you might actually be able to come up with some new ideas for this fight against him, but mostly, Cal, when was the last time you really had fun?"

He nodded once, like he was processing everything I'd said and then held out his hand. "Okay, lead the way."

I snatched up his hand, entwining our fingers and dragged him behind me. Fifteen minutes later, we were all down the street at Bruno's. After everyone put in their food and drink orders, Cal and I stood side by side and watched the folks shuffle across the floor.

I caught his eye. "I think we're gonna be the youngest people out there."

"And the rustiest." He looked nervous. The septuagenarians on the floor were killing it.

"Speak for yourself." I joined the line as soon as I saw an opening.

The dance instructor, a tall cowboy with blond hair and a close-cut beard, wearing the tightest jeans I'd ever seen on a man, came over and introduced himself. The way the jeans fit this man was provocative. I had a hard time keeping my eyes up on his face because, one, I was curious how he moved so fluidly in such constricting pants and, two, I'd never seen a guy with a butt that... full. Bubble butt, for him, was a flattering term.

He shoulder bumped me as we danced side by side, as a way of introduction. Kyle was his name. He was friendly and not even a tad flirty. He was the exact type Cricket liked, and I couldn't help noticing that his eyes were flicking in her direction.

"What's your name?" he asked me over the music.

"Cal," Cal said over my shoulder, surprising me so much I jumped and missed a step, causing me to stumble into him. He righted me and hip bumped me to get me moving into the right direction.

"I think he was talking to me," I said.

"Nah, he was talking to both of us, right, Kyle?" He tucked his thumbs into his waistband and spread his shoulders wide, like a peacock preening.

"I'm Sabrina." I purposefully stepped on Cal's foot, but he played it cool, showing no sign that he felt it.

"Welcome, Cal and Sabrina. Hope you enjoy the dances. Maybe you can get some of your friends out on the floor too." Again, his eyes flicked to Cricket.

My phone vibrated, and I glanced at my Apple watch to read the message.

Cricket: Kyle was my match. My good date.

Ohhh. "I'll see what I can do," I told him as we all shuffled down the line with three side steps and a turn. Kyle moved away to speak to another person, and I gave Cal the stink eye. "What's your deal?"

He nodded toward Kyle. "What's with pants that tight? He can't be comfortable, and if he is comfortable, then he can't be a man with man-sized parts."

"Oh, I hadn't noticed his front," I said. "I was too busy staring at his butt. That's probably the best butt I have ever seen on a man." This time, Cal stumbled, and I laughed. "What's the saying? I could bounce a quarter off that, it's so tight?"

"That ass is a trampoline—bounce a quarter, and never find it again," he snarked.

"You seemed bothered by this. Self-conscious about your ass?"

He flexed both arms, making his biceps pop. "And I've got scars. Chicks dig scars."

The song switched to a two-step, and without thinking, I put up my hands, and he took me into his arms like he'd done a thousand times before. He turned me around a full circle, then pulled me in as we glided across the dance floor instantly in sync.

"Puh-lease, everyone has scars. That there is a unicorn butt. A rarity." I was teasing, yet based on the sudden furrow of his brows he had yet to figure that out.

"I think you're in a vulnerable state right now; it's impairing your taste," he said tightly, his gaze avoiding mine.

The hand that had been gently caressing my hip suddenly tightened with tension. Two words came to mind: mixed signals. We'd had a great day at the community center and were now doing something we had loved to do as a couple. I was in his arms. There was chemistry between us. Yep, mixed signals.

"Hey, Cal?"

He finally looked at me.

"I'm going to say something that is up front and maybe uncomfortably honest. Okay?"

He nodded slowly like he was not sure he wanted to hear it.

"I think Kyle has a thing for Cricket. He can't stop looking at her. And he's her type. Your app matched them. So I'm thinking of how I can get them to talk. But that's not the honest part. Right now, there is no one I'd rather be hanging out with than you. This moment right here is better than good." I squeezed the hand that had our fingers entwined.

He visibly relaxed as he pulled me a smidge closer, his grip loosening. "Good, because there is no one I'd rather spend my time with than you." Then he rested the side of his face against my temple, and I melted into him.

And I decided to just enjoy this. Because right now was the exact feeling I'd been chasing for years, and who knew when I'd have it again?

Chapter Twenty-One
CAL

The ranch foreman's wife went into labor same day as the cows. Typically, there was little to do, as the heifers did all the hard work, but the foreman monitored the cows to make sure they were progressing, and I took on this responsibility when the foreman left. I used to help my grandad with this when he ran the ranch. Sometimes we'd spent the entire night in the barn, taking turns sleeping—the hay a soft bed—as we made sure all the heifers were okay.

Since the attack on my company started, I'd often asked myself who would I be if I lost my company, because if that happened, I would have lost my purpose. And who was I without that? I'd begun to think this little side trip to the ranch was showing me exactly that.

The day my dad had showed up at my hotel room in Vegas, I knew something bad was about to happen. There were storm clouds in the sky and a rancid smell in the air. When he'd laid out all the papers—his plans on what he'd do to Travis and Sabrina if I didn't walk away—I'd been stunned. For years, I'd raged against my dad, exclaiming that he didn't know me or what I wanted, but he sure knew that night. He hit a home run with his threat. His only mistake was to not attach the contingency that I work for the company. So I'd done as he asked and then disappeared from his life—from everyone's, really—disgusted with every part of what had happened and with myself.

It had always confused me that a guy who could not have cared less for his family was so determined to keep us close. Was it to hurt us? Yeah. To control us? For sure. And maybe also because he was a paranoid SOB, and whether he liked us or not, we were blood, and only blood could get his company. But I wanted no part of it and no part of him.

Sabrina was the first thing I had ever wanted and hoped for. And he'd forced me to give her up. And now he knew every whack he took at her was like a gunshot to the heart for me. That was why he was hitting her hard. I would have bet a part of him wanted me to keep my company. I rubbed elbows with some of the richest and most powerful people, and good old Dalton Beckett would see that as a benefit. Then we'd handed him my Achilles heel on a silver platter.

I rubbed my chin as I tried to separate my emotions so I could go at this strategically. I stared at nothing, lost in thought, as I sat on two stacked bales of hay and pondered. Then I noticed that Rod, next to me, was rubbing his chin as well.

I pinched my nose. He pinched his.

I faked a yawn, and he did the same.

I did an over-the-head arm stretch. "I am a weasel, and my name is Rod."

He'd started mimicking me before I finished the sentence. "Hey, I'm not a weasel!"

"Gotcha, though, didn't I? What's up with you?" This kid. He worked better than some of the hands, and he certainly knew the ranch well.

"What do you mean?" Rod lay back on the bale of hay with his hands under his head.

"Isn't tomorrow a school day? Don't you have homework? Why are you hanging out around here?" Since when do kids go outside and do stuff instead of staying inside, playing video games?

"You want me to leave?" He side-eyed me.

"Nope, you can stay."

"I don't have homework, and even if I did, I wouldn't do it, because school is stupid, and I don't understand why I have to go." Petulant, he grabbed up fistful of hay and tossed it to the ground.

"Wow, it's a little soon to be saying that. You're... what, first grade?" Had he not been pint-sized and young, he could have easily been mistaken for a rancher or ranch hand.

"Second, and it sucks. Everyone there is an asshole."

"Whoa, are you allowed to say asshole?" He'd definitely picked up the ranch language.

"Who's gonna stop me? My dad's not here." He looked away, his eyes shiny with moisture.

"I think Mrs. Claudia would not like to hear any bad words out of your mouth." What do I say to a kid whose dad needs to take a break from life a couple times a year without thought for his kid?

"Yeah, she would be ticked."

"And then she'd probably stop making all those good desserts." Mrs. Claudia was an exceptional cook and an out-of-this-world baker.

"Those are for you all." He eyed me warily.

"Nope, all for you. She won't let any of us touch them until you've had yours. She used to do the same for me when I was a kid. She does it because she wants to see you smile." I hadn't realized it then, but what Mrs. Claudia had done for me as a kid had only added to the magic that was this ranch, all an effort to make up for the one thing we wished we had: a loving father.

Rod smiled, his ears a little pink with embarrassed happiness.

"If she asks you if you have any favorites, tell her you want to try a Boston cream pie." That was my favorite.

His face scrunched up with uncertainty. "That doesn't sound good."

"It's the best. Vanilla cake with crème in between and chocolate on top." I licked my lips. "Crème is like pudding," I clarified in response to his curled lip.

"I thought you said it was a pie."

"Yeah, those Northerners name things weird, but trust me on this. It's good."

He eyed me suspiciously, then gave a nod. "You like Ms. Sabrina, dontcha?"

"I've known her a long time. She's a very good person."

Rod rolled his eyes. "Not like that, dumb-dumb. You like her the way Bobby Weyman likes Abigail Fetter. Only he's always trying to look up her dress."

I choked on a laugh. "Well, I think Sabrina would punch me if I tried to look up her dress, which is a pretty uncool thing to do, by the way—look up a girl's dress."

"She punches him, too, but he doesn't stop. It's really annoying." His stomach rumbled.

My watch told me dinner was soon. "Maybe tell a teacher." I didn't like that this Bobby kid was getting away with that kind of behavior. Respect and consent needed to be taught and modeled early.

"They tell us that we shouldn't tattle."

I stared at Rod and wondered how it was that kids grew up knowing anything when the message was mixed all the live long day.

"Maybe I'll ask the principal if I can do a presentation for the school and get the message across to this kid and any others like him." As I said it, I knew this was a good idea. I pulled out my phone and texted Paul to set it up.

"Seriously?" He sat up.

I showed him my phone. "Yeah, I just told my guy to work on it."

"That would be awesome." He glanced over my shoulder. "Oh, here she comes. I think she likes you too. She watches you like you watch her. Abigail doesn't like Bobby—I can tell." He raised his arm and waved. "Hi, Ms. Sabrina."

Sabrina crossed the barn, carrying a basket. "Rod, Mrs. Claudia is looking for you. Dinner is ready, and she made lemon meringue pie."

Rod slid off the hay. "That's my favorite." He headed out the door, getting his hair tousled by Sabrina as he went.

She was lovely, standing there in the evening shadow of the sun, her long hair flowing over her shoulders. Something had passed between us the other night at line dancing—a truce at worst, a fresh start at best. Whatever it was, I liked it.

She sat next to me and handed me the basket. "Dinner for you. How's it going in here?"

"There are seven new calves, and they've bonded with their mothers. I have two I'm watching to make sure they progress. They've been at it awhile now."

"How do you know when to intervene?"

"When they start showing signs of fatigue. Sometimes you'll see them stop trying for long periods, like fifteen minutes. Other than that, though, we try to let them do their thing. They know better what to do than we do."

"Which one are you watching?"

I pointed them out. I showed her the old-school clipboard we kept to mark progress.

"Mind if I stay out with you?" She chewed her lip as she waited for my response.

"I'd love that."

Sometimes I was caught off guard when I realized Sabrina was within reach. Like this moment. I'd never thought she'd ever be in my life again.

"How did you get into matchmaking?" I asked as I snacked on treats from the basket and watched the cows.

As she pondered the question, she twisted and untwisted a lock of hair around her finger over and over again. It was mesmerizing.

"I think being able to read people came from my dad. He was always talking about paying attention. Kind of like your situational awareness. But he always noticed different things, like the cut of their clothes or where their attention was drawn to. He looked for what they were trying to ignore. He was so good at it." She paused in her twirling, probably remembering something, because she smiled as she blew out a breath through her nose, then started the twisting again.

"But pairing people up...?" I asked.

She was next to me on the bale, leaning back on her elbows, one leg swinging out and in.

She shook her head at me. "You don't want to hear it." Then looked at the calves.

So it had something to do with me? Now I really wanted

to know. "I do actually." But she wasn't going to tell. "Did it have something to do with us?"

Her eyes swept over me, then she dropped her hand from her hair so she could push off the bale. She walked to the gated portion, where the mamas and babies were kept. "Yeah, it does."

"Okay, so...?"

She looked at me over her shoulder and grimaced. "We've just found good space between us. Talking about it feels like dredging it all up again." Her hair was falling all around her, and she kept pulling it together, twisting it, then tucking it over one shoulder. But it didn't stay like that for long, coming unraveled. She did this a few more times before pulling it into a ponytail, and I was hit with a flash of a memory I'd long forgotten.

"Come here." I crooked a finger at her. I patted the space between my legs. She came back to stand in front of me, so I grabbed her hand and turned her around, pulling her by the hips to sit. "I'll braid your hair."

And just like that, we were back in time, in college, at Christmas break during an unexpected snowstorm we'd gone out to enjoy. Sabrina had fallen on a patch of ice and hurt her shoulder. Highlights of that time included showering together and washing her hair, after which she'd taught me to braid to make things easier for her.

"Cal." She grabbed my hand to stop me.

There was a push-pull dynamic between us. I could feel it. I knew she could feel it too. Though we both wanted to push together, heartbreak made pulling back a natural reaction.

"Come on, maybe this right here—us reconnecting and healing the past—is the best revenge against my dad."

She narrowed her eyes as she thought about all that I was asking. It was old us meeting new us, and that didn't come without a little sadness. She let go of my hand, and I let her hair out of the ponytail.

"Tell me about matchmaking." I made three sections. I was not a master French braider, but I was decent.

"After you left, after I graduated, I really didn't know what I was going to do with my degree. One of the casino owners in Vegas offered me a marketing job, mostly because he was good friends with Dad. The owner said he felt like things were stale, so I pitched the idea of doing themes. Singles night, speed dating, romance-themed game shows— you name it. Because gambling on love is no different than other gambling, in my opinion."

She paused, maybe waiting for me to object. I didn't disagree.

She continued. "I was really good at pairing people up and word started to get out. A number of the couples I paired had married. And that's when the casino owner asked me to help him find a wife. Which I did. They are still married today. Then word of mouth happened, and all of a sudden, I was full with requests and clients. So I left the job and went back to Texas to be near Dad."

"So you fell into it? Why do I think there is more to it than that?" I'd paused my weaving, waiting for her to fill in the blanks.

She blew out an exasperated sigh. "Fine. After you left, I questioned whether love was real. Sure, my dad said he and my mom had the real deal, but I was three when she died. Who knows what time might have done to them? So I started these love-themed events to prove that love wasn't this magical thing that happened once in a lifetime, that it could be cultivated. That people with shared interests and of like minds actually made better life partners than those swept away by passion."

That had been us, swept away by each other, and it sure had felt damn near magical.

"And...?" I asked.

"And I was right. All that burning need flames out, and then you're left there standing next to someone who hums when they eat and uses a body soap that is too strong, and you wonder what the hell you've done and how can you escape and escape fast."

Is that what she thought of us? I had the urge to sniff my body to see if my soap was too strong.

"So you don't do it because you're a romantic?" I asked.

"No, not anymore. I'm very pragmatic about it."

"But Jace and Meredith?"

"Proof that heat and passion don't always have to be the first sign. Those two needed someone, and I could not see any better person for them than each other."

I picked up the hair tie and twisted it around the ends. She wasn't a romantic anymore. Logically, I knew it was because she'd chosen to have those beliefs, but it didn't give me comfort that I had contributed to the act that had made her question all that to begin with.

I was about to apologize when I heard, "Wait just a second! You can braid?"

We both turned to find my sister had come in and was holding a large thermos of what had to be coffee.

She stomped her foot. "All this time, you could braid, and you never once braided my hair? I'm insulted."

I smiled. "Do you want me to braid your hair now, Brynna? Would that make you happy?"

"It's a start." She tried to shoo Sabrina away.

"Oh, look." Sabrina pointed to a heifer. "A baby is coming, I think."

Brynna and I said the same thing at the exact same time. "That's not good."

I pointed to the heifer for emphasis. The calf was coming out the wrong way.

Chapter Twenty-Two
SABRINA

I would suck as a mom. The calves told me that—well, one in particular, and that calf knew because he was rejected by his mom. She even kicked him. Then he was handed to me, and he was not happy going from one bad mom to another. Obviously, I cared more than his mom did, but this calf knew I would probably drop him or feed him the wrong food or something just as heinous.

Cal said it was because I needed to relax. But it was hard to relax when one person said, "Oh shit, the calf is breech," and a second person said, "Is it breathing?" when the calf came out.

The answer was no, it was not breathing. Brynna did some crazy rubbing and cleaning out the mouth, and then the calf was breathing, and I was crying. Cal put the calf in the pen with the mom to nurse, and she went all Mommie Dearest on him. So I tried to feed him, and the calf freaked, and Cal took him, and I backed away, embarrassed because I was no help, then tripped over a bale of hay, because those were large and obvious, and twisted my ankle and landed in a small pile of poo. Brynna had to help me back to my room.

Freshly showered, I thought I could still smell the poo as I tried to put on my jeans. I was lying on the floor because it hurt to bear weight.

I was contemplating crying when Cal banged open the door. "Sabrina, I want to look at your ankle."

"Dude, ever heard of knocking?" My hands were on my waistband, pulling up, when he barged in. I only had a bra on. No shirt. My jeans were at my knees.

He stood at my feet and smirked down at me. "I said I would help once I got things situated in the barn."

I sat up to lean on my elbows. "I'm not incapable. I can do a lot. I told you that." I pulled my jeans the rest of the way up.

"I can see that."

He was staring at the small swath of red fabric exposed by the open fly. He watched me fasten the button on the jeans, and then his eyes traveled up to my bra. The charge had been stoked when he braided my hair, then primed when he'd walked in, his eyes sweeping over me and going dark blue with desire. I wanted him too.

"Red's always been a good color on you. I like that you still match everything." He moved to stand between my legs, towering over me.

I knew what he wanted, and I wanted it too. Just the touch of a kiss. He'd always been a good kisser. I wondered if that had changed. But the thing with us was that just kissing had been hard to do. Once we started hitting the bases, both of us always wanted a home run.

I cleared my throat, but my voice came out husky. "You left the door open. What if someone walks by? And I just got these jeans on. Do you know how much effort that took?" I looked between him and the door.

He knelt, his hands going to the floor beside my hips, and like every time before, I felt that invisible string that connected us, pulling us together. I hooked my legs behind him.

"I just want to know—"

"So do I," I said.

He moved to crawl over me, holding himself in a plank position, keeping our bodies apart but close. Those strong corded arms didn't even look like they were straining. I slid my legs up to his waist and dropped back off my elbows.

"The door," I said.

"No one will come by. One of the hands came to relieve me. Brynna went to her barn to work, said she was inspired by that mean mom cow, and my mom is in the kitchen. Lord, you are beautiful." He dropped a kiss onto the top of one boob that the bra was pushing up and out. Then he did the same to the other.

There was no hesitation. No trying to talk the other out of it. We'd both silently agreed and moved forward. I wrapped my arms around his neck and pulled him to me. When our lips touched, it was like going through a portal, spinning with craving, a yearning that had never waned.

He scraped my lips with his teeth, and when his tongue touched mine I gave it a quick suck. This sent him into a frenzy and me into a tailspin. He kissed me like there was no tomorrow and we might not get the chance again, which maybe was true. Each kiss he delivered was a declaration as he moved across my neck to the spot behind my ear. I was hungry for him, his touch, and from the way his hands swept over me, I knew he felt the same. I tried to draw him to me with my legs but ended up bumping my ankle and crying out in pain.

Cal jerked up and looked at me in question, a twinkle in his eyes. "That's never happened to me before."

I swatted his shoulder. "I hit my ankle."

He ran his hands down my thighs as he sat back on his haunches. He slowly moved toward my ankle. His touch was like silk, and I thought my eyes would roll back in my head from the sensation. I wondered what it said about my feelings for Cal that I found the swipe of his hands nearly orgasmic.

He swiveled and looked at my ankle. "Let's get you downstairs and get it elevated with some ice. Here, I'll take you down." He stood, scooped me off the floor, and headed for the door.

"I need a shirt first." I laughed.

Cal swiveled again and set me on the bed. He picked my T-shirt up off the floor and turned to toss it to me but then stalked toward me instead. He slid his hand behind my head and bent to taste me one more time, his lips sweeping over mine, his hand pressing me to him.

I put my hands on his waistband and pulled him closer. Kissing him was like everything I remembered and all that I had forgotten. I remembered how much I loved his touch and wanted to be with him, the feeling of being right where I was supposed to be. But I'd forgotten just how witless he rendered me. How small the world got because he was all I needed. How I sometimes felt like I could only breathe because his kisses were giving me air.

I pushed him away for a brief rest and took my T-shirt from him. His face was close, his breath on my cheek.

"Reenie?" He sounded uncertain, maybe scared and wondering if he'd gone too far.

"It's okay."

He moved to sit next to me. "Is it?"

"I just remembered how much I depended on you. How much I asked of you."

"It was never too much."

I slipped on my shirt. "Wasn't it?"

"Not for me." He met my eyes, and I knew he was telling the truth. Which made me want to ask the why again.

But I knew I'd get nowhere. He wasn't ready to tell me. And in this moment that didn't matter as much as the lesson I'd just taught myself, that I had depended on him for so much. Maybe more than I should have.

I took his hand. "I think I could use some meds too. My ankle is throbbing." And so were my head, my heart, and my girl parts. But Tylenol wasn't going to help me there.

I stuck out my hand. "Here, help me up."

He stood. "Piggyback or...?"

"Just fling me from the top of the stairs and put me out of my misery. This throbbing is wearing on my nerves."

He squatted down, his back to me, and I climbed on. He was like a powerlifter, standing right up as if it was no biggie that I was on his back. I really wanted to see the man's thighs. I would have bet they were the size of tree trunks. Instead, I closed my eyes and stuck my head into the crook of his neck to enjoy the comfort of his body and smell.

"Don't get too fresh there, or we won't make it down-stairs," he growled roughly.

I giggled as he grabbed me behind the knees. Then he looked at my ankle and gave a low whistle as if saying *Ouch*. He carried me downstairs and set me gently on the couch, then put a pillow under my foot as he raised it to rest on the coffee table, using the most tender of touches.

* * *

CAL

* * *

She looked around the living room, then shook her head. "Can you take me to the kitchen? I'm starving."

Her voice was breathy and soft, as if maybe my touch did to her what hers did to me. I wanted to test that theory. I met her gaze and watched her pupils dilate when I ran a finger down her arm.

"I can get you food. I can get you whatever you want." My eyes flicked to her lips. I saw a flash image of her lying on the floor in her panties and bra, jeans pulled up to her knees, her hair a black halo surrounding her. "I just got you here."

"Yeah, but what am I supposed to do?" she asked.

"You are supposed to let your body take time to heal. What's wrong with you? Can't you be idle? Sit and relax."

Earlier, when I was braiding her hair, had been the first time I'd seen her slow down. I thought she stayed busy because she was avoiding all the sadness the last few days had delivered. When the calf had rejected her, anguish had flashed across her face, the same anguish she'd shown when the adoption agency dropped her. It was the hurt of a loss. And she hadn't wanted to talk about it after that day. Even Cricket was worried, telling me Sabrina had clammed up and would tear up whenever Cricket pushed.

"Says the workaholic." She frowned at me.

"Touché. I can go get your laptop or something."

She pursed her lips like she was thinking about her options. Chances were high that she'd find something on the internet that would hurt her.

"If you actually let your ankle rest, it'll heal faster," I said.

She sat forward like she was going to push off the couch and opened her mouth to say something but was interrupted when the front door slammed and someone squealed.

"Where is everyone?" my sister cried out from the foyer.

"In the living room. What's wrong?" As I started toward the foyer, Brynna rushed into the room, holding a small glass bowl in the palms of her hands.

"Look, I did it. I finally did it. That evil cow mom helped me have a breakthrough." She thrust the colorful bowl toward me. The colors looked like various crayon strokes: bold and childlike with lines of gray and black woven in between.

"You made a bowl?" I teased, knowing she had made dozens of bowls of various shapes and sizes.

"No, jackass, it's the colors. I finally was able to make the pattern I wanted." She beamed at me.

Mom came into the room from the kitchen, wearing an apron and wiping her hands on a towel. "What's all the screaming for? Oh, Brynna, you made a bowl. It's lovely, dear —perky and fun—"

"But with a hint of sadness," Sabrina said.

"Yes." Brynna pointed to Sabrina. "You get it." She handed her the bowl. "I call it The Disturbed Childhood."

"Oh, Brynna," Mom said, a hitch in her voice. "That's so sad."

"But it's not meant to be fully sad," Brynna said.

Sabrina adjusted on the couch so she was on her knees, looking over the back, the bowl in her hands. "I see it. I see the happy and the sad. And the title *The Disturbed Childhood* to me means everything. Could be anything. A pet dying. Moving. Or like for me, losing my mother. Something that breaks from the norm. A disruption."

Brynna held up her arms in victory. "Yes, that's exactly the message I wanted to convey. It's the mix of those colors and dark lines that make us this smooth and round bowl open to taking in more. Filling us. We should put memories in this bowl."

My kid sister was impressive. We'd grown up in the same unhappy house, yet she had found a way to channel it into something beautiful. I was the first person she'd made something for. I dug into my pocket and pulled out my keys. From my keyring, I took off a square piece of metal with a multicolored glass circle in the middle and placed it in the bowl.

"That was one of the first pieces you made, Bryn. I carry it everywhere to remind me to look for the beauty in life like you do." I gave my sister a side-arm squeeze.

Mom walked up and put a small rose-gold band in the bowl. "We got that on our trip to Europe after you graduated, remember? It was the first piece of jewelry I bought myself after moving out of the house. It was empowering." She kissed her daughter on the cheek.

"I remember that because I met you both in Switzerland," I said. That trip had been enjoyable, something that was not the norm in our family.

The three of us shared the memory briefly before Brynna looked at Sabrina.

Sabrina shrugged. "Sorry, I don't have anything from my

past here except your brother, and he's not a memory I would I put in the bowl anyway."

She said it teasingly, but there was an edge in her voice. She looked between the three of us, and I knew she wasn't speaking about our past but about her present. Once I saw it, I couldn't not see it. I'd lived with it for years. It was loneliness. Here I was, standing in a room with my family, sharing a memory, and she no longer had that. For the first time, it dawned on me how alone she must feel at times like this.

Mom rested a hand on Sabrina's shoulder. "I think I can help with that."

Then she went to the giant bookcase near the fireplace and pulled out a large leather-bound photo album. She handed the book to Sabrina.

Chapter Twenty-Three
SABRINA

Morgan sat sideways on the couch, one knee pulled up so she could face me. "This ranch has been in my family for decades. It belonged to my mother's parents and her mother's parents before her, though it was little more than a cabin and some fences at that time. Every generation has lived and raised their family here except my mother. Well, I guess me as well, but we're here now." She looked at her kids and smiled. "Sit. You both will want to hear this."

I waited patiently for the story to continue. Cal took a seat next to me and Brynna in the oversized chair next to us. I handed her the glass bowl.

"My mother went away to college on the East Coast, and there she met and married my father. He became a professor at a university in Williamsburg, Virginia."

I straightened, surprised. "That's where my mom was from."

Morgan nodded and smiled. "Yes, I know. I grew up with your mother. That's why the first time I saw you, I said you remind me of someone I used to know. It's incredible how much you look like Rachael."

I sank into the couch, stunned. "You knew my mom?" Other than my dad and grandparents, I'd never met anyone who knew my mom.

Cal came in closer and rested an arm along the back of the couch and me. "Seriously, Mom? How come I've never seen this album before?"

Morgan held up a hand. "I'm going to tell you why. It's not the best story." She cupped her hands to her face "But I am so ashamed, so please forgive me in advance."

I looked to Cal, confused. He arched a brow. Clearly, he felt the same.

Morgan opened the album. Instantly, my eyes were draw to various pictures of two little girls.

"Your grandfather was a professor who worked with my dad. And we lived on the same block. A coincidence. My mother and your grandmother became good friends, and since Rachael and I were close in age—she was a year ahead of me—of course, we became good friends too. The best." Her voice dropped, thick with emotion.

She pointed to a picture of two little girls with Popsicles and tutus, their hair in pigtails, each with an arm thrown across the other's shoulders. "Rachael and I did dance classes together. We learned to ride horses together. We were cheerleaders at our high school. Not only was she my best friend, but I admired her too. She was kind and funny and pretty and so confident, and I had gone through this ugly duckling stage"—she flipped the pages and pointed to a picture—"and felt so self-conscious around her and, well, anyone I thought was pretty and had it together. Rachael never made me feel bad or anything. She wasn't like that. She was a good friend until the end. I, however, was not."

My mother's image was on these pages. I ran my hand down the page, touching each picture with Mom in it, tracing the lines, feeling her memory. "I've never seen some of these," I whispered.

Morgan let me turn the pages, explaining certain pictures as we went. She picked up her story when I came to pictures of them in college.

"Because our parents taught at William & Mary, we certainly didn't want to go there. How can you have the college experience with your father right around the corner? Rachael left for college the year before me. She went to—"

"Brown."

"Yes, Brown. Rhode Island was just far enough to be away from home but just close enough to drive home if we had to. Rachael had a good first year, and that gave my parents reassurance to let me go." Morgan chuckled. "Of the two of us, I was the one who was more impulsive, and I guess they thought Rachael was a good influence over me, and with her nearby, I would be fine. And I was. We were."

"Until...?" Cal asked.

Morgan gave him a watery smile and used the side of her index finger to dab away the tears. "Until we started going up to Massachusetts to Harvard. One of the girls Rachael had made friends with had a brother there, and they would invite us to parties."

"Dad went to Harvard," Brynna said.

"Yes, he did," Morgan said, looking at me. "He was desperately in love with Rachael."

"What?" Cal nearly roared as he leaped to his feet.

I was beyond stunned. My heart stuttered with disbelief,

and a cold wash ran over me. I put my hand up. "Stop. Give me a second to process this."

I looked at the album and pictures of my mother and felt as if I were seeing a part of her for the first time. In the albums at home were endless pictures. Dad had been the one to pass along the stories of my mom in an attempt to keep her memory alive. But never once had Travis Holloway brought up Dalton Beckett—not before I met his son and certainly not anytime after Cal had been to our house. I knew Mom had gone to Brown, that my grandparents considered it a way for Mom to spread her wings, and that they'd never once held her back. They had adored and supported their only child in everything. And in a handful of years following my mother's death, they had showered me with just as much love and devotion until they died.

"Mom, what do you mean that Dad was in love with Sabrina's mom?" Cal was a looming shadow over us. His eyes flashed with anger.

Morgan raised her hands in defense. "Calvin, calm down, and I'll tell you the story."

He looked to me and shook his head in disbelief. "I didn't know. I swear. I never imagined, and had I known, maybe things..." He wiped his hand down his face, looking shell-shocked, then turned and stalked to the fireplace, his back to us, his shoulders a rigid line.

"Maybe what things, Cal?" I asked. Did the history of our parents impact the future of us? When he didn't answer, I turned to Morgan. "What do you mean he was desperately in love with my mother?"

Morgan flipped the page, and there was an image of Rachael, Morgan, another girl, and three guys. She pointed to the girl. "That's Maggie. It was her brother Henry who was at Harvard." She pointed to the tall guy at the edge of the photo. "That's him. Moving inward is Matthew Thompson, and next to him and Rachael is Dalton."

Cal moved like a flash from the fireplace and snatched up the album. He stared down at the image. His face softened when he looked at me. "I knew you looked like your mom. I could see that in the pictures you had around the house, but in this one here, you guys could be twins." He handed the album back to me. "Matthew Thompson used to be Dad's lawyer, right?"

"Yes," replied Morgan. "They had a falling-out, and he left the company."

Puzzle pieces were falling down around me, and I was slowly putting them together, creating a scene that had at one time not made a lick of sense but was starting to become clear.

"So Dalton liked my mother? And how did she feel?" I asked Morgan.

The older woman leaned back into the couch and rested her head back against the top cushion. "At first, she thought he was funny and smart. Because that's Dalton. He makes a great first impression. It's once you get to know him that you see how he really is. We'd gone up a handful of times to parties, and one spring break, Henry said they were all going to Vegas and asked if we wanted to come. We did, so we went."

"My mom met my dad in Vegas." I looked at Cal. He knew the story. It was why we had gone there in the first place.

"She met him that weekend," Morgan confirmed. "I think it was our second night there. Travis was in a high-stakes game, and a crowd was surrounding him. We stopped to watch. Many of the others got bored after a while, but your mom—"

"She said she couldn't take her eyes off him. She said that for a guy sitting there with a lot to lose, he was still funny and kind and calm and... well, that's what my grandmother told me."

"There was just something about him, Rachael said. I think it was love at first sight for both of them, to be honest." Morgan smiled wistfully. "It was very romantic."

"Dad said that he almost folded so he could get out of the game," I said. "She was that distracting to him. But he stayed in and won, albeit a few hours later. He said when it was over, he gathered up all his chips and went up to my mom and said, 'I need to cash these in, but how about we get some dinner?' and she said, 'I thought you'd never ask.'"

On the page was a picture of my mom sitting on the lawn at college, dressed in shorts, her legs stretched out in front of her and a braid over her shoulder. I ran a finger over the image. In the place where memories were stored, I heard my father's voice telling me stories about them every night before bed. Our time with her had been too short. Our love for her had never waned.

"They were together from that moment on. Your dad would play at the casinos near college and see her whenever he could. He refused to let her quit school. All she wanted to do was follow him around. They were married the day after graduation."

"They eloped in Vegas," I added.

"With your grandparents present, of course."

Cal pointed at his mom. "Wait, that's how you recognized the picture of Travis the other day."

She smiled at him. "I thought then I had exposed myself,

and at the time I wasn't ready to tell this story. But after I saw that picture and thought about it, I knew you both needed to know."

Brynna snorted. "Wow, you missed that? For a guy in security, you really suck."

"I was distracted." Cal glared at his sister briefly before returning his attention to his mom. "What's dad's role in this? You said he was in love with Rachael."

Morgan sighed wearily and pressed her palms to her eyes. "All our lives, Rachael never led me wrong, and she was right about Dalton. I was just too jealous to see it." She removed her hands and grimaced. "Dalton kept trying to break Rachael and Travis up. She stopped going up to Massachusetts for the parties. She was with Travis every chance she got. I once overheard Dalton tell Matthew that he thought it was just a fling and she would get tired of Travis. Dalton said he wanted to marry her. Her and only her." Morgan snorted her derision. "He wanted her, and she wouldn't give him the time of day. It drove him mad."

"I bet." Cal moved back to the fireplace. With one hand on the mantel, he stared into the flames.

"Dalton was everything a girl was supposed to want. He was rich, good-looking, and going places. I once asked her why Travis and not Dalton, and she said Travis was more her type. It wasn't until I told her I was going to marry Dalton that she told me how she felt about him. I will never forget her words. She said, 'He may seem nice, but it's all a ruse. He's a man out only for himself. He isn't kind or generous and is selfish to the core.' She begged me to not go out with him. You see, he was using me to get to her, thinking that would make her jealous, but you can't make a person who doesn't care about you jealous." She pressed her shaking hands to her mouth. "I was such a fool," she said through her fingers.

"What happened?" Cal pressed.

Morgan dropped her hands. "We started to date, and a few months later, Rachael graduated and eloped, and I found myself pregnant with you. Rachael and I had stopped talking a few weeks earlier after she begged me to stop seeing him. I accused her of some awful things. Things I never got to apologize for." Tears slid slowly down her face. "She was right. She was so right, and I never got to tell her how much of a fool I was. I am so sorry, Sabrina. Dalton has had it out for your father ever since."

Pieces were clicking together, and I saw more of the full picture. As I studied Cal's face, he avoided my eyes. I had met Dalton Beckett once, a week before we went to Vegas. And I'd seen him there that night Cal broke up with me. Cal, who was supposed to be working for the family business but wasn't. Cal, who'd disappeared from my life as if he'd never been in it at all, without any rhyme or reason. Only now I believed I had the why. Everything made sense. I shoved the album at Morgan and pushed off the seat to stand, forgetting about my ankle, then wincing as I steadied myself.

"Look at me, Cal," I demanded. He ducked his head, and a ball of nausea ate at my stomach. "I swear to God, Cal; you owe me the truth."

He turned, his face a ragged mess of emotions, so many I couldn't parse them. "He said he would destroy both of you. Your dad had that big tournament coming up in Monte Carlo, and Dalton knew people in the IRS and customs, and he said he would stop at nothing. And he would have done just what he said. You don't know how he is. He would have buried you both. It would have been worse than what he's doing now." He pushed off the mantel and came to stand in front of me.

All I could do was stare at him, incredulous. "I can't believe this." I shook my head, then pressed my palms to my temples, trying to squeeze the circle of thoughts spinning like an endless round doodle on a page. "I can't believe this."

He cupped my cheek. "Reenie."

I put up my hand, stopping any more words from coming at me. "Nope. Nope. You do not get to say anything else. You have done enough." Not caring about my sore ankle, I pushed passed him and limped my way around the couch and the stairs.

"Where are you going?" he called.

"Home. I have to get out of here. I can't stand to look at your face right now. I am so mad at you."

He had changed the trajectory of our lives because of a threat his father had made, without even talking to me or my dad. He'd given up on us, our future, for what? He'd never given me a say.

I was right. I had been the one more in love with Cal than he was with me.

Chapter Twenty-Four
CAL

Sabrina limped around the room to the stairs, wincing, using the furniture and walls to support her.

"Sabrina, I know you're mad, but let's talk."

Heck, I was mad at myself for never digging into the why. I had assumed my father was making the ultimatum to try to control me. Sure, I knew Dalton wouldn't think the daughter of a professional gambler would be worthy of his son, which was ironic because Dalton didn't think I was worth much, either, but I'd never once thought my father's demands had anything to do with Sabrina or her father.

Travis. He must have known who my father was all along, yet he'd never said anything or showed any hint of animosity. I followed Sabrina, quickly catching up with her on the stairs. What were the odds that Rachael and Dalton's children would meet and fall in love? So low it would have been a fool's bet.

"Reenie, let me tell you about that day and explain it." I put out a hand to help her, and she slapped it away.

"Oh, now you want to tell me about that day—not when

I was crying and begging you. Noooo, not then." She leaned forward, grabbed a fistful of my shirt, and pulled me close. "I want to hurt you so bad right now it's not even funny. I want you to hurt like I did that day." She pushed me away.

"You don't think it hurt me to break up? I was doing it to protect you."

She snorted and hobbled up another step.

"I went to Vegas with every intention of marrying you," I said.

My mother gasped. She and my sister were watching from below, curious looks on their faces. Neither of them knew the story.

"And you left with every intention of never seeing me again, without any explanation."

"Because it was the best way to protect you and your dad."

She swung around to glare at me and put a finger in my face. Her eyes were spitting fire. Her mouth opened to say something, but the words never followed. This was the most pissed I'd ever seen her, but more than that, she had the same betrayed look in her eyes that she'd had when I left. She wagged her finger once, then curled it into a fist. I knew she would use it. And Sabrina had a mean right hook.

Yeah, I had betrayed her and our promises, and saying it had been to protect her and her father now sounded weak. But in the moment, it had felt very real. Devastating.

"I know you need space. Just don't leave. Take some time, and then let's talk."

She shook her head. "Why do we need to talk? Why can't you just make the decisions for me and tell me what you think should happen? Who cares how I feel or what I think? That seems to be your MO."

"Where are you going to go tonight?"

"I will go wherever Cricket takes me. As soon as I get to my room and phone, I'm calling her to come get me." She glared at me.

She rocked to the side to rest her weight on the bannister as she took another step. If I let her go, there might not be a hope of rekindling what we'd just started.

"Oh, for fuck's sake," I said, exasperated, and moved in front of her. "Fine. You want to go? Go. But you will hear me out first." I bent forward and grabbed her around the waist.

"What are you doing?" she screeched.

I flipped her over my shoulder, fireman style, pivoted on the stairs, and headed toward her room. "I can't watch you hobble up these stairs anymore. You're being ridiculous. I now see what I did was wrong. I get it, but we are going to talk about it. Ow! Why did you pinch me?" She'd gotten me on the back of my arm.

"For calling me ridiculous. You are the ridiculous one."

I felt her fingers on my triceps again, going for another pinch, so I slapped her on the ass. "Stop that!"

She gasped. "You stop that, you giant goon."

She wiggled like she'd rather fall to the floor than be carried another step by me, and I smacked her bottom again. When I made it to her room, I tossed her onto the bed like a sack of potatoes. Sabrina bounced, her hair flying into her face.

When she settled, she blew out her hair, moving what she could with her hands. "I hate you."

I stood before her bed, hands on my hips. "I know; you have every right to. But—"

"There's no but. You don't get a but."

"Okay, fine. I did what I thought was best in the moment

with the facts I had in front of me. It wasn't an easy decision by any means. And this"—I pointed to what lay outside her bedroom door—"is the first time I have ever heard of a connection between our parents. I just thought Dalton's actions were a way to control me. I told him then that if he made me pick, then I would pick you every time, and he said I really didn't have a choice. And where you were concerned, he was right. Leaving you was the only way to protect you from him. That's why I didn't want you involved in any of this nonsense either. You have always been a target of his. Now I know he's been gunning for your dad, and you, for forever."

"He can't touch my dad," she said angrily.

"Oh yeah? Look at what he did to you the other day when that article about your dad came out. You were devastated. You went right into defense mode and were on the attack. Now you have an IRS investigation. You have to hire a lawyer to help with the estate accusations. And what about the adoption?"

She flinched.

"He wants to take everything you love away from you— your hopes, dreams, and memories. He will wear you down and ground you into pavement if he gets half the chance. What are you going to do then?"

She stared at me with shiny, narrow eyes. Maybe I was finally getting through to her.

"You said you had no choice, but we always have choices."

"Yes, I could have talked to you and Travis. And you would have been by my side for sure. And then I would have had to watch Dalton destroy your family. How do we" —I pointed at both of us—"survive that? How do you not resent me? How does it not destroy us? You know it would have."

"It's not destroying us now."

"We're different people now. And your dad isn't here. I stood in that hotel room, watching him tear my world apart, and I wanted to kill him. I wanted to kill my own father, and I was horrified by that because the worst thing I could ever do is become a reflection of him. Then he told me what I was going to do next, and I had to walk away." Best thing I ever did was not go to Harvard but to the University of Texas instead. My father refused to pay for school, and I was fine with that. I didn't want to be in debt to him. Becoming self-sufficient gave me the option of walking away from my family, so I did.

"I saw no other way to protect you than what I did. There was no way in hell I'd give that man anything he wanted. So I walked away from it all. And make no mistake: I will burn my company to the ground before I go work for him. Before I give up Mom and Brynna, this ranch, or a chance with you."

Her lower lip trembled. "My dad loved you. He never understood why you stopped being a part of our lives."

I brushed a hand down my face and wondered if I should tell her the rest. Would she find peace in the heartbreak? But I couldn't keep any more secrets.

"Yes, he did. He knew." I met her gaze and watched her work out my words.

She shook her head again. "No. How?"

"That time you came to Seattle to see Dr. Rasmussen. I saw him there." Now she would know it all.

"I didn't see you." She pulled her legs up under her on the bed, looking confused.

"You were in the waiting room. I talked to Travis in the patient room. Dr. Rasmussen had been a client of mine. He had been more than happy to agree to my request."

Her mouth went slack, and I could see her working out the timeline.

"You are why we got in to see Rasmussen, aren't you? We were told the wait list was years." She clutched her hands in her lap and stared at me, her eyes large.

"Jace told me about Travis's diagnosis. I mentioned it to Nigel—Dr. Rasmussen. He said he would see Travis. So I reached out to your dad and told him to take the appointment and I would explain everything. I asked him not to mention it to you." Getting Travis in to see one of the world's best oncologists was the least I could have done.

"Why?" Her one word was broken and chipped.

"Because your dad was dying from cancer. Because you were already dealing with too much. All I have ever wanted was for you to be happy. How confusing would it have been to have me pop back in to try to help? I'd never wanted to hurt you the way I did, and if I had a chance to help, I was going to take it. So I did."

"This doesn't make any sense." Sabrina put her hands over her face and refused to look at me.

"I have letters from your dad. I have them here if you want to see them."

Her hands fell to her lap. "Seriously?"

I nodded.

"Okay," she whispered.

I went to the door.

"Where are you going?" she asked.

"To get the letters."

She waved me back over. "I'm going with you."

My lips twitched with a repressed grin. "You think I am going to my room to hastily craft some letters from your dad because this is all a ruse?"

"I don't know what to think anymore. That's why I am going with you." She continued to wave me over. "Pick me up. We'll move faster if you do the walking."

I did it without argument and, once in jmy room, placed her on the edge of my bed. Then I went to my closet and came back with a small accordion-style envelope. Inside were three handwritten notes from her father. I handed it to her.

She gently removed the letters and started to read. By the second one, she was quietly sobbing. I was ripped in two, watching her. I dropped to my knees in front of her, my hands beside her on the bed.

"Reenie." I used a thumb to brush away her tears.

"After he died, I was so alone. Even with Jace and Meredith and Nick and all my other friends, I was alone. I wanted you. I needed you, but I..." She shook her head and looked away.

"I'm sorry, baby. I am so sorry. I wanted to be there."

"But my dad asked you not to." She held the letter up. "He was on your side."

Placing both hands on her face, I swiped away the heavy flow of tears. "No, he was on your side. He knew my dad was an awful person. He didn't want you to have to bury him and fight my dad at the same time." I leaned forward and kissed her on the forehead. "My family has made a mess of your life. I have made a mess of it too. All I ever wanted was for you to be happy and safe. Watching you hurt, like you are right now, kills me, Reenie, and knowing I was the reason is excruciating."

I kissed her temple as her hands came to rest on my shoulders. She dropped her head to my chest, leaned into me, and cried.

"Everyone's making decisions for me except me. No one thought to give me a choice. Am I so fragile that I need to be this protected?" She pushed away, my shirt fisted in her hands as she gently shook me. "Did both of you not trust me?"

I stood, eased her fist from my shirt, then went onto the bed next to her, and pulled her into my lap, wrapping her in the tightest hug I had. "It wasn't about trust. It was about love. You had already lost so much with your mom and grandparents and now your dad. Why would I add more to that if I could avoid it. We never wanted to see you hurting like you are now. This is what I wanted to avoid. And I thought, and your dad thought so too, that what we did was going to avoid all this. In the moment, it really felt like the right thing. Now I see what we did was wrong. I'm so sorry, baby. But when given shitty choices, picking the one that does the least amount of damage is the best I could do."

As I held her, she unraveled. And she unraveled me. I wrapped a hand around the back of her neck and delivered small kisses to the top of her head, hoping it was some comfort. Though too many years too late, I tried to give her the hug she'd needed after she buried her dad. I held her for the hurt I'd given her, for the loneliness she'd felt, and for every day over the last ten years I'd ached to hold her one last time, though I'd known there was no such thing as one last time. I would always want more.

Chapter Twenty-Five
CAL

There was a shift between us. A good one. There were no more secrets, and I felt like I had a better picture of my father and his motives. Once she got all the tears out, Sabrina and I lay in my bed and talked for hours, starting with my description of the night my dad had shown up in Vegas with all his threatening promises. He'd laid out his attack for me and spun the tale of how much Sabrina and her father would hate me, how they'd see me as the bad-luck streak that had invaded their lives.

I could have Sabrina hating me for being an asshole; I could come back from that. Pain like that could be healed. But if her life had been decimated, along with her father's, because of me, how do we overcome that? The strain and hurt would have eventually shredded us to pieces. And that I could never come back from.

Then Travis had gotten sick, and I knew I had to say something. He had to know.

As she snuggled up next to me, her swollen ankle propped up on my leg, she made her declaration. "You were right, you know. To do what you did." She looked up at me, and expecting to see acceptance, I saw hurt in her eyes. "I'm lying here, thinking about how I just want all this to go away. How I'd kill for a fresh start to figure out what we should do next, me and you, but I know we can't do that. Your dad is out there with attacks already in the works. I'm tired and I'm scared and I try to picture what life would look like had you told me that day in Vegas and I can see the cracks. I can see how it could have destroyed us. And I for sure know I couldn't have withstood this sort of attack while my dad was sick. Even now I don't know if I can handle more blows."

I ran a hand over the top of her head, pushing the hair out of her face. "Okay, what do you want to do?"

"That's just it. I don't think it matters what I want to do. I think now that I'm back on your dad's radar, I'm gonna stay there regardless. What happened between him and my parents is unfinished business to him, and now he has a chance to finish it. He's not going to stop, no matter what I do—what we do."

She was right, of course.

"He's taken away my one dream." Her voice was raspy from unshed tears.

"Actually, I was thinking about this. He's taken away one avenue toward your dream. But I was doing some research, and there are other routes to adoption."

"But once he finds out about that, he'll attack me there."

This was also true.

She sat up and stared down at me. "We have to see this through to the end, don't we? Not just for your company and app but to even have a chance at living a life without his interference."

This was the part I hated. I must have always known this

battle with my dad would have to have a grand finale. A final battle.

I nodded and picked up a lock of hair to wind it through my fingers. "We're stronger together. I see that now."

She studied me as she worried her lower lip, then gave a clipped nod as if she'd made up her mind. "Okay, then. We need to up our game. We need to stop playing like there are some rules to this war, because he's not doing that. I think we can punch back harder and still keep our ethics."

And then she laid out a plan.

When we shared it with Paul, he loved it. I spent the morning making the rounds on the morning show via satellite. I told the world that my father was behind the attack and smear campaign, and I explained how our app would be different. How the app conception had begun because of Citra's sister. I talked about Casey at the community center and how the app gave her a solid checklist of ways to protect herself. And I had friends in the industry back up what I taught about personal safety, though no one was willing to back me up personally, and I got that. It hurt, but they were scared of it affecting their businesses, which fed their families, and that was understandable. Cowardly, but understandable. Standing up and taking heat was not a pleasant experience. Ask me how I know. I ended by explaining how my company's goal was other people's safety, and how the smear campaign had endangered other people.

We ended the shows on a high note when they asked about Sabrina. I wasn't going to declare my feelings on TV before I could say them to her, but as people scrolled through her Instagram feed and asked questions about us, I didn't have to say much—the pictures spoke for themselves.

One female host clutched her chest and swooned when I

said, "Some things are meant to be. They don't always come easily or freely, but they come. Sabrina is my meant to be. She always has been." And then I went on to slam my dad's attack on her father.

Afterward, I stood at the corral's fence and fed my horse an apple. Sabrina came up beside me and leaned against the fence. She was wearing yoga pants, a sweatshirt, and one of my heavier jackets as the fall wind was blowing in. Her ankle was wrapped, and she wore slip-on shoes.

"How's the ankle?" I handed her an apple from the bag at my feet, and she held it out to the paint she'd ridden.

"Almost like new." Sabrina beamed. I got a contact high just watching her. "It's like waiting for the war to break out, isn't it?" she said. We'd picked up our weapons and pointed them at my father. Now he was either going to flinch or fire. "Can you even guess what his next move might be?"

I shook my head. "I think he wants to take things away from me. I think he's going to come after you more."

She shrugged. "I don't see how. He's already hit me hard."

"I think we need to open our imaginations and come up with some wild ideas before we say he can't do any more harm."

One of the ranch's SUVs pulled up close to the house, and Rod jumped out of the back before the vehicle had come to complete stop. I glanced at my watch. School had two more hours before letting out. Mrs. Claudia came to stand out on the porch, and Rod took one look at her, turned, and ran to the barn.

"Was his shirt ripped?" Sabrina asked.

I thought I'd seen blood on his face. We looked at each other, and I bolted toward the barn. I stopped briefly to wait for her, but she waved me on. When I got into the barn, Rod was on the hay bales where we'd sat the night before. He was crying.

I sat down next to him, and he turned away. I didn't know what to say. This felt more like a Sabrina situation than one I could deal with. So I sat next to him and let him cry.

She walked in a few minutes later, eyed us both, then took a seat on Rod's other side and started rubbing his back. He flinched at first but settled when she moved from stroking his back to his head.

He was wearing a flannel shirt in muted fall colors, so the blood on the sleeve wasn't hard to miss. Neither was the tear at the shoulder. Who does this to a seven-year-old, and if it's another kid his age, what the actual fuck is wrong with people?

"Did I ever tell you my dad was a professional gambler?" Her voice was soft and soothing. She didn't wait for him to say anything. "After my mom died, we moved around some. I think it was hard for my dad to stay in one place because then he would think about her. We moved to this small town in Texas called Brewster. Cori is from there." She looked at me. She was telling us both the story. "My dad always liked high-stakes games, but after my mom died, he avoided them, like maybe they reminded him of her, or maybe he thought his luck had run out or something. He never said. In this town, there was this really mean girl named Cami. I think she was around my age. Her dad was one of the wealthy guys in town. Big fish in a small pond."

Rod's sobs had subsided.

Sabrina continued to soothe him. "She was really mean, and I hated her guts. She was always saying terrible things to us, like how Cori's teeth were ugly and made her look like a crazy rabbit. This was before she got braces. Or how it must be hard to know how to be a girl with no mother around. It was like she knew what would hurt the most. I wanted to smack her in the face."

Rod picked up his head. The tears had streaked a path on his dirt-and-sand-covered face. His upper lip was busted, and he had the beginnings of a bruise on his right cheek. "Did you?"

She shook her head. "I didn't slap her. I clocked her upside the head with my book bag. She'd pushed me too far that day. She said terrible things about why my mom died. And to this day, I can't even bring myself to repeat them even though I know she was wrong. Just pointing out the fact that my mom was gone was terrible enough."

"He said my dad left because he couldn't look at me. That I was the reason why my mom was dead." Fresh tears ran down his face.

Rod's mom had died in childbirth.

"When he said all that, what did you do?" I asked.

"Nothing at first. I tried to walk away because my dad says it takes more courage to do that than to fight."

"But...?"

"But he followed me and wouldn't shut up, so I just turned around and charged at him like a bull. I knocked him down. Then I hit him."

Sabrina scooped him up and tucked him into her lap. "You know that's not true, right? About your mom and your dad."

"He's not here, is he?"

Rod's statement was too mature for a kid his age. When I was seven and my dad would let me visit, I'd spend at least the first twenty-four hours trying to be the perfect son—a solid day of me trying to win his love and affection before the anger and rejection set in. It was a wonder I hadn't gotten into more fights.

"Do you think your dad loves you, Rod?" Sabrina asked.

He nodded. "I guess. It's hard when he's not here." He moved his hands to his lap, and I saw that his thumb was swollen.

"That's all you have to know. Hold on to that. Who knows why he's not here right now? Only he can tell us, and maybe he doesn't even know. Being an adult is hard too. Mrs. Claudia says he loves you, and as we know, Mrs. Claudia never lies."

I pointed to his hand. "What happened here?"

"I tried to punch him."

I was not one for violence. My whole job was to prevent it the best we could. But I was in favor of protection, and that started with people protecting themselves.

"With your thumb tucked into your fist?" I asked.

Rod nodded.

I stood and scooped him up. "Come on. Let's go inside and get you cleaned up and put some ice on that hand. Then I'm going to show you how to punch. Never tuck your thumb in your fist. Ever."

Rod nodded.

"But I think you know that now," I said.

"Is punching something we need to learn?" Sabrina stood too.

"Rod's dad is right. Walking away is far harder, but there might be a time when you are going to have to punch someone, so you'd better know how to do it right."

Rod wrapped an arm around my neck. "Mrs. Claudia is gonna yell at me."

"Only because you scared her," Sabrina said. "But I bet she makes a dessert you like."

His eyes went large, and he looked at me. "I asked for Boston cream pie."

I smiled and started for the door. "Attaboy."

"That's your favorite." Sabrina fell into step with us. She poked me in the biceps. "Did you put him up to it?"

"I maybe mentioned it, and Rod wants to try new things, don't you?"

Rod nodded. "It has pudding in it. I like pudding."

Crème, pudding—I wasn't going to split hairs.

"Nice job, by the way," I said.

"Nice job for what?" she asked.

I did a small nod toward Rod. "You calmed him down instead of making him cry. Much better than how you were with the calves."

"Oh, shut up." She punched me in the arm. But she was smiling, and I knew that was exactly what she'd needed to hear.

Chapter Twenty-Six
CAL

No more letting the app suggest our dates. When you knew someone like I knew Sabrina, sometimes you had an idea that nothing suggested by the app could match. I had put together a real date for us, and excitement had me whistling as I set it up.

Our love for each other had that special something that people dreamed about. Our love was the kind that stuck forever. All this time apart, and it hadn't waned. Now I just wanted to say how I felt, out loud. I really wanted her to say it too.

Looking back, I realized that the day we'd had to share a horse and I'd told her what I wanted to do with her—to her— I hadn't done it to scare her away. She'd been sitting there, her legs over mine, so close and looking at me with the bright-blue eyes of the Sabrina who loved me, and I'd been body-slammed with the realization that I'd missed her so damn much. Then she'd looked at me like that again at the community center, and it had all just clicked. We needed to start making new memories, happier ones, and working on dismantling our walls.

Sabrina was in my office, talking to LA about her documentary. She'd spoken to the director and was now on the phone with the actor. Things didn't sound like they were going all that well. All the more reason to take her out and get her mind off the parts of our lives that were unraveling.

I stood outside the door, waiting for the right time to interrupt. These last few weeks had been a whirlwind, a complete one eighty in my life. In Peru, I certainly hadn't wondered what came next and then pictured myself at the ranch, drafting a plan to win a woman's heart.

I stepped into the office and caught her eye.

"Hang on, Nick." She raised a brow in question.

"Thought maybe you might want to go see the waterfall near No Man's Lake."

Her face lit up. "Yeah, I totally do." She glanced out the window. "Isn't weather coming in?"

I nodded. "We've got time. But we have to leave now."

She quickly ended the call. "Let me change, and I'll meet you outside at the barn."

I pointed to the stairs. "Go. No horses today. We'll take an ATV. Mom's packing some food for us too."

She took off up the stairs with a laugh and the slightest of limps. I hadn't been fully cognizant of how exhausting our constant push and pull had been until now. It was much easier to stop resisting. I went outside to prep the ATV, caught my sister as she was coming in, and admired a vase she'd just created.

Sabrina bounced out of the house a few minutes later and stopped short when she saw me. "Where's the other ATV?"

"I thought we would just take one. It's easier."

"Where are you all headed?" Brynna smiled

"To see a waterfall," Sabrina answered.

Brynna swung her eyes to me , and her smile widened "The one at No Man's?"

I couldn't look at my sister. She knew the falls were secluded and romantic, which straight-up told her my agenda. So I just nodded.

Brynna chuckled. "Have fun. Do all the things," she called over her shoulder as she headed up the stairs.

Sabrina came to stand beside me. "We should post something. It's been a few days since Cricket's article came out. Let's feed the fire." She moved in closer and held out her phone. "Smile for the camera."

I moved behind her, making her the little spoon, and snaked one arm around her waist to pulled her in tight. I rested my other hand on her hip. Then I bent and tucked my face into the crook of her neck.

"Smile for the camera," I whispered as I nuzzled.

My breath made a path along the crook and onto her shoulder. She leaned fully into me like a limp noodle, and dang it all, holding her felt so good. Maybe the waterfalls were too far away. Maybe I should just take her into the woods, propose ravishing her, and see if she agreed. I had a feeling she would.

I stepped back, keeping one hand on her elbow to hold her steady, picked up the Stetson she'd dropped, dusted it off, then plopped it on her head. I tweaked her nose because I didn't know what else to with my hands. Well, I did know, but I wasn't going to do that without Sabrina's consent or here in the yard for all to see. So nose it was.

Her nose crinkled up. "Well played, Calvin." She

adjusted her hat, and I noticed a slight tremor in her hand. I'd stuffed mine into my pockets so she wouldn't see they were doing the same.

I dipped my head once. "Let them narrate that." I climbed onto the ATV and patted the seat behind me. I liked rattling her. I liked being rattled by her.

"Hey, the waterfalls aren't an option on the app's dating suggestions," Sabrina said.

"Yeah, I know. It's my idea, not the app's."

"Well, you should tell the IT team to add a box for others to help the algorithm."

"Reenie, this isn't an app date. This is an us date. All I care to share about it right now is that picture." I pointed to her phone, then patted the seat behind me a second time.

She blinked up at me, then bit her lip. "An us date, huh? What kind of stuff can people do at these falls, Cal?"

"Get on, woman, and I'll show you." I wagged my brows.

Sabrina laughed, but her expression said it all. She looked besotted and horny. Exactly how I felt.

* * *

SABRINA

* * *

The drive out into the mountains had been fun. A shift had happened between us. A good shift—toward healing. I couldn't put my finger on when it had happened, exactly, but after the night of airing all the truths, we were able to finally move forward instead of circling the drain like we'd been doing.

I didn't think I'd fully processed what Morgan had said about my mom. On some level, it felt like she was talking about someone else because so much of it was new to me. And though my temper still flared when I thought about Cal making the choice he had that night in Vegas, I was coming to terms with it. Begrudgingly, I understood.

Cal himself was merging the two Cals I knew—the old and the new. And I liked this blended version of him. Besides the fact that he was galactically hot, the self-awareness and confidence he'd developed over this last decade were freaking intoxicating. He'd always been self-assured, but now there was an edge to him that he'd never had before. A fuck-around-and-find-out mannerism. Each day, the hurt from our past faded a little more.

Perhaps this was what forgiveness looked like. And that picture we'd just taken—yeesh, taking it had made me so hot I nearly burst into flames. I got weak in the knees and almost fell getting on the ATV. Cal with his damn swoony kiss.

I rested my head against his back and gave in to the moment, enjoying the now. Everything was perfect, even with all the bullshit going on. I looked over his shoulder at the vast stretch of land. It made me feel like a tiny dot in the Wyoming landscape, but not in a bad way. It was like the camera lens zoomed out, taking in more of the picture, which felt like a metaphor for our lives. Everything was about seeing the big picture.

I held on to his waist, my hands on his hip bones. He picked one hand up and kissed my palm, then worked his way down to my wrist. My nipples puckered with want. That was what this man did to me.

Cal pulled up to narrow path and shut down the ATV. He pointed to a dark cloud far in the distance. "We have a couple of hours. Let me show you the waterfall. I brought some food, too, so we can picnic."

Cal was beside the ATV, the soft cooler in hand, by the time I removed my helmet and stood. He was stupidly handsome. All he had to do was flash me a grin and I became witless. I wanted to say something but didn't know what. That I wanted to jump his bones. That the closeness of the ride out here had done it for me, revved me up. But he didn't give me a chance to speak, tugging my hand to draw me onto the path, which narrowed quickly, the forest too dense to ride through. We didn't talk until we broke through the trees to the opening of the falls.

I gasped at the sight. All the naughty thoughts that had been simmering fell away. A pool slightly bigger than a hot tub lay before us, with a waterfall about ten feet high dumping into it. We were in the valley of the mountains. Ponderosa dotted the landscape.

"It's beautiful." I touched his arm, and static electricity crackled between us, sending heat up my arm. Yeah, I was in trouble. If a touch was making me hot and bothered, I'd probably orgasm with just a kiss. I glanced at his mouth but looked away when he caught me.

"We just missed the crimson by a few weeks. It adds a lot of color here." Cal pointed at the cloverlike ground covering.

"How do you not just want to stay here forever?"

Cal chuckled. "Mostly because I get hungry, and sometimes indoor plumbing is a perk. This is one of the best places to come and work out what's on my mind."

"If you duck under that swath of trees you'll see some mini falls." He held a hand up to his knees to tell me the height. "And there's a hunting cabin about half a mile up the trail. If you sit quietly at the cabin, you can see all kinds of animals come to the falls. It's magical."

I swung my eyes to him. "Bears?" A few years back, Jace had been attacked by a sick bear.

Cal pointed to his pack, which was on the ground. "I have bear spray in there. And I have never seen a bear at the falls. Besides. any noise we make will scare off the ones that might be there."

I did some rapid clapping to let the bears know we were here.

Cal laughed. "And now any animal within a half-mile radius has been scared off by that noise. Come on." He snatched up his backpack and nodded for me to follow.

My phone vibrated in my vest pocket. "Weird. I'm getting a signal." I took it out.

"Yeah, there are some parts that get service. Some cell towers hidden in the trees. You can never actually get away from civilization."

Cricket texted.

> His dad may have some media in his pocket, but the public opinion is on your side. Check out these comments.

She'd linked to an Instagram page. The page took much longer than normal to load, but when it did, the pictures were of the community center event. People were praising Cal and his work.

He stopped to look at me and the page, and I beamed at him.

"What?" he asked.

"You're getting some love for what you do. People are

finally coming out to defend you." I tapped to access the Instagram notifications and saw there were already over a hundred comments. I scrolled through them. "Oh, hmm."

"Okay, what does that mean?" He stepped closer.

"That picture we took earlier. Some haters have come out."

"Haters?" He reached for the phone, but I pulled away and turned to keep him from getting it. "They're sad that you're dating me, they don't think I'm good enough, and a lot of women have called you a snacc. With two cs."

Cal's brows knitted in question.

"Good enough to eat, you sweet morsel, you." I slapped him on the shoulder. "It means they want to sex you up immediately, and, you know..." I gestured toward his boy parts.

"Considering the word is snacc, I'm guessing eating each other out is part of the sexing up."

Instantly, my cheeks flared with heat. I slapped my palms to them to hide my blush.

Cal chuckled and then straightened like a peacock, spreading his shoulders wide, preening. "Good to know I'm such a hottie."

His feigned arrogance quickly diffused my embarrassment.

I rolled my eyes. "Don't let it go to your head, or I'll have to drown you in the falls."

"Well, they're wrong." He relaxed his chest and smiled big.

"No, you are very much a snacc."

"I meant they are wrong about you not being good enough. It's me who isn't good enough."

He held my gaze, and my body went warm from the sincerity I saw. But I caught a glimpse of something else before he winked, then ducked away to spread out a blanket he'd taken out of his pack. Was that guilt?

"Cal, you are not your dad. What you do for others is amazing. No one's life is free of mistakes or regrets. It's what you do after those mistakes that counts. And you have done so much."

He dropped everything onto the blanket and studied me. "Does this mean you forgive me?"

I glanced at the fast-moving clouds above us. "I think I forgave you when I found out about how we got to see one the best oncologists in the world because of you, or maybe it happened when I signed up to help. I dunno. Maybe this is forgiveness."

He stepped up to me and placed his hands on my shoulders, his thumb gently caressing the area near my collarbone. "I'm sorry for everything."

"I know."

"I've never stopped wanting to be with you." His eyes were a shimmering sapphire color, bright with earnestness.

This was it—the moment I'd thought about a million times over the years. It wasn't closure I had wanted or revenge either. It was a chance to have Cal back. Maybe I was stupid or pathetic, but our time together had been so good. And though I told myself that what we'd had was over, I'd still been holding on to it all these years, never really letting go.

I missed him. I wanted him. And he was telling me he wanted me. Still. And my head was asking my heart if it was sure it wanted to take this leap again.

"Reenie?"

There I stood, half of my body numb, afraid, and the rest quivering with anticipation. And the response my brain came up with was embarrassing, but I let the words out anyway because I had nothing else.

"Cool. Great. Awesome."

Chapter Twenty-Seven
SABRINA

Cool? Awesome? That's what I said? Even thinking about it made me want to cringe. I wanted to jump him right then and scream, "Yes!" in his face. Instead, I'd said, "Cool."

Cal's lips twitched with restrained laughter, which triggered my flight-or-fight response. I scurried away like a scared bunny, exclaiming, "Oh, I want to go to the top of that waterfall!"

Everything went downhill from there. Twelve minutes later, I was on the ground, sprawled out across the rocks that made the edge of the waterfall, soaking wet. I tried to push up, but my hand slipped on the wet rocks, and I got nowhere.

Cal held out his hand, offering to help me. His eyes danced with merriment.

"Don't you dare say *I told you so*." I slapped at his hand.

"I don't have to; you just did." A smirk popped up, but he had the good sense to wipe it off his face before I threw a handful of mud at him. "Can you stand?"

All I'd wanted to do was stand near the falls and put my hands in the water. Cal had warned me that the rocks might be slippery and advised against it. His words, "I advise against it, Reenie." So cocksure. So bossy.

I had proceeded with caution and gotten to do exactly what I wanted and had been feeling super smug and cocky only to fall on the rocks as I was trying to make my way back to the not-as-slippery grass. My previously injured ankle was still weak, so when I'd started to slide, the ankle had offered no support. My butt—my entire backside really—was soaked, and my ankle was throbbing.

"Don't you dare laugh at me. Busting my ass isn't funny." I slapped my hands against the shallow water in frustration.

He gave a clipped nod. "Though it was a spectacular busting of the ass. How is it you can look pretty, falling?"

The spray from the waterfall had dampened my hair, and now strands clung to my face. I was muddy and wet and knew my face had to be a hundred shades of red. But his words were sweet.

"I'm not so vapid that calling me pretty will make me feel better." Mostly. It did make me feel a little better.

"I never thought you were vapid. It was simply an observation." His arms were akimbo as he studied me.

"Thanks, though. I appreciate the compliment."

"Can you stand?" He was still on the safe grass at the edge of the rocks.

I tried to adjust to stand, but my hands lost purchase. "I think if I flip over to my knees and crawl, I can get off the rocks. How humiliating is that?"

Cal opened his mouth to say something, a flash of lightning lit the space, followed by an ear-deafening crack of thunder, which shook the ground. Have I been sitting in the water so long the storm caught up? I had been careless, and he had been right, and now I was going to get struck by lightning and die out here. At least the backdrop was lovely. But the universe had to hate me if it was going to let Cal Beckett be the last person I ever saw before I'd had a chance to jump Cal version 2.0 and see what that was like.

Irony, thy name is karma.

There was another flash, and hand to God, I thought maybe the bolt had struck near us. The boom that followed made the water tremble. I looked at Cal as I butt-scooted toward him, my hands and feet sliding. I had stayed back from the edge of the falls because I knew that had to be the slipperiest, but when I caught air, I'd landed right on the edge.

I was literally living on the edge, constantly fighting the rush of the water as it maniacally ran toward the precipice to create a waterfall. Though the drop wasn't that high, maybe ten feet, I did not feel like taking a plunge. It was bad enough that my jeans were wet, the feeling of such grossed me out.

But getting struck by lightning while being in a pool of water made wet jeans look like a nonissue. Getting electrocuted would dry those jeans right up, like a speed cycle on high heat, and my clothes and I would be cooked.

Cal looked in the direction of where I'd thought the lightning had struck, and he then stomped out to where I was but stayed away from the edge. "Give me your hands!" he barked.

I did, and he pulled me toward him. When I was closer to him than to the drop-off, he scooped me up, one arm around my back, the other under my knees. And he did it so effortlessly. He didn't even need to toss me slightly to readjust me. If I had been standing, I would have swooned.

Fat raindrops began to pelt the earth.

"Please don't fall," I pleaded as I clung to him.

If we got stuck out here, would we have to fight off wildlife. I'd heard stories about elks attacking people. And there were bears. Oh, my word, bears. Cal might not have seen any, but that didn't mean they weren't out there, because why else would Cal have bear spray?

He made getting back to not-slippery land easy. In three large steps, we were there. "We need to get to the shelter. I don't want to be out in this. Can you stand?" he asked.

Our faces were so close, and his body was so warm. Mine was cold from the water. Goose bumps covered my skin. "I think so," I said.

He eased me down to a stand. "You really twisted your ankle when you fell."

I tested putting equal weight on both feet and gasped in pain, lifting my injured leg up immediately as I used his chest for balance. "I think that's a no on the standing."

Truth be told, as embarrassed as I was, if a girl was going to get hurt in the woods during a thunderstorm, there were worse people to be stuck with. My friend Nick for one. He had zero survival skills or instinct. Then there was Jace. He would be very confident in this situation, as he'd been raised in this forest, and so would most of my friends in Wyoming. So okay, maybe it was no big deal that Cal was with me. I was lucky I had so many capable friends. But regardless, I was glad Cal was here. Protecting me was where he excelled, and I felt like I needed some protection.

Lightning flashed. He turned his back to me. "Hurry, get on."

I climbed him like he was a tree, scurrying right up like a squirrel looking for a hole to hide in, and held on for dear life, burying my face into the crook of his neck as the thunder rolled across the land. "We're going to die!" I cried.

I didn't know why I was so scared. I lived in Texas. Hurricanes, hello. But I was usually indoors and wearing warm clothes during those.

Cal chuckled but didn't waste a second getting out of the open space. He paused only long enough to grab his pack and cooler before heading farther up the trail. I looked up to see where we were going, and ahead of us was a worn-out-looking hunting shack. If I were honest, shack was too good a word for it. He made good time, and we only had to endure two more flashes of lightning before we were in the cabin and Cal was latching the door behind us. The place smelled musty and a little like body odor, a remnant of all the dirty hunters who had passed through.

He pressed my back against a wall for support. "You can get down now. But hold on to me so you don't have to put weight on your ankle."

I slid down him like rain on a window, slow and clingy. I put my hands on his waist as I balanced myself. He dropped the stuff he'd been carrying, did a half turn, and flung a long arm over my head to rest against the wall.

When I stopped wobbling, he turned fully and placed his other hand on my hip. "You good?"

My hands were on his waist, and his face was close as he bent down to hear me over the heavy raindrops beating against the wood shack. I moved my hands to his shoulders and looked up, meeting his gaze. His brow was knitted with concern, his eyes dark and questioning. Where his fingers steadied me, heat moved like a current from him and surged through my body.

Am I good? Hard to say.

Parts of me were fine. Small, insignificant parts. Other parts, like my racing heart and my mind with its naughty ideas, were out of control.

A drop of water rolled down the side of his neck, and without thinking, I licked it off him, dragging my tongue along his skin. Cal groaned and not in a way that said he was annoyed. As I pulled back, his hand brushed away wet strands of hair stuck to my face. I shivered with longing.

"You cold?" His voice was a hoarse whisper. One hand held me steady as the other brushed up and down my arm, trying to warm me and chase away the goose bumps that textured my skin.

I shook my head, unable to speak.

He swiped his thumb across my lower lip. "You have goose bumps, and your lips are pale."

"That's not why I shivered."

His eyes flared with heat. "We have to get this boot off you to look at your ankle."

"It's just an ankle. I have another one."

He smirked. Leaning in, he whispered gruffly, "I might have to take your pants off to see the whole ankle." His hand brushed against my leg, going under my knee. "Let the wall support you." He lifted my leg, running his big hand up the back part of it, and held it up.

If I'd been limber enough, I would have thrown that leg over this man's shoulder, because I suddenly wanted his hands everywhere, not just on my leg. I sagged against the wall, letting go of his shoulders to place my hands on the wall behind me.

The hand on my hip slid up and under my wet shirt. He shifted toward my injured leg and moved his hand to my ankle, sliding into my boot, my calf on his forearm. He didn't even look like he was straining from the weight.

"Maybe we should leave all this on. What if keeping the boot on is helping with the swelling?" His fingers lightly probed my ankle.

I hissed, and his eyes went to mine. "Just tender," I said.

Then his eyes dropped to my lips, and he leaned forward and lightly brushed a kiss across them. A wave of desire slammed into me so hard I gripped the wood wall, my nails digging out splinters. This man, this idiot who'd broken my heart and left behind an emptiness I hadn't yet found a way to fill—he simply did it for me. There was no greater truth than that. It was the way he moved smoothly and with ease, the touch of his hands, soft yet firm, and his outdoorsy yet manly smell with a top note of cedar and a down note of bergamot.

"I'm so wet," I said. Heat flushed my face when his gaze snapped to me. "My clothes. My clothes are wet from my shirt to my jeans. It's not comfortable."

His hand was still under my thigh as he slowly straightened, holding my gaze. "I don't want just this, Reenie. This one time. I want no regrets. I want to put my hands on you so damn much it's making me insane. But I want us to be on the same page."

I'd seriously underestimated my feelings. I'd thought time had dulled us to a pale black-and-white. But the last few weeks together had painted over the old us with new, shiny, bright colors, and in this space, with him so close, his hands on my body, I could barely breathe for wanting him.

"We are on the same page," I whispered.

"It might kill me if you change your mind."

"I won't. I have never regretted you, Cal, and I have no regrets now, nor will I tomorrow."

His breathing was shallow, his pupils dilated. "You are so fucking beautiful."

He slanted his mouth over mine hesitantly, but when I raked my teeth across his lower lip, he went all in. He kissed me like there was no tomorrow. As lightning flashed outside, our hands reacquainted themselves with each other's bodies, finding all the favorite parts and making hasty reintroductions. He dropped to his knees, bracing my leg against his shoulder, and undid the buttons to my shirt. He spread it wide.

"I have to get a condom." His mouth grazed my belly button.

"You brought condoms?"

He stared up at me. "I was hopeful."

I bit my lip and smiled. "There's one in my front pocket."

His nostrils flared, his eyes going wide.

"What?" I said. "I was hopeful too. Though I'm not really worried about getting pregnant, and I haven't been with anyone in a long time. Clean doctor reports. In case you were wondering."

I ran my hands over his shoulders, then made hasty work of releasing all the buttons. He pulled both his flannel shirt and T-shirt off. His chest, no lie, was unreal—all defined muscle. To say he had a twenty-four pack would be an exaggeration but would paint the correct picture. The man was ripped.

He had beautiful carved muscles and tanned skin. I ran my hands across the hard planes, pausing at the healing wound, which was a healthy pink scar. I dropped a kiss onto it.

"Same, though I'm certain I can't get pregnant," he said with a chuckle.

His eyes asked the question, and I nodded. Consent.

In a flash, he'd flipped out the blanket and had me on the floor in the middle of it. Cal knelt between my legs, drew off my shirt, and tossed it to the side. His hands went to my boobs and cupped them. "I love when you wear red. Holy fuck, I missed these."

And he buried his head between them. All I could do was cling to him for dear life because I was spiraling out of control. He pulled away and put his hand on my thigh.

"I have to take the boot off." He cupped my booted foot. "If you want to take those wet jeans off."

The way he said wet was so dirty I nearly unraveled and tore my jeans from my body like the hulk rips off his shirt. "Hurry," I said.

And in one swift motion and a hiss from me, he tugged my boot off and eased my leg back down, rubbing my calf to take my mind off the ache. I'd taken the other off at the same time. I went to the snap on my jeans, but he knocked my hands away.

"I do that." His voice was gravelly. "Please."

"But you're going so slow," I whined.

"I want to savor every moment." He undid my jeans and slid down the zipper, his eyes on me the entire time.

I watched his every move, biting my lower lip at how erotic being stripped by him felt. With his talented hands, and my skilled mouth, we explored like two lucky people who had found the hidden holy land. My vision swam as he clamped his mouth over one nipple and sucked, wrenching a moan from me.

"You are everything," he whispered as he traveled kisses to my other boob, then gave that one the same attention he'd given the other, showing me with his mouth and tongue how much he needed me.

"My pants," I whimpered. He reached for the wet denim, and I arched to help him take them off. His warm hands grazed, down my thighs as he worked off my pants and I dug my nails into his shoulder from the pleasure of his touch. Then he took my hands, placed them together, and held them over my head with one hand. He was in charge, and this was all for me. That was what holding my hands away, not letting me touch him, meant.

Plus, it drove me wild. When Cal loved me, he loved me right. I felt worshiped and cherished and was desperate to show him the same.

His free hand slipped between my legs, and when he touched me, I was electrified and bucked. I wrapped my legs around his waist to draw him in closer as I ground into his hand.

He moaned, "Lord, I've missed you." His voice cracked with emotion, his lips on my neck as his trembling hand spun magic with his knowing touches.

And when I couldn't take any more, I begged for him. Then he slid into me, his hands lifting me from underneath to change the angle and push his hips into mine, going deep as he filled me.

Sex with Cal had been one reason why losing him had hurt so badly, and for so long, because with him, I was complete. No one had ever loved me like this. Sex had never come close to being an out-of-body experience like it was with Cal. So much was right with the way our bodies fit together, how he knew what angle to tilt my hips to hit my hot spot. I choked back a sob at the tremendous pleasure of it all.

He fisted one hand in the back of my hair, and the other stayed under me as we moved together, Cal saying my name over and over again. And as the thunder crashed outside, the lightning between us combusted, sending a forceful current through us as we took each other to the place we'd both longed to go from the moment our eyes had met in his office.

Chapter Twenty-Eight
SABRINA

We had multiple rounds of sex all through the storm and only left when day was giving way to evening. We didn't want to get stuck in the shack overnight. Not that I would have minded, but I was getting cold, and the temperature was going to drop.

Putting on my damp clothes was worse than awful. When we got back to the ranch, Cal carried me to my shower before doing anything else. Brynna gave us a knowing wink. My ankle hurt like a son of a gun, but that wasn't where my focus was. I wasn't ready for us to be apart.

"I don't know if I can manage this by myself," I said when he plopped me onto my bathroom counter, then stepped to the shower to turn it on.

"Then, of course, I have to stay and help," he replied, already peeling off his T-shirt.

Bless the person who'd designed the shower with its bench seat, because straddling him put no pressure on my ankle and good pressure on all the right parts. With his big hands on my ass, he helped me ride. All it took was his knowing hands soaping me up, and I was propositioning him. After the shower, he wrapped me in a towel and carried me to the bed, propping my foot up on pillows. He returned later with a tray of food, pain relievers, and promise in his eyes. Which he kept in spades.

In the wee hours of the morning, he tucked me up against him, his finger tracing a lazy path on the side of my thigh. He broke the silence. "You know, Jace asked me once if I had a death wish."

His breath was on my neck, and I was right where I wanted to be. "Do you think you did?" I asked.

"No. I really did trick myself into believing that I was happy. Or maybe content. I knew I couldn't have you, but I believed that was how it was going to be, so I tried to recognize that I had everything else I needed. But I was wrong." He nuzzled my neck and left a path of featherlight kisses across my shoulder. "I needed you."

"Did you not realize that you were cutting out your sister and mom too?"

He grunted. "I thought seeing them occasionally when they went on trips was sufficient, and if we didn't see each other much, my dad would forget about them. Mom had moved out, so I knew Brynna was in a better home. But I see now how much Jace was right. I may not have just been throwing myself into situations that were high risk; I was also burning myself out."

I rolled toward him and put my leg over his. "High risk? Like getting shot?" I kissed the wound on his shoulder.

"Yeah." His voice was scratchy with emotion.

He slanted his mouth hard against mine and flipped me on my back. Conscious of my ankle, he lifted my leg to his waist, and I followed with the other leg, wrapping both around him as I wove my hands into his hair.

"I missed you," I said. "So much. No one else ever felt right."

He raked his teeth across my lips, pausing to suck on the lower one before responding. "There was this one time you were dating a doctor, and it looked like he made you happy. I took a protection assignment out of the country. It was grueling and a fit punishment for me. I didn't come back until Jace told me y'all broke up."

"We dated for eight months." I met his kiss with one of my own as I clung tightly to him.

"One of the longest eight months of my life. And I hated myself for wanting to take out a doctor. Didn't he do something great like..."

"Orthopedics. He never made me feel like you do."

"Tiny dick, huh?"

I laughed. "Why is it always about the size?"

"I'm right, though, aren't I? Not that I like even thinking about you and him."

I slid my hand down his chest to below his hip to stroke what was pressing against me hard.

The next morning, he piggybacked me to the car and took me into town to see the doctor. I texted Cricket to tell her we should meet up. I was waiting on the cold patients' table with that stupid paper on it. Every time I moved, it crinkled or ripped as it stuck to the back of my legs. Cal leaned up against the wall, checking his phone.

Bryce Jacobson, Hannah's husband and the town vet,

walked in wearing a white lab coat, with a stethoscope around his neck.

"Ha, ha." I said. "Did Cricket send you? I don't need a vet. I need a doctor."

He held up a hand and smiled. "Sorry, not Bryce, just his twin, Bryant. People get us confused all the time. Even our parents."

I leaned in close and could see no difference. He had the same face, laugh lines and all. The good doctor waited patiently, his hands in his pockets allowing me to survey him.

"Seriously, and you're a hot doctor?"

He nodded, rocking on his heels from my compliment. "I moved here about six months ago. Bryce kept talking it up, and after my divorce, I figured a fresh start would do me good."

"Oh. I'm sorry."

He shrugged it off.

Bryant was the cliché of the handsome country doctor, and I would have bet cold hard cash he was being heavily chased by the local women. Hot, educated guys like him were prime pickings. In the years without Cal, Bryant would have been on my 'consider pursuing' list. He was the kind of guy that checked all the right boxes.

"I bet you are insanely popular in town," I said. "Probably get a daily visit from one of the church ladies professing an ailment they don't have, but they do have the phone number and a pitch for their single granddaughter."

Bryant sat on a stool and rolled toward me, then took my foot in his hands. They were soft and warm. As I'd done over the last ten years when an attractive man touched me, I waited for a reaction—a fluttering of the stomach, a piqued interest. But nothing came. Only one man did it for me and always had. I gave Cal a smile, and my heart skipped a beat.

"How did you know?" the doctor said with a laugh. "Oh. Wait. Sabrina, right?"

I nodded.

"You're Hannah's matchmaker friend. I have heard all about you." His smile widened. "You're not going to jump into the mix with the church ladies, are you? Call me old-fashioned, but I'd like to meet the next Mrs. Jacobson by chance." He flashed me a grin, then studied my ankle.

"Nope, I only work with people who want it." I winced, and Cal took a step closer.

Bryant apologized and slowly started to move my foot, rolling the ankle. "Tell me when it hurts."

We did this for a cycle of three, and Bryant wrote something on his notepad. "You going to be in town long?"

I shrugged. "That all depends." I glanced at Cal. We were waiting for his dad to make the next move, and we hadn't really talked about what came next for us.

Bryant looked between me and Cal. "How do you two know each other?"

"College," I said.

"She's my girlfriend," Cal said at the same time.

* * *

CAL

* * *

Okay, a man knew when another man was sizing up his woman. And that was what the doc did when he came into the room and saw Sabrina. His posture straightened, his smile widened, and I caught a glimpse of him breathing hard in his armpit, probably checking his breath.

Then he saw me, paused midstep for half a second, and decided to take a gamble and try his hand at winning her attention. Poor sap. He was out of luck. Not that Sabrina and I had declared our intentions and had the *Where do we stand* talk, but I expected we would have it soon. Maybe even before the sun set. And this nitwit was reading the room all wrong. He was flirting and touching her. Granted, he had to touch her to look at her ankle, but still, his hands lingered a few seconds too long.

I ground my teeth to keep from growling at him. This would play out, and we'd get a good look at what kind of guy the doc was. I didn't like the idea that I might have to snap off the good doc's hands, beat him with them, then toss them into the fire.

I wiped a hand down my face. Goddamn. I was stupid crazy for this woman. So I understood where he was coming from. But when the good doc asked his question about her status, I thought it only fair the man knew the playing field.

"You an orthopedic doc?" I asked, thinking of our conversation earlier.

Sabrina stifled a chuckle, and her eyes met mine. I stuck my hands into my pockets and shrugged. I'd loved any memory of that doctor right out of her. Mission achieved.

Sabrina returned her attention to the doc. "I'm sorry— your question. I thought you were asking how we met. Which was college, but yes, we're dating."

Bryant looked between us. "And you've been dating since college. Impressive." He said it like he didn't mean it, as if I were stringing Sabrina along with promises of forever.

"Off and on," Sabrina said.

"Not so much off," Cal said.

Sabrina snorted. "He was out of the country a lot."

"All in the name of safety."

Bryant looked at me and snapped his fingers. "That's right. You're that securities expert. Hannah said what you did at the community center was fantastic. I've seen you on TV before. Sorry about the beating you're taking in the news and about them taking away that Pinnacle award. Why shouldn't you be awarded for something you did that they said was awesome but now are scared because of the press? Chickenshit, if you ask me."

Sabrina sat up straighter, looked at me in surprise, then searched her purse for her phone.

"You left it at the house," I said.

She narrowed her eyes, and I knew what she was asking.

"Paul told me about it when we got back. It's like the good doc said. They're afraid of bad press." Just one more thing my dad had taken away from me. I hadn't even told her about the award to begin with, mostly because I had forgotten about it with everything else going on.

She leaned back and crossed her arms. "Assholes."

Sabrina was watching me, so I gave her a small smile and a shrug, then looked at her foot, hoping to hide my anger. "Paul is on it."

Dr. Bryant, quick to pick up on the vibe, stopped looking at Sabrina with his romance eyes and moved into doctor mode. He reached into a drawer and pulled out ace wrap. "I don't think it's broken, but let's X-ray it real quick to rule that out, then depending on what we find, I'll wrap it to help with stability and swelling and give you something for pain and inflammation." He smiled at Sabrina. "I'll grab the machine.

Hang on." A few minutes later, he was in the room and taking an X-ray. "You've got some good tears in there. This is a pretty severe sprain, but nothing is broken." He finished wrapping her ankle and inspected his work.

"Thank you, Bryant," Sabrina said.

He tapped a notepad. "You want me to call these into the pharmacy in town? Are you set up there?"

She nodded. "I am. Thank you."

He stuck out his hand. "It was a pleasure to meet you, Sabrina."

And then he turned to me and put his hand out for a shake. "And you as well, Cal."

The guy was all right—decent. I kind of liked this guy.

Sabrina and I left the appointment, with her on crutches, and went to meet Cricket in the town square. "When were you going to tell me about this award?" she asked.

"I'd honestly forgotten about it."

She paused a few blocks from the square. "Help me get to this bench. Can you go get Cricket and tell her I'm here? I'm too tired to hobble my way there."

"Tell me her number, and I'll text her."

She shook her head. "I need to get away from you for a minute. And when we get home, I'm going to talk to Paul. Getting answers from you is like squeezing water from a rock."

I chuckled. "You need me to help you get away from me?" I picked her up and carried her to the bench.

"Yeah, it's a new fresh kind of hell. I get so frustrated with you for not telling me things. Is losing this award a big deal?"

I wanted to tell her it wasn't, but she'd see through that right away. "Yeah, it is. They don't give it out every year, just when someone does outstanding work, and we were being recognized for our work on school safety. Paul's pissed because it would have helped with the launch of the new division and the app. I'm more pissed because I think Hitchens had his hand in this. Not giving it to me because I don't deserve it? Fine. But don't take it away because of outside pressure." I bent and kissed her on the forehead. "But I'll go away, and then you can miss me when I'm gone."

She swatted my arm and still looked pouty.

"Babe, seriously, Paul will brief us when he knows more." I kissed the pout right off her lips.

Then I walked over to get Cricket. When we were coming back, we arrived just in time to see a woman slap Sabrina across the face and witness Sabrina return it with a punch.

Chapter Twenty-Nine
SABRINA

I was sitting there, minding my own business, waiting for Cal and Cricket to come, when a woman approached me. I'd seen her when we came out of the doctor's office, and she'd given me a filthy look. She waited for Cal to walk away before she approached. At first, she just stood near me and stared—or more like glared.

I ignored her. What else was I supposed to do? I scrolled through my watch, checking messages, but scrolling on a watch was its own sort of torture. Cori had sent some photos. They were pictures of us at the community center and line dancing, and they showed a closeness, a bond. More than our attraction.

There was one with Cal, me, and Jace that reminded me the way we'd been in college. The divide starting with that event in Vegas could no longer be seen. The beauty we'd had in college existed today, and the only thing to change was our age.

"I know who you are." The woman moved to stand to the side of the bench, like she'd been trying to look at my phone.

Damn, my situational awareness blows.

"And exactly who do you think I am?" I shouldn't have asked, because I could smell the anger rolling off her and knew that was trouble.

"You're one of those assholes that did that program at the community center."

"And that's bad because...?"

Shut your mouth, Sabrina. I should have excused myself and hobbled away. Put space and some crutches between us.

"Because you all walk around like you live a good life when you don't. You ain't any better than the rest of us. That man of yours has it all wrong. Showing a girl some attention ain't bad. Sometimes they mean yes when they say no."

I felt a flare of pride when she called Cal my "man," but it had been extinguished quickly with the next remark. "You're a woman, and you're saying that?" I asked. "Not to sound cliché, but no means no. It literally means to refuse, not sorta kinda agree."

A kid Rod's age walked up and stood next to her. He had a sucker in his mouth and a red mark on his cheek.

"Well, that nurse said yes to my sister's boy, and then when she thinks she's too good for him, she tells the poh-leece that he's harassing her."

It took me a moment to connect the pieces, but I believed she was talking about Casey.

"All he wanted to do was give her some good attention. Ain't nothing wrong with that." She pointed to her kid. "And this one gets in trouble at school just for exercising his amendment rights. All he did was say the truth. That feral Jamison kid jumped him and marked up his face. He's as worthless as his father."

So this was the kid who'd hassled Rod. It totally made

sense. I'd had enough. There was no point in engaging in a conversation with this person. I pushed to a stand, got my crutches underneath me, and was three steps away before she rushed to stand in front of me.

"What? You don't like what I have to say? You think because you live out on a fancy ranch you are better than me —than us?"

This woman was all over the place with her accusations. I didn't know anything about her, yet it was hard not to make assumptions. What I did know was I needed to get away.

"Please step aside." I used my firm teacher's voice, but it didn't work.

She put her finger in my face. "You think you can just do what you want, say what you want, without repercussions? My nephew was arrested. My kid is in trouble, and he's only in second grade. And it's all because of you all thinking yer better than us, that we're here to serve you."

"You ever think that it's a you problem?"

Before it left my mouth, I knew it was the wrong thing to say. Her eyes were crazy with anger, and up close, I smelled whiskey on her breath. But apparently, I was exactly who she accused me of being, because I'd just said what I wanted to say.

My gut told me I'd pushed her too far and was about to get hit. I had to let go of my crutches and put my wrapped foot on the ground to try to block her, but I was a few seconds behind when she delivered a heel punch to my temple. That surprised me. I'd totally thought she would be a fist-punch person.

"Now it looks like you have a problem. What are you going to do about that?" she asked.

Honestly, I made the decision before I was even

cognizant of it. My weight had shifted to my injured ankle and my right fist had pulled back. I made sure my thumb wasn't tucked, like Cal had told Rod. And I socked her in the eye.

"That's what I'm going to do about it." I shook out my hand and shifted back to my uninjured ankle because, holy crap, the pain in both my ankle and hand was powerful.

She reared back, her hand over her eye, and moved into feral mode. She brought her arms up like she was going to claw me to death, and my heart sped up. I would have to use a crutch as a weapon.

Suddenly I was in the air. Cal picked me up by the waist and spun me away from her, using his body to block me from her. "What the hell?" I cried.

She charged but came to a dead stop when she collided with him. He didn't even wobble. He was a brick wall.

I dangled a few feet in the air and tried to look over my shoulder to see what was going on. The woman was on the ground, having bounced off Cal and fallen back. He offered her a hand to help her up, but she snarled, one hand still over her eye.

"Ma'am," he said.

"She hit me." She pointed at me.

"You hit me first," I retorted. Oh my days, it was like being transported back to the playground.

Cricket joined the fray. "Kathy, what the hell is going on?"

The woman glared at her.

"Can you put me down?" I asked Cal.

He took me to the bench and lowered me to the seat. "How's your hand, slugger?" His voice was quiet. He held my chin in his hand as he inspected my cheek. "You got a nice welt."

"I think she had a ring on her finger."

He brushed his thumb across it, then picked up my hand and checked out my knuckles. "I always did say you had a mean right hook."

"Because I know to keep my thumb out."

"Good girl. Though I'd rather you not punch people."

"Me too. Her son is the one who Rod got in a fight with, and I think her nephew is the one stalking Casey." I kept my voice low so as not to trigger her.

Fort joined us. He looked between me and Kathy.

"Arrest her. She assaulted me." She jabbed her finger in my direction several times.

Fort sighed. "Well, now, let me ask you if you hit her first. Because just in the short walk here, five different people —we'll call them witnesses—told me what they saw, and they all said you started it."

"You're on their side. I should have known."

A deputy rushed up and handed Fort two bags of ice. He handed one to Kathy and one to Cal, who put the bag gently on my face. "Five minutes, then switch to your hand. Five on, five off."

I nodded.

"Look over here, Kathy." Fort pointed to the lamppost next to the bench and then a few more on the path. "And there and there. There are cameras on all those. All I have to do is watch the film. So I'm not sure if you can claim assault and know that Sabrina might be able to claim self-defense, but we'd have to get lawyers involved and all that. You want to do that?"

The disgust slid from her face replaced with worry. She shook her head.

Fort nodded. He turned to the deputy. "Take Kathy and Bobby to the diner and get them some coffee and food."

The two of them were hustled away.

Fort raised a brow at me. "How ya feeling, Rocky?"

"Foolish. I really feel badly. I hit her in front of her kid." The awfulness of it all was starting to come into clarity. I had a hard time meeting Fort's eye.

"Sadly, it's not the first time," he said.

I groaned and covered my face. "That makes it worse."

"You wanna press charges?"

I shook my head. "No. Of course not. Not that I condone this, but I get the feeling there is more at play here."

Fort took a seat next to me. "And you would be right." He looked at Cal. "Remember Casey from the community center?"

"Her nephew is Casey's creeper," I supplied.

Fort nodded again. "Apparently, some of Casey's family members talked her out of doing most of the suggestions you gave. Said you were being dramatic. No outdoor-motion sensors. No house alarms. But she did add a safety latch to her door, so when he showed up the other night and she wouldn't let him in, he lost his shit. It took a while for him to kick down the door. Gave her enough time to hide in a closet and call us. He's got a record for this sort of stuff in two other states."

Cal gave a low whistle through his teeth. "This is what I mean about my dad affecting my credibility. Someone other than me is gonna get hurt—did get hurt." He tapped his watch, and I moved the ice to my hand.

"Take me home," I said to Cal, who wasted not a second scooping me up. Fort handed him my crutches.

"I can walk. I just meant that we should leave." I laughed.

"I'm a little shaken here, Reenie. I didn't like seeing you get hit. Even if it was by a woman."

"I'll text you to reschedule," Cricket said.

I felt foolish being carried like a bride. "No, come to the ranch if you can. We can figure everything out there."

She nodded. "I'll be right behind you." Then she took off.

"Listen," Fort said before turning away. "I've got a bead on Jamison's whereabouts. I'll let you know if it gets confirmed. Looks like he took a trip to Mexico."

I sighed. "And the day started out so promising."

Chapter Thirty

SABRINA

We weren't back at the ranch ten minutes when Cori pulled in. She'd heard what had happened in town from her husband.

"You didn't have to come all the way out here," I told her. We were whispering over her sleeping baby.

"The baby sleeps in the car, so it was really more for me than you." She smiled, but it faltered quickly. She moved the baby, still sleeping in the car seat, to the floor.

"You look exhausted," I told her.

Cori slumped onto the couch.

"Kid's not sleeping well, huh?" Cricket asked.

"No, and Fort has been called in every night, and my in-laws took Tabby for a couple days to Cheyenne to give me a break. Joke's on them. This one"—she pointed to the cupid-faced baby—"has turned into an evil dictator and has been a straight-up asshole since they left." She leaned forward conspiratorially. "It's like she knows."

Cori's eyes strayed to the stairs.

"Why don't you go up and catch a nap. We've got her.

273

My room is the third door on the right." I jerked my head to tell her to go.

"Do you mean it?" She sat up, full of hope.

Cricket and I nodded in harmony. Cori leaped up and thrust her diaper bag at me. "The front pocket has a freezer back with six breast milk storage bags. She will probably wake in another twenty minutes to eat."

Cori had come prepared.

"You know you could have just asked us." I grinned.

"You have a lot going on. I felt bad asking." Then she was up the stairs and out of sight.

"She totally played us," Cricket said.

I shrugged.

Cal came back into the room with an ice pack. He handed it to me and nodded toward my knuckles.

"Fighting is stupid." I placed the pack on my sore hand.

A Facetime request popped up on my phone, which, coincidentally, was right where I'd left it when we went into town. On the coffee table.

Nick Trask. I accepted the request. It was not unlike Nick and me to Facetime, but maybe because the day had taken a shitty turn, I couldn't ignore the tinge of apprehension coiling in my stomach.

"Hey, what's up?" I asked.

Nick's normally jovial face and easygoing manner was gone. He leaned closer to the screen and looked over his shoulder, then back at me. His brows were knitted in anger. My heart sank. It looked like he was sitting in his car.

"Goddamn producer."

I told myself this wasn't a big deal, but the world suddenly felt small and claustrophobic. "What happened?"

But I thought I already knew. Maybe I'd been expecting

it, because what else was there left to take from me, other than Cal?

"He said he wanted you off the project. Said he loved the idea, and I was perfect because—no, duh, dipshit—we were going to do this without a show, so it's not like he's casting me in a role. Asshole. But he wanted to use a different matchmaker."

I exhaled.

"I'm fucking raging right now," Nick said.

I dropped my head into my hands, using the tips of my fingers to push back the tears. "I'm sorry."

"For what? I was only on board because you were. I don't need this. And I told him just that. I told him he could stick his proposition up his ass and forget ever working with me again. I also told him he was going to regret this. Then I walked out, caught his assistant in the copy room down the hall, and asked her what was up. Took me making a personal happy birthday video for her sister to get the details, but apparently, some conglomeration called Beck Group funded that asswipe's pet project on the condition he dump you."

Cal sat down next to me and came into the phone's field of vision. "That's my dad's company." There was no mistaking the apology in his eyes. I put my hand on his and squeezed.

"Dude, he's jonesing to take you out. I have a friend in the press who's been good to me, so I drop him leads every so often. He called me right before my meeting and said there's a reporter, a bad actor, named Smith, who's digging around, trying to find some dirt on me and Sabrina. Trying to say we've been having a secret love affair"—he sang the last three words with a hint of anger but still holding on to his sense of humor—"since before Melissa died."

"Oh, Nick, I am so sorry." Nick was very protective of his deceased wife and their relationship.

He waved me off. "I got my lawyer on it. He's a shark. He'll tear Smith apart by ripping off his head and spine, then beating him with them. He's already gathering the info to show it's part of your smear campaign. This Smith is a dimwad who doesn't do a good job of covering his trail. But I really just called to say I'm sorry. The news is gonna break soon, and I wanted you to hear it from me first."

"I'm sorry you've been dragged into this."

"Shit, Sabrina, you know I've been through worse. This is nothing."

And he had. He and Melissa had been childhood sweethearts who'd met while living on the compound of a cult their parents belonged to. The cult was known for its wicked disciplining practices. When they were sixteen, they ran away and started fresh. But none of it had been easy.

"In other news, I punched a person." I held up my hands and showed my bruised knuckles.

"Damn! This, I gotta hear." He grinned at me.

I filled him in on Rod and my ankle and how they all led to the approach from Kathy.

"I would pay good money for a picture of that or a video. I'd make it a screensaver on all my devices. It would be the gift that keeps giving."

"Oh, shut up," I said.

But something he'd said bothered me. I looked at Cal, then Cricket. Even though Nick was not in the room, he was quickly on the same page.

"There's no video of that, I hope," he said. "Smith gets ahold of that, there's no telling what the spin will be."

Video? Heck. How about a personal interview from the woman herself?

Cricket stood up. "I'll call Fort and give him a heads-up." She rushed from the room.

"Listen, doll. I'm in the car, and I think people are starting to recognize me. I've got a woman standing two cars away, giving me sideways glances. Oops, out comes her phone."

"We can talk later. Thanks, Nick. Love ya."

"Back atcha." And he ended the call.

Cal had straightened next to me. I squeezed his hand and brought it toward me as I entwined my fingers with his. He didn't look upset, just unsure.

"Nick and I met through Melissa, his wife. She was dying around the same time Dad was. We were on some charity boards together. She was the love of his life. Like you are mine. So when Dad and Melissa died, Nick and I were there for each other. He doesn't have any family." I told him about the cult. "He's like a brother to me, and I don't know how I could have made it without him after Dad died."

He searched my face, then gave me one nod before leaning in to kiss me on the forehead. "Then I will forever be grateful to him. Now, about this documentary..."

I shook my head. "I am so angry right now, I can't even process what's just happened. Or what to think of it. Can we talk about it in a bit?"

"Of course."

Cricket came back in with Paul following behind her. "Fort says they've locked down any video."

"We can't ask her to sign an NDA because that will tip our hand. Maybe no one finds out and approaches her."

The baby started to fuss. Cricket tried to soothe her by

rocking the car seat, but that didn't work. She took the baby out of the carrier and handed her to me. "I'm going to warm up the milk. Hold her a second."

I greedily took her and buried my face in her neck, giving her kisses and talking soothingly. She smelled so good, like baby power and soft fluffy balls. Her crying began to pick up in intensity.

"Grab me the binkie," I commanded.

Paul tossed it to me, but little baby Layla got even more pissed when I offered it to her. I held her up and sniffed her butt. Nope, all good there. Her face was getting red as her wails increased.

"She's probably hungry," Cal said.

I looked over my shoulder for Cricket. "Want to test that theory?"

Cori had said Layla wasn't being easy, so logically, I knew to not sweat it, but after the calf thing, well, I had some doubts. I held the crying baby out to Cal. He took her in his arms and held her just like I had. He offered her the binkie. She fussed for a few seconds longer, then took the binkie and started to calm down. She batted her pretty blue eyes at Cal.

The doorbell rang, and he tried to pass the baby back as he stood.

"Give her to Paul," I grumbled, knowing Layla only fussed for me.

He did, and Layla continued to work the binkie with no complaints. Cal went to answer the door, and Paul stood over me with Layla.

"I should make some more calls about this Smith guy." He handed off the baby.

She wasn't in my arms for fifteen seconds before she

popped out the pacifier and began to wail again. I let my head fall back to the couch and looked up to the ceiling.

Irony, amirite?

Fort entered the room and took his daughter, who quickly quieted. Cricket came back in and handed off the bottle.

"Don't sweat it, Sabrina," Fort said. "She's all about the fellas right now. Something about how babies like our features. She's giving Cori a tough time, too, and that's her food supply."

What he said seemed to be true, but I wondered if Cal had told him to say something to make me feel better.

"Is Mrs. Claudia around?" he asked, his daughter tucked contently in the crook of his arm. There was something seriously hot about a man in a uniform, a gun strapped to his side, feeding a tiny baby. And as insecure as I was about babies, it still made my ovaries perk up.

"She was in the kitchen a minute ago," Cricket said.

Fort rubbed a hand down his face, looking weary. My trouble radar spiked. Cal's must have as well.

He stepped toward Fort. "What is it? Is it about Rod?"

Fort nodded. "His dad was killed in a car crash this morning. A guy he was with, the only survivor of four, says they were headed back here. Apparently, Jamison told them he had to get home, but if they wanted to come with him, he knew they could get jobs working the ranches."

A wave of shock and grief swept over me. Maybe, eventually, knowing his dad had been headed home would bring Rod comfort. "What happens to Rod?" I asked.

"Because there is no legal guardian or relative, he has to go into the system."

Of all the things I'd heard that day, that piece of news was the one that broke my heart.

Chapter Thirty-One
CAL

We were all sitting out on the back deck. Someone—probably Jace—had started a fire in the firepit. A bottle of whiskey was going around, and when it got to me, I poured a finger into my glass.

Rod had fallen asleep, crying in Sabrina's arms, and Mrs. Claudia had carried him off to bed. So much had been lost, but watching that kid's heartbreak was the worst. Fort was working on getting Mrs. Claudia set up as a system caretaker to keep Rod here and with as little disruption as possible. What was hard was not being able to answer his questions about what would happen or make any promises. The system was the system, and it wasn't a good one.

I handed the bottle to Jace. Sabrina was sitting next to me, her foot elevated, a blanket over her lap, her hand entwined with mine. "I might be in the system. I've had a background check and all that. Maybe I could take him. Maybe I would be a faster alternative."

"In Texas you are. Not here."

She blew out a weary breath, and I kissed her temple. She squeezed my hand and scooted in even closer. My girl.

Paul cleared his throat and rubbed at his scruffy chin. "Not to be indelicate, but I have to…" He looked at me. "I need to know if you're going to cancel your attendance at the gala. Not only are they assholes for canceling the award, but they're cowards, too, because they're scared you might show up and create a scene."

Jace barked out a laugh. "That means you should go."

"I should." I took a drink. It would serve them right. Part of me wanted them to have to look at me, knowing they had caved. A little discomfort went a long way.

"And you know what else?" Jace leaned forward, the glow from the fire showing his devilish grin. "You all should get married. That would really piss off the old man. Make his head explode."

"What?" Sabrina and I said in unison.

She sat up. "Are you seriously suggesting a revenge marriage? If I had something to throw at you, I would."

Jace put up his hand before I could speak. "I've known you two forever, right? And I have to say, if you are sitting here, pretending that you're just taking it slow and figuring things out"—he spoke mockingly—"then you're both stupid. For a decade, you two have been pining away for each other. And now you're back together, and really, it's just a matter of time before you tie the knot anyway. Besides, what more can that piece-of-shit father do to you?"

I shook my head. "I feel like every time someone says that, it jinxes us."

"It would really piss him off," Brynna said.

"But you don't get married to spite someone."

Jace snorted. "You get married because this is a forever

thing, nitwits." He wagged a finger between me and Sabrina. "The spite is the extra bonus. Like a wedding gift to yourselves. He has tried to rule you, ruin you, and keep you apart, and he has failed. Fuck him."

"Fuck him," Brynna said with a chuckle, then took a drink of her whiskey.

"Every day you aren't together is another day he wins," Paul said.

I looked at him, surprised. "You agree with this?"

"But we are together," Sabrina said.

Jace nodded. "Sure. We all know that—those of us here. Everyone else sees a couple dating. A couple seeing if it might turn into something more. Which means it could go either way. You're like a reality-TV show. Will they, won't they, and people are taking bets whether when all this is resolved, you two will still be together. They don't know what we know or see what we see. If there ever were two people meant to be together, it would be you two. Hell, even the universe got involved and said, 'Enough of this bullshit; these two should be together.'"

Meredith put her hand on her husband's thigh. "You can be such a romantic," she said breathily.

He leaned over to kiss her. "You like that? I'll show you a little more of that later when we're alone."

She giggled and kissed him again.

When they were done, Jace turned to the crowd. "I forgot what I was saying."

Brynna gave an envious sigh.

"Tomorrow is the anniversary of the day your parents met. Did you know that?" Mom asked. All this talk of marriage and forever had her beaming bright as the sun.

Sabrina pulled out her phone and checked the date. She

nodded, then smiled at me. When we had run off to Vegas, we'd picked our wedding date to be the same as her parents'. And to be honest, I was thinking we'd maybe make that happen next year and the date we'd originally picked could still be our date. But now Jace's suggestion was on my mind.

A few hours later, I piggybacked Sabrina up to my room because Fort and Cori were staying in hers. Jace and Meredith were in the remaining spare bedroom. No one had felt like driving home.

Sabrina was flat on her back in bed, her hair around her in dark waves. I knelt between her legs as I helped her get out of her clothes.

"This is my favorite part." I pulled down her pants and eased them over her wrapped ankle.

She arched a brow. "This is your favorite part?"

I gave her a lecherous grin. "My favorite part of the foreplay. Getting you naked is a natural high for me."

She sat up and pulled off her shirt.

I gave her my sad face. "Why'd you do that? What a buzzkill. I like to undress you."

She laughed and leaned back on her elbows. "You were taking too long with all your talky talky."

I ran my hands up her legs, then dropped a kiss on the inside of her thigh. I did another when she shivered with pleasure.

"Well, bad news, babe, because I've got a lot of things I want to say." I crawled up her, planting little kisses on her body along the way.

Sabrina grabbed me by the shirt and pulled me close. Her eyes dropped to my lips, and she licked hers. "Can it wait until later?" She kissed the corner of my mouth, flicking her tongue across my lips.

"I guess, but I thought maybe you'd like me to tell you about all the things I'm about to do to you." I met her gaze. Heat flared.

She dropped her hands to the fly on my jeans. "Well, in that case, you should get started."

And I did, in very explicit detail. I was a man writing a how-to manual, not forgetting any step. I even included some footnotes on alternatives that could be used. When I finally slid into her, we both groaned with pleasure and relief. It was good to be home. And I didn't leave until she called out my name and collapsed in bliss.

Afterward, she snuggled up next to me, her hand making lazy loops on my stomach. "This feels surreal. Like I'm going to wake up from the best dream I have ever had." She placed a kiss on my right pec.

"You know, Jace isn't wrong."

Her hand didn't stop with the patterns. "About what he said tonight?"

"Yeah."

She said nothing.

"Do you disagree?" For a moment I wondered if I'd been reading it all wrong. I had hurt her pretty badly. Maybe she would need more time before she would be ready to have me forever.

She looked up at me and smiled. "No."

"Then why were you so quiet just then?"

"Because I was thinking of all the time we've lost. His advice would have been good ten years ago."

I kissed the top of her head and pulled her closer, almost on top of me. "We can't do that. I did what I thought was best then. I'm not convinced it would have all turned out okay if I had done otherwise."

She pushed up onto her elbow and looked down at me. Goddamn, this woman is beautiful. Her eyes told you every-thing. And at the moment, they were telling me she was a little bit horny and a little bit...

"You're right. We needed to have all the information about my mom and your dad. I'm not sure my dad would have told us."

Acceptance. That was the other thing I saw in her eyes. It was the best gift she'd given me besides forgiveness. And her body, of course. She was no longer reliving the past but looking toward the future. Speaking of the future...

"I have an idea."

"So do I." She climbed on top of me.

I was already hard. In one second, she held me in her hand as she lowered herself onto me, then she bent forward and angled her hips back to take more of me in. I groaned from the heady pleasure of it.

"Before I lose you." She leaned forward and whispered her idea into my ear.

Did I say how much I loved this woman? Damn, she's a dream.

Chapter Thirty-Two
CAL

In the morning, we made our plan with Paul and our friends. I'd be lying if I said a part of me wasn't hesitant. It came from years of trying to protect her. I didn't mind taking risks; I was good at that. It was my job. Risks with her, though, I preferred not to take. It wasn't that I didn't have faith in us. It was just that I'd never been able to predict my father, and I didn't like that. I didn't like to see her cry because of what he did to her. I didn't like that she was the bait.

The only obstacle to our plan was Sabrina's ankle. "We need to solve the entire problem of walking and weight bearing," I said.

Sabrina's eyes lit up with an aha moment that shone brighter than a million-watt Q beam. And that was how I ended up back at the doctor's office with Sabrina getting a cast put on while my jet was preparing for a flight.

"Okay," she said, putting her phone back in her purse. "My connection is having a bunch of dresses delivered to the hotel."

"Remember when I said the X-ray didn't show a break?" Dr. Bryant asked her. "That didn't mean you should be doing this. It's bad enough that you should stay off it. Since you won't listen, this will help protect your ankle, but even then, try your hardest to do minimal walking."

"Maybe we should wait until you have time to heal a little more," I said.

She shook her head. "The gala is perfect. When will we have that chance again?"

She was right, of course.

Two hours later, we were in the air with a final destination of LA, making two quick stops on the way, one in Vegas to tie up loose ends and the other in Seattle to pick up my tux. I'd changed out of my jeans and flannel shirt and into dress pants and a button-down. Business attire. I was sliding back into the Cal I'd been before she came into my office, and though I didn't want to give him up, I didn't want to ignore how different I'd felt since being at the ranch.

Sabrina sat across from me in a pretty navy dress that complemented her red cast, with her foot in my lap and my hand over her toes to keep them warm. My long legs were stretched out, capturing her other leg between them. The collar on my shirt felt tight, and I tugged at it in hopes of stretching it.

Sabrina chuckled.

"What?" I asked.

"That day in your office, you were all buttoned up. Now, after some time living your cowboy life, it looks like buttoned up might not really suit you anymore."

I smirked. She could read my mind.

"What?" she asked.

"I did stay away too long. I realize how much I missed it —how important the ranch is to me and how it suits me."

"So much good has come out of all this." She smiled, but I saw the sadness of her loss in that smile.

I leaned forward and captured her chin in my hand. "Hey, any time this feels off and you want to bail, we will. We don't have to do this gala thing. You get a bad vibe, let me know."

She shifted so she could lean forward and take my hand. "I love that you don't want me to get hurt and that you're worried. But we're in this together. Stop trying to be a one-man show. Ask for help."

I barked out a laugh. "What? Did you just meet me?"

She dissolved into laughter. "Right!"

We made our two stops and arrived at our LA hotel as the sun was setting. I'd reserved a suite that overlooked the hills. The living room and kitchen were the central space, with a mirrored wall that a bar backed up to. The mirror reflected the setting sun. A rack of dresses were waiting for Sabrina to try on in the bedroom.

I ordered room service, and while Sabrina was in the other room, trying on the gowns, I called a former client in the jewelry business to line something up for the next day. Sabrina would need some accessories. After dress picking, we would eat and review the plan. Having a plan and acting on it felt good.

Sabrina tried on a handful of dresses, each one sexier than the last, and was leaning toward a hot red number with a V-neck and thigh slit. The dress matched her cast well enough to offer it some cloaking. All plans for room service and reviewing went out the window when she came out of the room in the last option. The dress hit mid-thigh and looked like it was vacuum sealed onto her. The material was sheer with a nude-colored liner that, at first glance, made me think I was looking at skin. The dress left just enough to the imagination.

"Holy shit." I stood. Her legs looked like they went on for miles, and she wasn't even wearing heels.

"Clashes with the cast, for sure. It's a cute dress but a no."

I took a step toward her and put my hand over my racing heart. "Cute dress? You clearly don't see what I do."

She took my breath away. Her hair flowing over her shoulder, her smooth thighs—yeah, I loved Sabrina for more than how she looked, but all her assets were the cherry on top, and at that moment, I wanted to put that cherry in my mouth and tie a knot in the stem.

"You don't like it?" She looked confused and did the cutest little hop turn to see it from different angles.

"Reenie," I growled.

She caught my gaze in the bar's mirror. "Why are you looking at me like that?"

"Like what?"

"Like you're the big bad wolf and I'm Little Red Riding Hood with a basket of cookies." She hopped around to face me as she put a hand on her hip.

Her mouth—jeez, those cherry red lips were hinting at a smile. She knew what I was thinking. Heat flared in her eyes.

I glanced at my watch. "We have a little more time before the food gets here, and I'm craving cookies."

"Well then, we'd better hurry." She opened her arms, and I rushed to her and lifted her up by her sweet ass.

"Hurry? What are you saying? They can leave the cart by the door."

She wrapped her legs around my waist. "I should take the dress off."

"Oh no, darling." I stalked to the bedroom. "Can't we keep it on?" Then I kicked the door closed. My one goal to make her happy.

The next evening I'd made Sabrina cry before we even left for the gala.

* * *

SABRINA

* * *

As soon as we walked into the ballroom, we were accosted by a tall, lithe man with thinning gray hair, thick glasses, and a left-eye twitch.

"Cal, what... why... we... we weren't expecting to see you," he sputtered, spraying us with spittle as he ran his hands up and down the lapels of his tux.

Cal—looking stupid hot in his tuxedo and black cowboy boots, making me think of spy movies and sex in cloaked public places—clasped the man on the shoulder. "Nelson, it's good to see you. Let me introduce you to my wife, Sabrina Holloway." He paused to look at me with his shit-eating grin. "Holloway-Beckett."

I put out my hand to shake his, and of course, I picked the one with the stunning diamond ring he'd given me earlier that had made me cry and forced me to redo my makeup.

Damn straight, we'd made a quick stop in Vegas and taken ourselves to the courthouse to tie the knot. It was what we'd planned initially, and though we would have liked our friends with us, we didn't need them to be. We had each other. We would have a party when we got home.

Home. We'd decided that would be the Wyoming ranch. It made sense. All the people I loved the most were there except Nick. Cal said he wasn't worried about his company; he could run it from anywhere.

Nelson stared down at my ringed finger and became even more flustered as he went from rubbing his lapels to gripping them white-knuckle style.

"Sabrina, this is Nelson Maher, head of GSI," Cal said.

Nelson didn't look ready to shake anyone's hand but took mine lightly with his fingers and gave me a damp, tepid shake. I returned my hand to Cal's arm, subtly wiping my fingers on his jacket. Other than the shake and a jerky nod, Nelson barely registered me. His eyes were on Cal.

"But, Cal, you heard about the award?"

Cal waved a dismissive hand. "Yes, Nelson, I did. I'm here because I'd like the board to tell me to my face why they withdrew the award. You understand how this withdrawal has devalued the award and the committee?"

Nelson's ears turned pink. His left eye twitched four more times before Cal clasped him on the shoulder again. "Relax, Nelson. I think my presence is causing enough of a scene."

The man visibly relaxed in front of us, his eye spasm slowing down. "It's not that. I was worried you'd be upset. It's the most ridiculous thing, isn't it? But I was outvoted."

"I appreciate that, Nelson." Cal shifted his weight so I was leaning more on him and off my foot. Only ten minutes into the evening, I could feel a dull throb coming on.

Nelson nodded several times and stuck his hands into his

jacket pockets, making the coat tent around him. "It is good to see you, Cal. For what it's worth, Hitchens is the one who started the cancel campaign." Then he shuffled off to greet other people.

I blinked in surprise. Terribly nervous Nelson outing another person like that spoke to his respect for Cal. "I read him wrong. I thought he was horrified when he saw you here, when he was actually worried you'd be upset."

"Nelson's a good guy, and he won't start spreading word of our marriage, so we need to find the gossips."

We mingled, moving slowly around the room with occasional stops to let me rest. Cal was approached by a lot of people who all seemed to not only like him but admire his work as well. One guy waxed poetic about the initiative they'd pushed out to colleges, regarding updated plans and procedures for school shootings.

"Standing here in a formal gown and talking about how to prevent school shootings feels like a weird juxtaposition," I said.

"Mm, I can see that, but part of change starts here. Sadly, it's not always a given that people will do what's best unless there is an incentive behind it." He glanced at my foot. "How ya doing?"

I waved away his question. "If someone needs an incentive to do the right thing when it involves keeping people, especially children, safe, they should be... I dunno, but something bad should happen to them."

"Thankfully, those people are the minority." He brushed a lock of curled hair behind my ear. "I'm glad we came. I often wondered what it would have been like to have you beside me at things like this. Now I know."

"A lot of work, huh? With me leaning on you so much. It

makes me think of that terrible saying, 'the ole ball and chain.'"

"I think that's more about being shackled. And I'd pick you to be shackled to every time."

"Such sweet words," I cooed.

"We'll give Dalton another hour to show up before we bail. Think your ankle can take it?"

"Of course. What if he doesn't show up?"

"Then he'll send a proxy. We need to show them we aren't rattled and we're ready to rumble."

"Okay, I'll go sit at the bar and see who approaches," I said.

"And rest your ankle while you're at it."

"Win-win." I brushed a kiss across his mouth.

Cal's phone chimed, and he checked the text message. "Paul's contact in Vegas said someone from the Beck Group called to confirm the validity of our nuptials."

The gauntlet had been thrown. Now we would wait.

Chapter Thirty-Three
SABRINA

From where we sat, Cal and I had a sight line on each other at all times. He wanted to come up with a hand signal in case someone came to bother me, but I reminded him that I was more than capable. Just let one fool mess with me, and I would show him my heel strike.

Cal was easy to find in the crowd, taller than most and larger, too, like a clean-shaven lumberjack who carried whole tree trunks on his shoulders. He had that badass look like he'd gotten into the trenches when there were trenches to get into. Everyone else was split into two groups, either rich executives with flawless tans from having never shown up to work or dedicated workers with their pasty white skin from never leaving their desks.

Sometimes when Cal was talking to someone, he would look only at me. I could feel the heat from his gaze from across the room.

Word was getting out. Some of the women were casting me sideways glances as I sipped on my flute. A flutter of excitement tickled my stomach. We. Are. Married. Legit. For real. No takesie backsies.

There had never been one thing that felt righter than this. I adored him and felt adored by him, and as much as I hated his overwhelming need to protect me to the point of putting me into a bubble, there was no mistaking how safe I felt with him. Even with my heart. He was the love of my life. There had never been another. I was not scared of relocating. I was not scared about all the obstacles coming our way. And they were coming.

Together. That was how we would handle it.

"Can I get you a drink?"

The man asking was tall with shaggy blond hair cut in the style popular with teens. A broccoli cut, I thought it was called. Though he wasn't a teen. He tossed his head to move the curly bangs out of his eyes, and it became clear why he sported the style. He thought the hair flick made him look... coquettish. Yep, that was the best word for it.

His bright white smile was large and full faced, only it didn't reach his eyes, which had a predatory gleam. And no crinkles. Botox.

He held up his glass to remind me of his question.

"No, I have one. Thanks." I held up my flute of champagne.

"You're with Beckett, right?" Leaning on his elbow, he turned toward me, the position putting us eye to eye.

"I am."

"You're the matchmaker, right?"

His eyes scanned me up and down. He was a letch. He stopped at the large diamond on my finger.

The ring was not obnoxious by any measure, but it was stunning. Cal had said, "Oh, I have an accessory for you."

Then he'd slid the ring on to my finger and professed his love. He'd also borrowed a large pear-shaped diamond necklace that hung from a platinum chain, where it lay two inches from my cleavage. Which was where Blondie's eyes were now fixed.

"I am a matchmaker. I don't exactly know who the matchmaker is." I snapped my fingers to draw his attention, and he dragged his eyes up.

"Think you could match a single guy like me?"

"Are you seriously looking?"

I knew he wasn't, even if he didn't know it. I knew his type better than they knew themselves. Trust-fund guy who'd slid into the family business, reaping the benefits without doing a lot of the work. I never took clients like him. Next, he was going to say something about how he was seriously looking now that he'd seen me and ask if I ever matched myself with clients.

"I wasn't seriously looking until just now." He winked. "How about a you and me match?"

If I had a fistful of money for every time that happened, I'd be able to retire. I'd have adopted a dozen kids by now. I put down my glass. I wasn't going to be sticking around. I would find a new stool.

I gave Blondie my full attention. "That's the best you've got?"

"What do you mean?"

"That's the best pickup line you could come up with? I should hope not. I mean, I'm in the business of love. I have seen amazing declarations of love, grand gestures. You name it, I've seen it. I've seen people connect, and it wasn't over some poorly thought-out pickup line. I mean, put some effort into it."

"You don't like a little flirting?"

"That's not flirting. Flirting is mutual. That's bothering someone, and it's disrespectful. Plus, you knew I was married to Cal. You asked and looked at my ring. So propositioning me also speaks to how little respect you have for me and him and probably yourself."

That got his attention. He placed his whiskey glass down with a bang and turned fully toward me. He tried to continue his casual appearance as he continued to lean against the bar, but his face had gone tight—or maybe that was the Botox—as had his shoulders.

"It's never been a problem before."

I rolled my eyes. "I seriously doubt that's true. You asked me three questions and then hit on me. You didn't introduce yourself. You didn't give us a chance to get to know each other, to see if maybe there could be something between us."

"What if I want something casual?"

"Then you don't need a matchmaker; you need an app that specializes in hookups."

Cal made his way to us, a slow stroll with one hand in his pocket. He arched a brow in question. I gave him a large smile to show I wasn't uncomfortable. He came up to the bar next to me, ordered a drink from the bartender, then turned around to face the crowd.

"How's it going, babe?" Cal nodded to the blond toad. "Hitchens."

Toad nodded back. "Beckett."

I shifted so I could see Cal better and pointed to the guy he'd just addressed. "*The* Hitchens?"

"His father. But they are like minds."

"Ah, got it. Well, Mr. Hitchens, here, was asking me about matchmaking."

Cal smirked. "I doubt that's what he's really interested in."

"Me too."

Hitchens held up his hands in defense. "Hey, I was just trying to get to know you. You guys have had a lot of press lately." He sneered. "You can't blame a guy for his curiosity. Besides, she is the prettiest thing in the room."

I bristled at being called a thing and was about to say something when Cal moved in behind me and wrapped a possessive arm around my waist.

"Don't talk about her as if she's not right here, and don't refer to her—or any women or person, for that matter—as a thing." His tone was cold and steely.

Hitchens chuckled. "Whatever."

"Sabrina has an impressive right hook. I'm confident she'd like to show it to you."

I leaned back against Cal. "Hmm, among other things. Like that handy knee thingy you taught me."

Hitchens seemed unfazed. "A bit of a scrapper, huh? I guess you'd have to be, growing up in casinos and gambling dens."

The way he said "casinos and gambling dens" was laced with disgust. And he clearly thought this might get a rise from me. This guy had been trying to push my buttons from the minute he had my attention, from flirting to insults, like he was going through a checklist of keynotes to hit.

"I'm not ashamed of how I grew up."

Hitchens shrugged. "Too bad you can't right hook the IRS. I bet it's frustrating to have them dig back through your dad's winnings. Or was it you who didn't file the taxes on his estate? Like father, like daughter maybe?"

Cal's body stiffened behind me, and his hand gripped

my hip. I pressed a hand to his as a cue that Hitchens's words didn't bother me. Then I noticed that the gentleman behind Hitchens had turned as if he was trying to listen. His smartphone was on the bar, closer to Hitchens than himself. It took about three beats before I figured out who he was and what the game was. I slid off the stool and moved quickly around Hitchens to the other guy, who jerked up, surprised by my sudden appearance next to him.

"Mr. Smith, is it? Wasn't that how you introduced yourself at the press conference? Is there something you'd like to ask me, Mr. Smith?"

I glanced at Cal. Anger burned in his eyes.

At first, the man had the decency to stammer, but then he gathered himself and puffed up like a rooster. "There is a lot of dirt in your backyard, Ms. Holloway, and I plan on exposing it."

"And you call yourself a writer. I'm not sure exactly what you mean about dirt. There is nothing in my past that I am ashamed of."

"Everyone says that, but they always lie. I will expose you. I will show the world who you really are and what you come from." He grabbed his iPhone.

What I came from? He'd said it like my roots were a bad thing, which was ridiculous. But then something dawned on me.

I leaned in close to Mr. Smith and pretended to dust lint off his shoulder. "Tell Dalton Beckett that never once in my mother's short life did she regret her choices. She knew what type of man the forever type was and what type of man was a loser, and that's why she picked my father over him. That, Mr. Smith, is what I came from."

The reporter leered and leaned in. "You can fling your

insults, but we are only just getting started. You haven't seen anything yet." He narrowed his eyes.

I wondered if Mr. Smith had a personal stake in this fight. I made a mental note to find out. But my guess was he just liked being mean.

"We're not scared," I said.

"Well, you should be."

I was done with this conversation. I held out my hand to Cal, who took it and tucked my arm under his with my hand resting on his forearm, and we walked away.

"How soon do you think we'll see your dad's counter-strike?" I asked.

"Any minute now."

Chapter Thirty-Four
SABRINA

Our presence at the gala did exactly what we'd set out to achieve.

- 1. We faced the backstabbers—Hitchens, mostly —and stared them down. Which in the end only helped Cal, as many came out in support of him and with offers to work on projects together.
- 2. We announced our marriage at the gala and with an Instagram post of our hands entwined with our wedding bands. Then we did a second with my engagement ring bright and shiny.
- 3. We spurred his dad into making a strike.

Cal was right—we were woefully unprepared for the counterstrike from Dalton. Our imaginations had not been good enough. He made us wait, which Cal said was an attempt to create a false sense of winning. On the surface, it looked like the narrative was swinging our way with the exception of a few comment jockeys who accused us of faking the marriage. We didn't care about them. And while all that was playing out we moved forward with entwining our lives. Making Wyoming a hub for us both. Fort had set up an appointment with child protection services as we wanted to start the process to get custody of Rod, and I made plans to have my Texas home maintained on a schedule; leaving it empty unsettled me. Turning it into our vacation home felt very bougie, I told Cal on a laugh. This house was more than just a place I loved. It was a part of my history and held so much of me and my family.

But under the waters, a riptide was developing. We'd collapsed into bed late and fallen asleep after some slow, tender loving, only to be woken up an hour later by my phone. The number was for Flower Mound Police Department. It was three in the morning, West Coast time. Flower Mound was where I lived.

"Sabrina Holloway?" the voice asked.

"Yes."

"Do you own the property on 257 Grapevine?"

"Yes." I sat up and switched the phone to my other ear.

Cal turned on the bedside light and studied me.

"Ms. Holloway, my name is Detective Pham. I'm calling to say there has been an accident at your home."

"What sort of accident?"

"A fire. Looks like it started in the garage. Your neighbor called it in. We need you to come do a walk-through with us."

"There's been a fire at my house," I told Cal. "I need to go home."

"Was it arson?' he asked as he reached for his phone.

"Was it arson, Detective Pham?" I asked.

He cleared his throat. "That will be looked into. We

need you to meet with the fire inspector. How soon can you be here?"

"I'm currently in California. I have to look at flights—"

"I'll have the company jet ready to go in an hour," Cal said.

"I should be there in about four hours," I told the detective. "Is it bad?"

"It's not good."

We made plans for me to call the detective as soon as I arrived, and he and the fire inspector would meet me at my house. While I was throwing my clothes into my suitcase, I called my insurance company. Cal was on the phone, coordinating the plane.

We were in the car, heading to the airport, when I said, "I have a bad feeling about this."

Cal rubbed the back of his neck. "I'm not one for believing in coincidences, but maybe that's what this is."

I knew he wanted that to be true. The guilt would be huge if this could be traced back to his father.

"You are not responsible for the actions of another person." I took his hand and squeezed. "I love you. Whether it was an accident or not is irrelevant because all of us are safe. That's all that matters."

He was leaning in for a kiss when his phone rang. It was Morgan. He put her on speakerphone. "You're up early," he said.

"Cal, there's been a fire in Brynna's barn. An explosion really." Her voice quivered with emotion.

"Is everyone okay?" He met my worried gaze with one of his own.

"One of the hands was in the pasture with some cows when the barn exploded. He was hit with debris. He has some burns and a head injury. He was airlifted to the hospital in Cheyenne. Fort is on his way with a fire inspector. Brynna is devastated."

"You have to go home," I told him.

He was torn, but a person couldn't be in two places at once. "After we go to your house."

"That's not all," Morgan said. "I was served papers last night. Your father has filed for divorce and is asking for the ranch." She choked back a sob. "The nerve of that guy."

Cal filled in Morgan about my house fire. I gave Cal the look—the one that said he needed to be with his mom more than he needed to be with me.

"He's splitting us up. You see that, right? I think he wants you to be home alone," Cal said.

"Then I'll ask Nick to come with me. Just because we aren't together doesn't make us weak," I said.

"You'll take Nick and a bodyguard. And, Mom, I'm sending a few people to the ranch as well. He's not taking the ranch today, but he has taken away our sense of safety, and I can fix that immediately. I'm headed home, Mom. Don't do anything until I get there."

As he disconnected the call, I was already on my phone, calling Nick. I gave him the quick rundown and asked him to meet me at the airport. He was already headed to his car when I made my request. That was how good a friend he was.

Cal called Optium and had two executive protection agents sent to the ranch and one sent to me. The plan was that as soon as I talked to the inspector and could leave, I would head back to the ranch. Cal was worried about all of us not being together.

Then, just when we thought it couldn't get worse, a

video of me socking Kathy in front of her child made the gossip sites. The image was not from a leaked county camera but captured on someone's cell phone. I became an instant meme and GIF. Neither of which were flattering. The vitriol was awful. Many questioned how I could ever think I should be a mom when I'd done that in front of a child. I had to admit, that hurt. It wasn't something I hadn't thought myself. Not only was Dalton pulling us all in different directions physically, but he was pulling our attention into all directions as well.

At the private airport, Cal waited for Nick to arrive before leaving me to catch a charter. "I don't like this," he said, pulling me into a tight hug.

"We've been through worse. Physical distance is nothing so long as we're on the same page."

"Let me know as things unfold, and get out as soon as you can. I know that's asking a lot, but I would feel a lot better being with you and knowing you're safe."

"I would question whether your dad could stoop so low, but I remind myself that nothing is off-limits to him."

We kissed goodbye, and Nick and I boarded one plane while Cal went to board another, and we went in opposite directions.

Exactly four hours later, I was standing in my yard with Nick, Detective Pham, a bodyguard, and the fire inspector looking at my mostly destroyed house. The fire had caught at the garage, and both the garage and my SUV were toast. No pun intended. Or heck, maybe the pun was intended because the space was nothing but charred remains. Unlike toast, the burned parts couldn't be scraped off to salvage the space.

The fire had taken my home office, which included guest

quarters for clients and consisted of a kitchenette, bathroom, living room, and bedroom space. When clients were leaving everything they knew and had opted for an arranged marriage in search of freedom, I tried to make that transition as comfortable as possible. It wasn't the loss of the space I mourned but the pictures I had put on the walls—images of happy couples, some with their children. Proof that what I did actually made people happy and gave their lives meaning. And losing that felt symbolic, like Dalton was trying to destroy all of it.

From there the fire traveled into my bedroom and living room. My kitchen was the only room with four walls.

I had to prove to the inspector that I had been out of town for the last ten days. Seeing as there appeared to be evidence that the actual living space of my home had been ransacked before the fire was started added evidence to the findings of arson. He walked me through where the fire had begun and how it had progressed.

"Do you know what they were looking for?" Detective Pham asked.

I shook my head. We did several walk-throughs, and with such a mess, there was no telling what might be missing.

"It's going to take weeks to get this squared away," my insurance guy said. "But it's a total loss. I'm sorry, Sabrina. I'll leave you to it."

Though I wasn't sure what *it* was supposed to be. Should I mourn? Cry? Rage? I decided on all the above.

I stood in the burnt-out garage and stared. Everything was replaceable. That was what I told myself. Maybe I'd lost pictures, but most of them, I'd stored in the cloud. But I'd lost other things: the first saddle I'd had as a child, which my mom had picked out. My dad's favorite blanket. The records he and my mom had collected in their short marriage. That was what I couldn't replace, and it would take seeing those things in pictures to realize they were gone. So Dalton had taken away my desire to have those memories or maybe just added an ache to them.

"Maybe I should go through the house again to see if I can find anything worth saving. Maybe I missed something the first walk-through."

"I'm sorry." Nick's voice was heavy with empathy as he looked around. He squeezed my shoulder in comfort. "You know all this can wait. You two shouldn't put off a honeymoon in order to take care of this." He gestured to the charred space. "I bet disrupting that was part of the plan."

"It is hard to think about going away. It's too much to process right now. I lost so much." I turned to the left and pointed in front of me. "That wall was all decorations. Christmas, Halloween. My tree is gone. All the ornaments I made for my parents. The ones I collected over the years. All those keepsakes are gone." I turned to the right and pointed. "On that wall, I had my dad's tools and car-washing stuff, and even though all that can be replaced, I'm still so sad about losing it that I..." I wiped tears off my face. I couldn't sum up how I felt and was at a loss for words.

Dalton knew how to cut deep. The house, I could rebuild. But the items that would trigger memories were gone forever.

"What do you think they were looking for?" The house being ransacked told us that much. Why take the time to go through a house when starting a fire and getting out of dodge only took a handful of minutes.

I shrugged. "And do you think they started the fire because they couldn't find whatever they were looking for?"

"That's my guess."

Nick walked over to the pile the fire inspector had made when he'd done his investigation. It consisted of a metal box the length of my forearm and a foot deep, my SUV's license plate, and a few tools. "What's in this box?"

I pulled my attention off the loss and onto the box. I couldn't place what I had used it for. Maybe the fire had discolored it and I was too far into my trauma response to put the brain power into figuring it out. "I'm not sure."

"A fireproof metal box. Do you have so many you can't remember them all?" Nick reached for a tool. "Mind if I open it?"

I shook my head. "I have three, but I don't remember any of them being in the garage." I began to search through the remains for anything worth keeping.

"Sabrina." The tone of his voice made me look at him. He was staring at me, slack-jawed. "It's some papers of your dad's. There's an unopened letter addressed to you in this box."

"What?" After the funeral, I'd gone through everything... hadn't I? I walked to Nick and looked into the box.

"Does any of this look familiar?"

I shook my head. All of my dad's important paperwork had been in my fireproof safe inside my bedroom closet. Well, the closet was gone, but the safe was still there. Fortunately.

"I don't think I ever saw this." I turned back to the space where the wall of decorations used to be and tried to picture it.

"You know, after Melissa died, I had to go through all her stuff. At one point, I hit a wall and couldn't do it anymore. So I stopped. A few years ago, I was in our closet and realized I hadn't cleaned it out. Her clothes were still there. Her shoes and purses. So much of her, and I had lived with it all there because I didn't want it to go away, as if taking out her stuff would really and truly mean she was gone for good. After Travis died, did you even think of going through the garage?"

I shook my head.

He picked up the letter and handed it to me. "Maybe Travis even forgot it was out here. Maybe he meant to do something with it, but you know how hard those last few months were. He and Melissa weren't themselves."

At the end of both Melissa and Dad's lives, it had been about pain management. I flipped the envelope over. It was card-sized. His penmanship on the page was even and easy to read, which told me he'd written this before things got really bad.

I slid my finger under the flap, opened the envelope, and withdrew three pieces of paper. One was a letter from my dad to me, and the other was a note from my mom—well, more a bullet list than a letter—and it explained the third piece of paper.

"She lists out things like you do," Nick said as he read over my shoulder.

I unfolded the third piece of paper, and we both studied it. "Holy shit," we said in unison.

Chapter Thirty-Five
CAL

I was supposed to go to the ranch, but after Sabrina took the flight back to her house and I was jogging toward my charter, I was struck with a random thought. In my business, there were the things going on around you. These were typically in your face and consumed a lot of energy, but there were also undercurrents. The undercurrents were what I was trained to interpret. They were what packed a punch.

In Peru, the asset had been the target of a loud group of activists who opposed him on everything. They made his life difficult, and being out in public tended to get contentious. They'd resorted to flinging paint and disrupting vacations. That was their agenda in Peru. But the undercurrent was the husband of the woman the asset had an affair with, and of course, the asset had never told us about said affair. The husband had used the activists as a cover when he drew his gun and aimed at the asset. And though I wasn't a fan of the asset's personal life and practice, the job offered a much needed change of environment, the sole reason I'd taken the job. And it ended with a bullet hitting me.

At the stairs to the charter, I paused and pulled out my phone. At the moment, a lot was happening on the surface, but there had to be an undercurrent, a hidden agenda. I called Spoon and had him dig into Dalton's schedule and current business deals. My gut told me to pause my flight, which I did while I waited for Spoon to do his magic.

Twenty minutes later, he had a list of Dalton's appointments and deals in the works, the biggest being a ribbon cutting on a new hotel in the Vegas area. The land itself was prime, and though construction had started, the Beck Group had not announced the project until earlier that day.

"Who are the investors?" I asked Spoon.

"Still working on that. Also, it looks like he's doing a deal with a media conglomerate that's been struggling. I'm guessing this is where he found Smith and got him to do some dirty work for him. The deal should close soon once it's through the FCC."

"Why did we not know any of this?" I was frustrated.

"Because this stuff doesn't get out until the paperwork is filed, which happened yesterday. Listen. I was talking to that reporter in Wolf Creek. She's sharp. She has been going through the town's video and looking at the area where someone filmed Sabrina's altercation. She thinks she found a car and is sending me the images any minute now so I can narrow it down. I tapped into the woman's email account—what's her name, Kathy—and she did receive a payout to confront Sabrina and make a scene. I'm putting all that together too. We're starting to get a step ahead here. Your mom will be able to use this to her advantage in the divorce.

And Paul can show the media all this to help with the video's narrative."

Who knew how long the divorce would drag out? The worry alone would beat down Mom. But that wasn't the main point. I needed to put my finger on what was.

"I think Dalton's getting desperate, to have fires started and my mom served. If we can trace the arson to him, then he's looking at being charged. That's very reckless." And very unlike my father. Everything he did was measured.

"Maybe it's because what was in the media was your happiness and not you guys falling apart. He thinks you aren't feeling all the punches?"

Yeah, we'd done a good job coming together. All the hits we'd taken hadn't shaken us. In fact, we were stronger than ever. I wasn't going to lie; the hits had hurt. But when you had people to pick you up, love you, and give you therapeutic hugs, the pain just seemed more manageable.

"What time is the ribbon cutting?" I asked.

Five minutes later, I was having the pilot change the flight destination to Vegas. I texted both Sabrina and my mom about my change of plans. I was going to crash my father's ribbon cutting. How nice of him to have scheduled media coverage. My instincts told me Dalton expected me to rush to Mom or be with Sabrina. He would not expect me to be at his ribbon cutting.

During the flight, I had Paul release a statement about the fire that had destroyed Brynna's shop, which made her work rare as her shop was out of commission for the foreseeable future. Her prices tripled instantly simple due to the limited supply. I bet Dalton hadn't considered that.

I had a few hours to kill before the ribbon cutting, so I asked my mom for Dalton's password and spent the time reading all his email. It really was pathetic that his security was so lax. And how entitled he was—so much so that he was sloppy. There was no smoking gun about the arson but very clear exchanges between him and Smith, the journalist and the person Smith paid to hack the adoption agency, and exchanges outlining the deal between him and my former employee turned tailcoat.

Sabrina and I were able to connect when I landed in Vegas, and she told me what she'd found in the box. She and Nick would be meeting me there.

At the ribbon cutting, I stood behind the gathering crowd. I wasn't trying to hide my presence but wanted him to seek me out. I wanted him to think he'd bested me, that I was hesitant but here. I was in jeans, a flannel shirt, and my boots. I crossed my arms so my wedding band was clearly prominent.

"Son!" he boomed to tell the gathering investors about my presence, a large smile on his face as he walked toward me.

Dalton was tall, with silver-gray hair and broad shoulders. He looked like a tycoon. But he also looked peaked. An unhealthy pale-yellow tinge tinted his skin. It was only noticeable when the sunlight hit him just right. But I noticed it. Mom was right. He thought he could will himself into being healthy.

Then he caught sight of the ring, and his smile faded into a sneer. He got close and said in a low voice, "You are a fool. I bet you didn't even have her sign a prenup."

"Why would I? What do I have that I wouldn't give her? Or give up for her?"

"You can have all this." He waved his hand toward the

construction site. "I have built an empire, and you've thrown it away for a piece of ass."

His words were meant to rile me, and they did. I wanted to punch his smug face. But I wouldn't stoop to his level.

"But what is all this without love? Buildings? Land? See, that's where we're different. Reputation, power, and money are what you value the most. Not me. For me, it's family. None of this matters without them."

"Like you weren't bothered by my accusations in the press. Your reputation is important to you."

I raised a brow. "Wow, nice of you to admit you started all this. Sure, attacking my reputation bothered me. But then I just had to trust that those who worked with me would lean on that more than some lies. And that actually turned out to be true. Getting my award canceled at the gala didn't affect my relationships whatsoever. That's the point you're missing, Dalton. You can have all this. But when you're alone in the hospital from a heart attack"—I tapped his chest—"who will be there with you? No one. At least, no one you aren't paying to be there."

Nick walked up and clapped me on the shoulder, giving me his A-lister smile. Time for the second phase of the plan. He gave my dad finger guns as a greeting. His presence was drawing a crowd, including media, including those not employed by my dad.

"You are such a disappointment," Dalton snarled.

"What bothers you the most? That I won't join the family business or that I got the girl and you didn't?"

His eyes narrowed.

"Yeah, I know all about you and Sabrina's mom."

"Whatever you heard has likely been exaggerated. We

knew each other in college. That's it." He turned to walk away, but I followed him.

He went to where his investors were standing, waiting for the ceremony to begin and to get their recognition. He signaled for the mayor to meet him at the ribbon, and his assistant ran up to hand him giant scissors. I stood to the middle, keeping his attention on me.

The mayor gave a speech thanking the Beck Group and its investors for bringing more jobs to the area with the new hotel and entertainment space. As if Vegas needed more of that. But this plan was different, apparently. The hotel would be more like a resort with excursions, a bubble for the rich to get lost in without having to hop from location to location. A lot of money had already gone into the project.

Everyone was beaming and congratulating themselves when Sabrina stepped out of the crowd. "Excuse me." She had to say it a few times to get everyone's attention. When she had it, she continued. "I'm sorry. I have a question. What happens if the Beck Group isn't the rightful owner of this land?"

"That's impossible. A title search is done before permits are handed out," the mayor said.

"Except that I am the rightful owner of this land. I filed the paperwork today." She handed the mayor a card. "This is the name of my lawyer. He can answer any questions you might have. And it's very suspicious that permits would have been allowed, considering the Beck Group wasn't the rightful owner. Makes me think shady things are going on in city hall."

Sabrina stepped up to my dad and handed him what I knew to be a copy of the deed he had gifted her mom all those years ago. "My mother left this to me. She didn't know its value, but my dad did. He made sure my ownership was all legit, with the proper paperwork in place. All that was left was for me to file with the city, which I did earlier today. My dad was very thorough. He was like that with his taxes too. Which was never the threat you thought it was. You lost, Mr. Beckett. You lost all those years ago with my mother, and you lose now."

To the investors, she said, "I'm sorry about your financial loss."

An older woman with gray hair, wearing a pantsuit, stepped out of the crowd and up to Dalton. "Mr. Beckett, consider yourself served." Then she handed one to each of the investors.

"I'll see you in court," Sabrina said.

His response happened so fast that I was one second behind. I didn't know why I hadn't seen it coming. Sabrina had single-handedly brought the Beck Group to its knees with her lawsuit, though, she wouldn't have had to do it had Dalton not been a crook.

He lunged at her. "You're as stupid as your mother!" he raged as he grabbed her by the front of her shirt.

And my girl—well, she didn't take shit from people. I'd taught her well, if I do say so myself.

"Take your hands off me, and step back," she said.

But that just made Dalton pull her closer. "I will destroy you."

She leaned in and grabbed his shoulders while shifting her weight onto her uninjured foot. She was quick as she delivered a knee to his groin, making him drop like a sack of potatoes. "You're lucky I didn't show you my right hook. But I am so tempted." She pulled back her arm, preparing to take a swing.

I grabbed her around the waist and swung her away. "You got him, killer. Figuratively and literally. He can't even breathe."

She wrapped her arms around my neck and stretched up to kiss me. "Thank you for teaching me self-defense. You were right. I did have to put my hands on his shoulder."

I kissed her back and let her slide down to the ground. "Ready to get out of here?"

"Let's go home," she said with a smile.

Nick moved to stand next to us, and with his phone held out in front of him, said to Dalton, "That's considered assault, brother, putting your hands on a person like that. We all got it on video in case you question the accusation." He patted Dalton on the head.

"Hey," Sabrina said, grabbing Nick's arm. "Come back with us. I think you'd like the ranch and possibly some of the people there."

I took her hand and let her out of the crowd. "What did you mean when you said that to Nick?"

She tucked in close to me, putting more weight on me as she limped and smiled. "You'll see."

CAL AND
SABRINA
FIRST LOVE • TRUE LOVE

Epilogue

SABRINA

Two Years and a Few Months Later

The all-out decorations the town did for Christmas were my favorite, no matter how cold the actual temperature was, and the previous year, it had been really close to freezing. The ambience, the warm lights, the large, decorated tree, the carolers, the roasted chestnuts, and the hot chocolate warmed even the coldest person. I knew this because Kathy Weyman was laughing and smiling —as she did every year. That was the magic of it.

Of course, having a steady job and warm place to live had gone a long way toward helping her too. That had been all Fort and Cricket's doing. They'd seen a town member in pain and offered to help. Kathy accepting it had been the first step. Letting go of grudges had been the second. She'd been happy to go on a morning talk show and admit how Cal's dad, via Jonathon Smith, had paid her to provoke me.

All of us had been letting go of the ugly. Morgan's divorce from Dalton had been finalized a few weeks earlier, and she was glad it was behind her. Dalton's greedy reach for the ranch had proven unsuccessful. As had his fight against me and the land deed. Bribing a city official and banking that the land deed he'd gifted my mom had died with her had been a dumb gamble. Just because she'd died young didn't mean she hadn't had a will that had left the land to me. Dad had told me about it in his will, but in my grief, I'd forgotten, only to be reminded when the fire happened.

Funny that. Had Dalton been less controlling or greedy, he might still have his company—not be bankrupt—and be the owner of a resort. Who knew when I would have found the paperwork in that box?

I stood by a large bouncy house with Cori, drinking chamomile tea and watched the littles inside. There were three houses, one for older kids, one for kids three and younger, and one for the in-between kids. The in-between house looked like *Fight Club*, with all the kids bouncing around, their limbs out of control. Not one came out unscathed and without tears on their faces.

Cori's attention bounced between the in-between house and the one with the littles. "You'd think after taking an elbow to the lip, Tabby wouldn't go back in, but she did, and I'm worried it's to throw some elbows of her own." She chewed her lip.

I glanced over to where Fort was looking in the mesh window, pointing at a kid, and using his cop voice. I caught Rod by the arm as he dashed by with a giant elephant ear in his hand. "Hold up. How many of those have you had?"

We'd had the talk before coming into town. Just because all the food was free didn't mean he had to eat all of it.

"One." He focused on something over my shoulder, his

tell. He was lying. His friends had stopped, too, and were all looking at the ground.

"Is that your final answer?"

He sighed. "All right, this is"—his eyes flicked to mine— "my third. But they're really good, and I haven't had any other dessert, and Cal said I could."

"That's because Cal's not paying attention." He was busy helping with the sleigh rides. "I'll make you a deal. I'll let you have half if you give me the other half. And you have no more after this. You're gonna get a stomachache."

He narrowed his eyes. "You want the whole thing, dontcha?" He held it out. "You just don't want to stand in line."

Cori chuckled. "He's got ya there."

She adjusted her baby boy in the sling she was wearing. She and Fort procreated like bunnies. This one was only a few months old, and they were talking about another, not because they wanted one but because they knew that no matter what they did toward prevention, it would fail. Layla, now a bossy two-year-old, had been the result of a failed IUD. Baby Beau in the sling had been conceived while Cori was on the pill. Fort had been worried that if he got a vasectomy, they might have twins. Only Tabby, their oldest, had been planned, but all of them were wanted.

Rod waved the elephant ear. "If I give you this can, I have one all to myself?"

He drove a tough bargain. And the truth was, I did want the whole thing, and I didn't want to stand in line.

"Deal." I took the treat. "One more, and that's it. Or at least try to fit in something like a turkey leg or a potpie in between, please."

"I'll try," he said with an eye roll. After the handoff, he ran back toward the treat vendors.

"Your mom is cool," one of the kids with him said as they ran off.

Rod gave me a look over his shoulder and a smile. The adoption had been final a year now. He was ours, and we were his, and we didn't need names like Mom and Dad to make that official. But that didn't mean I didn't like it when people called me his mom.

I blew him a kiss. I loved that child with all my heart.

"Heads up. Here they come," Cori said, and I turned to watch two little girls, holding hands, slide out of the littles' bouncy house. They jumped up and ran to us—her Layla and our Simone, both fully embracing the terrible threes.

While Cal was doing a job in North Africa, he'd found Simone at an orphanage in a small village. He had taken one look at her and called to tell me he wanted to bring her home. There was no question that she was Daddy's girl.

"Bite," she said, looking up at me and the elephant ear, her hands wiggling in anticipation.

"Just one." I held it out to her. She took the largest bite possible, this crafty girl of mine.

Fort walked over, holding Tabby's hand. She had a scowl on her face.

"I hate these stupid bouncy things. Every year, I say we shouldn't do them, and every year, we do. Next year, I'm saying no. They're a liability. Jonah Shepard just bit someone, and I think the Billings kid might have broken his arm. Parents signed release forms, right?"

Cori patted his arm. "Of course. Everyone knows it's play at your own risk."

"I wasn't done, but Dad made me get out," Tabby said.

"You screamed in Jonah's face. Those houses make kids monsters, and you are not exempt."

"He jumped on my foot." Her chestnut hair was sweaty and clung to her forehead. She looked so much like her mother.

"It's packed like sardines in there. Everyone is jumping on everyone else," Fort groaned.

"Jonah's getting out anyway." I pointed to the exit slide, where Jonah ran off toward his brother Nathan, Rod, and some other kids.

Tabby tugged her hand out of her father's and gave her mom a questioning look.

"Yes, you can go over there, but we aren't here much longer. Twenty minutes, and don't get mad at me when it's time to go."

Tabby said nothing but ran off to catch up with the boys.

"Why did you let her go? She's gonna terrorize them." Fort bent down and scooped up Layla.

"Babe, she's got a crush on Jonah. Let her be."

Fort nearly dropped Layla. "She's in third grade. She's too young for a crush. And of the two, why did she have to pick the wild twin?" He caught sight of someone in the crowd and yelled, "Hey, Shepard, I want to have a talk with you!" before stomping off toward Jace and Cal.

I put my hand out for Simone's. "Come on. Let's go see Daddy and get a sleigh ride."

She took my hand, and we followed Fort to the others, where he was giving Jace a hard time about his son.

"It's not my fault I had boys and you had girls," Jace said with a laugh.

"I have a son," Fort said, pointing to Beau.

"Yeah, but those girls of yours are gonna kill you before

you can enjoy him." Cal picked up Simone. "Want to sit in the front of the sleigh?"

She nodded, and he placed her on the front seat and handed her the reins. "How about you, Layla?" When she nodded, he took her from Fort and set her next to Simone.

"Hey, Mama." Cal snaked an arm around my waist and drew me near. "How ya feeling?"

I held up the elephant ear. "Fine. I have this."

He laughed and took a bite. Then his hand gave a loving stroke down my arm and came to rest on my stomach. "And how about these guys?"

"They were kung fu fighting earlier, but now that I've had some food, they're resting." In four more months, we would meet our next two miracles. Our twins. Because, like Cal said, why do one when you can go big and do two? Of course, he wasn't the one who was going to have to birth these giants, who already were weighing in at the top of the scale.

I took in my friends, my small family, and the town and felt the warmth of each surrounding me. Home wasn't a house; it was people. It was community. It was the town throwing Rod an adoption party and telling him how happy they were he was not going anywhere. It was community of people rallying to build Brynna a new shop so she didn't have to wait months for a contractor. These people were everything. I had so much, and the best way I could express it was by saying, "My cup runneth over."

I wove a hand in Cal's hair and kissed him once, twice, and a third time. "Thank you."

There was no need to explain what I meant. He knew.

"Thank you." He returned the kiss. "Oh, Paul's staying

through New Year's, by the way. You wouldn't have anything to do with that, would you?"

I looked at the dance floor, where Paul and Cricket were dancing. I wasn't sure if she was over Deke yet or if she ever would be. But something seemed to be brewing between her and Paul that had potential.

"Mm, no. It's not them that I've been giving my attention."

I'd given up matchmaking as a profession after the smear campaign, not wanting to be away from Rod. I now worked for Cal's company, helping with women's and children's safety education. One of my favorite jobs was talking to schoolkids.

"What do you mean? Who's getting your attention?"

Past the dance floor, near the Christmas tree and the large ball of mistletoe hanging off a street lamp, sipping on mulled wine, were Brynna and Nick. She was laughing at something he'd said, and he was staring at her like he'd never seen anything more beautiful. Nick had been spending more time in Wolf River because the town acted like he was a nobody, and he loved that. But the real reason was Brynna. It had taken a while for these two to see each other, but now something real was happening that was healing for him and awakening in her.

I couldn't wait to watch love happen. How could it not? So much of it was all around us.

Open your phone's camera
to scan the QR code and
SAVE

Link will take you to
KristiRoseBooks.com
Buying from me means a
deal for you.

Books by Kristi Rose

The Wyoming Matchmaker Series- Whether marriage of convenience or star crossed lovers, everyone earns their happily ever after in this series.

The Cowboy Takes A Bride

The Cowboy's Make Believe Bride

The Cowboy's Runaway Bride

The Cowboy's Second Chance Bride

The No Strings Attached Series- A flirty, fun chick lit romance series

The Girl He Knows

The Girl He Wants

The Girl He Loves

Beach Town Love- boxset

Audiobooks

Samantha True Mysteries- These laugh out loud, action pack books take place in the Pacific Northwest. Join Samantha, an adult with dyslexia who's hid behind photography, on her adventures in her new life as a Private Investigator. A job she inherited when her new husband died unexpectedly and left behind a mess and another wife.

One Hit Wonder

All Bets Are Off

Best Laid Plans

Caught Off Guard

Two Time Loser

Dodged A Bullet

Audiobooks

The Cold Case Mystery Series:

Bone of Contention

Bone to Pick

PERFECT PLACE: A Liars Island Suspense

Perfect Place

Audiobook

Campus Murder Club- The dead are not forgotten

Campus Murder Club

The Meryton Brides Series- A wholesome romance series with a Pride and Prejudice theme

To Have and To Hold (Book 1)

With This Ring (Book 2)

I Do (Book 3)

Promise Me This (Book 4)

Marry Me, Matchmaker (Book 5)

Honeymoon Postponed (Book 6)

Matchmaker's Guidebook - FREE

The Second Chance Short Stories

Second Chances

Once Again

Reason to Stay

He's the One

Kiss Me Again

The Coming Home Series: Boxset of the above short stories

Love Comes Home

About Kristi Rose

Hey! I'm Kristi. I write romances that will tug your heartstrings and laugh out loud mysteries. In all my stories you'll fall in love with the cast of characters, they'll become old, fun friends. **My one hope** is that I create stories that *satisfy any of your book cravings.*

Here are 3 things about me:

- I lived on the outskirts of an active volcano (Mt.Etna)
- A spider bit me and it laid eggs in my arm (my kids don't know that story yet)
- I grew up in Central Florida and have skied in lakes with gators.

I'd love to get to know you better. Join my community and fire off an email and tell me 3 things about you! Not ready to join? Email me below or follow me at one of the links below. Thanks for popping by!

facebook.com/KristiRoseBooks

instagram.com/kristirosewrites

bookbub.com/profile/kristi-rose

Care to leave a review?

Dear Reader,

I am so honored that you took the time to read my book. If you feel so inclined, I would appreciate it if you left an honest review. You don't have to say much. Put the stars you feel it deserves and a few words. Some folks don't even put words. Reviews go a long way in helping authors in all sorts of areas including marketing.

Click here to find the store for your review!

Thanks again. You're a rock star!

Have a great one.

Kristi